Praise for *Deviants*

"A deliciously dark, harrowing world, brightened by dazzling characters and sparkling prose."
—Kelley Armstrong, *New York Times*–bestselling
author of the Darkness Rising trilogy

"A tense thriller with a strong, beating heart at its center."
—Diana Peterfreund, author of *For Darkness Shows the Stars*

"McGowan launches The Dust Chronicles with a bang, painting her post-apocalyptic world with a dark brush and featuring a strong-willed and determined protagonist."
—RT Book Reviews

"Keeps the suspense throbbing . . ."
—*Kirkus Reviews*

Praise for *Compliance*
*Winner of the NJRW 2013 Golden Leaf Award
for Young Adult Fiction*

"McGowan has topped the uneasiness of *Deviants'* dystopian story with *Compliance'*s psychological tension . . ."
—*CanLit for Little Canadians*

"I can't wait to read what will happen next."
—*Step Into Fiction*

"I love this series."

—*The Reading Cafe*

GLORY

The Dust
Chronicles

BOOK THREE

GLORY

maureen mcgowan

SKYSCAPE

SKYSCAPE

Published by Skyscape, New York

www.apub.com

Amazon, the Amazon logo, and Skyscape are trademarks of Amazon.com, Inc., or its affiliates.

ISBN-13: 9781477817261 (hardcover)
ISBN-10: 1477817263 (hardcover)
ISBN-13: 9781477847978 (paperback)
ISBN-10: 1477847979 (paperback)

Cover design by Jeanine Henderson

Library of Congress Control Number: 2014901588

Printed in the United States of America

First Edition
10 9 8 7 6 5 4 3 2 1

For my aunties Ruth and Grace Dafoe.
He rules the world with Ruth and Grace.
I love you.

Chapter One

FREEDOM PAINTS THE ILLUSION OF SAFETY, AND I WANT
nothing more than to yield to the fantasy. Surrounded by forest,
fresh air, and friends, it's easy to feel safe. I'm not even wearing
my dust mask.

My brother, Drake, leaps onto a boulder and squawks, flap-
ping his bent arms and repeatedly jutting his chin. Jayma copies
him, and she's so fragile, her bird impression trumps Drake's
gangly stomping, especially if I imagine my friend's red hair as
feathers and her dust mask as a beak.

Grinning, Cal shakes his head. "What in Haven's name are
you two doing? You look ridiculous."

"We're chickens," Jayma says, her cheeks pink from the sun.
"Haven't you seen one yet?"

"Nope." Cal moves his dust mask to the top of his head. "I've
eaten the meat, though. Tastes better than rat."

"What *doesn't?*" Drake crows like a rooster.

Laughing, Jayma spins toward me. "Your turn, Glory."

Leaning against a boulder, I raise my hands. "I'll leave the imitations to you experts."

Jayma slides down her mask, and its edges leave a crease on her freckled cheeks. "What's wrong?"

"Nothing. I'm great." I look up to the sky through pine boughs and encourage the corners of my mouth to smile. The trick lifts my mood—to a point. Today has all the ingredients for happiness, and they're mixed in the right proportions, yet tension binds my shoulders and refuses to let go. I shake out my arms, hoping to release it.

Jayma tips her head to the side. "Are you worried we'll get in trouble for coming this far?" She looks toward Concord, the newly chosen name for the settlement we live in. "Is it against Concord's Policies & Procedures manual to leave?"

"No way!" Drake leaps off the boulder, and a cloud of dust rises to his ankles from the carpet of pine needles. "There are no rules in Concord."

"Really?" Jayma replaces her mask and adjusts the straps to make sure it's tight. The asteroid dust that killed off most life on Earth three generations ago is sparse here—but still a risk. And Jayma hasn't been outside the domed city of Haven for long.

"Concord's not like Haven," Drake says. "There's no Management running things. No P&P manual. We can do whatever we want. Go wherever we want."

"And exactly where are we going?" Cal asks him.

Drake wags his finger. "What part of 'surprise' did you not understand?"

Jayma looks back though the woods. "What if we get lost?"

"Look." Drake traces his fingers over a mark on a tree trunk. "The last time I came out here, I scraped some trees. We've been following my trail since we left the water's edge."

"Did you hurt the tree?" she asks.

"I don't think so." Drake's brow furrows. "Trees don't feel pain like we do."

"You know so much about the world Outside." Jayma touches the scarred bark.

"Give it time," Drake says. "It's only been three weeks. You'll learn, too." He reaches for her mask. "Come on. Take that off." Drake's wearing his mask on the back of his head.

"No!" She backs away from him. "It's not safe Outside without a mask. Not for me." *Not for a Normal* is what she means. Not for her or for Cal.

"Don't be scared." Drake smiles. "There's hardly any dust around here. Nothing but pine needles and rock." He gestures around us. "You can take off your mask. Trust me. No one else is wearing one."

My heart warms with pride as I watch my barely fourteen-year-old brother reassure my friend. It's hard to remember he's two-and-a-half years younger than Jayma and I. Four years younger than Cal.

Jayma tentatively pulls the mask away from her face and raises it to rest atop her forehead. Drake nods in encouragement, and she draws a shallow breath.

"You can do better than that," he says. "Like this." Drake bends, then stretches back, arms over his head, as he draws in a lungful of air. "It's great to be alive!"

She laughs, but then her nose wrinkles, and she claps her hands over her mouth and nose.

Drake crosses his arms over his chest. "Do I need to do my chicken imitation again?"

She drops her hands to reveal a grin, then mimicking his movements, she stretches back and yells, "It's great to be alive."

"Louder!" Drake bends back as he pulls in a long breath. "To fresh air and freedom! Say it!"

Jayma tips her face toward the sky. "To fresh air and freedom!"

"That's better," Drake says as if he's her GT instructor. He had to quit General Training when he was only ten, after I accidentally hurt him with my Deviance and his legs became paralyzed, making him a parasite inside Haven. After that, he had to stay hidden to avoid being expunged by Management.

Jayma closes her eyes as she draws another breath. She twirls, arms stretched wide, and on the third rotation, one of her arms swings into Drake.

She laughs. "Sorry."

"It didn't hurt. You can touch me anytime." His cheeks redden.

She looks up at him with a half smile and full-on adoration—almost like the way she used to look at Cal's younger brother, Scout. My brother steps a little closer to Jayma.

Drake and I were separated for less than four months while I was back inside Haven helping to save other Deviants. But the combination of fresh air, hormones, and freedom created the perfect storm to transform my brother from boy to young man—smitten young man. Then again, he always liked Jayma.

"Have you ever seen a pine cone?" he asks her.

"What's that?" She takes a small step back.

"Nothing dangerous." He grins. "Pine cones hold seeds. Let's go find some." With one hand on its trunk, Drake spins around a tree and then heads into the woods. Jayma follows.

"They're cute together." Cal steps up beside me. "Jayma's coping well."

Shading my gaze from the sun, I look up into his blue eyes flashing below the dust mask on his forehead. "Does it bother you?" I ask. "Seeing her with Drake so soon after . . ." My mouth goes dry. His brother's death is recent and raw, and I see a hint of pain as he tries not to frown.

"Scout would be glad to see her happy."

"Still"—I nod toward them—"Scout and Jayma were dating partners. Are you sure you're okay with this? Whatever this is?"

"Yeah, it's fine."

I lean against the boulder again, studying Cal. Sunlight gilds the whiskers on his jaw and sharpens the angles of his face. Even the crooked bump where his nose was broken can't mar my ex-boyfriend's good looks.

In fact, I think the nose break made him more handsome. More rugged. And in spite of all that's happened, I want to reach my fingers across the distance that parts us. But it wouldn't be right. Not even to comfort him. The comfort would be short-lived and unfair.

"How are *you* doing?" I ask.

He straightens his shoulders. "Better. Good. But I miss Scout. All the time." He takes off the pack that holds his weapons—two long swords and a few knives—and sets it down on the forest floor with a clang.

"And what about Mrs. Kalin?"

His jaw shifts. "I *hate* her for what she did."

"So you *don't* think that Scout's death was for the best?" I ask quietly. "She wasn't justified?"

He turns to me. "Don't worry. Mrs. Kalin's not in my head anymore. I can't believe she ever convinced me that her torturing and killing my brother was for the greater good—for science."

My fingers graze his hand. "None of it was your fault, Cal. Zina caused the accident, and Scout was already hurt when he went into the Hospital. And later, Mrs. Kalin messed with your mind. She planted thoughts to make you accept it. There's nothing else you could have done."

He nods stiffly.

"How do you like Concord?" I ask.

"It's great, but I'm not used to being idle. I want to do more to help." He taps his foot against his weapon pack. "I should have gone on that Freedom Army mission."

"Cal, the FA unit left the day after we got here."

"Burn went."

At Burn's name, my heart stutters and my hand goes down to the knife he gave me, stashed on my belt. "That's different. Burn's been in the FA since he was a kid—and he didn't just lose his brother."

Cal stares at the ground. "The FA doesn't trust me because I was in COT."

"So was I."

"Yeah, but you were working undercover for the FA."

"The FA will trust you, too," I tell him. "In time."

Nearly the entire Freedom Army is away on missions, leaving only a few members to man the guard towers. And Cal's right, they don't fully trust him, yet. Suspicion was cast on me, too, when the FA first found out I was in Compliance Officer Training.

"Once Rolph, the FA Commander, is back," I tell Cal, "I'll talk to him for you. He's with the FA unit that left right after we got here." I gesture to the forest around us. "In the meantime, why not enjoy this break? Relax. Have fun."

"You're one to talk." He raises his eyebrows.

"What?" I tip my head and squint against the sunlight. "I don't think I've ever been this happy. Not since I was a kid."

"You *are* a kid." He nudges my foot with his boot. "Sixteen. Don't try to be so grown up already."

"I'll be seventeen in three months. And you're only two years older than I am." I poke him in the ribs.

He pulls back and grins. "I'm serious, Glory. You're the one who deserves to loosen up and have fun."

Cal leans on the boulder I'm sitting on. I slide over to give him some room, then stretch back, my arms over my head. A slight breeze rustles the branches high above us.

"Some days I have to remind myself how safe we are here."

"If we're so safe," Cal asks, "why did you tell me to bring weapons?"

"Just a precaution. A Shredder hasn't been spotted near Concord in years, but it's smart to be armed. And Drake told me that two men from Concord recently saw a crazed animal they think was a bear." I shiver.

"Don't worry." Cal's voice deepens. "I won't let anything or anyone hurt you." He turns toward me and it's all I can do not to kiss him.

Jayma shrieks. I leap to my feet, reaching down for the knife, but by the time I spot her, she's giggling and Drake's chasing her around a tree.

I smile, watching this bond build between my brother and best friend. Cal's brow furrows.

"You're not alone, Cal," I say softly. "You have a family here in Concord. So does Jayma. You two are part of our family now. With me and Drake and Dad."

Cal wrinkles his nose. "Do you mean I'm like a brother to you?"

I wince. "Not my brother, exactly. My friend."

"Friend, I'll take." He bumps me with his shoulder and moves his lips near my ear. "For now."

My face heats and I'm about to respond, but Drake races toward us, Jayma trailing behind him, wearing her mask again. I step away from Cal.

"Come on, you two." Drake beckons. "It's this way."

Chapter Two

THE SKELETON OF A STONE BUILDING STANDS DEFIANT close to a sloping shore. The lake's much smaller than the one next to Concord. Or maybe it's another section of the same lake? I can't tell.

"Does someone live here?" Jayma grabs Drake's arm. "What if it's a Shredder camp?"

"I was here a few days ago," Drake says. "It's cool." He races ahead, vaults through a window, and disappears. Jayma rushes forward and leans through the opening.

Drake jumps up and she screams—then laughs.

Cal pulls out a long sword made from recycled metal and scans the area as he walks cautiously toward the ruined building, his weapon raised like we learned in Comp training. Leaving him to evaluate the danger, I walk toward the lake bed.

In the distance, what's left of the lake glints in the sun, and I try to imagine what this place looked like Before The Dust. A few feet before the land starts to slope away, rocks are lined up in a semicircle. They're carved off at their tops and arranged precisely, almost like a long bench. BTD, would the water have touched my toes if I dangled them as I sat on one of these rocks?

I sit and close my eyes, tipping my face up to the sun. Drawing deep breaths, I unsnap all the tight bands inside me. I get why Cal wants to go on an FA mission. Part of me does, too. But I'm not a soldier.

And I want time with my family. I'm disappointed that Dad wasn't in Concord when I returned—he had no idea I'd be coming—but I hope he's back soon from his FA mission.

Banning all negative thoughts, I close my eyes and lean back.

"Whoa," Cal says as my head strikes his legs.

"How long were you standing there?" I ask.

"I just walked over."

"Guess we should join the others." I leap up.

"What's the rush?" Cal touches my arm.

His fingers are hot on my bare skin, and I yank out of his grasp. Hurt flashes in his eyes.

"I'm sorry." I stare at the ground.

"No. I get it. We're just friends. No touching." He turns toward the building.

"Cal." I reach up to place my fingers lightly on his back. "You're allowed to touch me. I'm sorry. I just don't want to give you the wrong idea." I made my choice between Cal and Burn—choosing neither.

"Drake! Be careful!" Jayma shouts from inside the building.

Cal and I head back, scrambling over a pile of rectangular stones at the edge of the ruined building. Carved stones lie in piles all around, but the original shape and a few interior walls are clear. On the far side, I recognize what's left of a fireplace, way bigger than any of the ones in Concord. This was once a grand building but for what purpose? Why would someone put a structure like this in the middle of nowhere?

Looking up, I see why Jayma was shouting. Drake's standing at the top of a stone wall. He jumps across a gap and tips to the side to catch his balance.

"Drake!" I shout. "Get down!"

He rises onto his toes. "Great view from up here. I can see the lake."

"You can see it from down here."

Cal steps toward the wall. "Come down. I'll help you."

"I want to check out the construction—see how they built this place." Drake walks toward the corner where two walls join. "Construction techniques from BTD are cool. It's amazing how they fit all these pieces of stone together like a puzzle."

His step wavers. I gasp and jump forward. The armor on his upper body rises, covering his bare arms with metal. Like most Deviants, Drake can't hide his fear.

"Careful." My heart's beating way too fast, pushing every ounce of blood and every molecule of adrenaline straight to my head. My body trembles, but I manage to keep my Deviance under control. "Get down. Please!"

He steps off the still-wobbling stone. "I'm fine."

Jayma's mask is on top of her head again, and her hands cup her cheeks as she looks up at him. Excitement mixes with fear in her eyes. She leans close to me. "Drake's so strong. Who would believe his legs were paralyzed for so long?"

Guilt drapes over me like a heavy black cloth. Drake forgave me for accidentally causing his paralysis, but even now that he's got the feeling and movement back in his legs, I can't forgive myself.

Cal moves alongside my brother, ready to catch him, but what if Drake falls on the other side? His armor will protect some of his body but not his head—or his legs.

Balancing on an unstable rock, Drake shifts his body back and forth, like he's dancing. The rock slips.

Tiny bits of concrete, or whatever's binding the rocks, crumble down. Cal shades his face to keep from being hit. Jayma rushes to Cal's side, just under Drake's perch. "Come down," she says. "You're going to hurt yourself."

"Okay." Drake winks at Jayma. "Your wish is my command, fair lady." He leaps off the wobbly rock. It loosens and tilts forward, right toward Cal and Jayma.

I lunge. "Look out!"

Time seems to slow as the heavy stone falls toward my friends.

Jayma looks up and raises her hands.

It's going to crush her.

Cal, too.

Jayma swings her arm.

She strikes the falling rock, and it flies to the side, landing with a crash nearly twenty feet away. Cal falls back onto the dirt and stares up at her. Drake sits on the top of the wall, twists, then lowers himself to the ground. My legs won't move. I can't believe what I saw. I'm sure my heart stopped, but now it's racing.

Drake gets to Jayma first, and she wraps her arms around him. After a moment of shock, he hugs her back with such ferocity I fear he'll break her, especially since his armor's still up.

"I thought I was going to be crushed," she says. "What happened?"

Drake leans back. "You pushed the rock away."

Her eyes are wide, her face pale. "No . . . No. What? No." She looks toward the rock. "It must be fake." She rubs her arm where the rock struck.

My body and mind reawaken, and I run to the rock and try to lift it. Straining with everything I have, I can't budge it. It must weigh more than two hundred pounds. I slowly turn back to my friends, and they're all staring at me.

"It's not fake," I say.

"Adrenaline?" Cal asks as he gets up off the ground.

"Jayma, you're a Deviant!" Drake's beaming.

She steps away from Drake, bumping into the wall behind her. "No I'm not."

"My dad didn't know he was a Deviant until he was exposed to dust," I say. "Maybe you're the same."

"I am *not* a Deviant." Red spots flare on her cheeks, and Drake flinches like he's been slapped.

"Because being a Deviant is so terrible," I say, hurt more for my brother than myself.

"I—" Jayma looks down. Her whole body trembles. Her knees buckle and Cal leaps up to support her.

"Your Gift is pretty amazing," he says. "You saved our lives."

"Gift." Her tone is hard. "You mean *Deviance*."

"That's Management's word," I say. "We don't need to use that word outside of Haven." I glance at Drake, who uses it all the time. "It's a *Gift*. You're *Chosen*." I choke on the last word, remembering Mrs. Kalin's twisted meaning for the term.

"See if you can lift the rock again," Cal says to Jayma.

"I'm not a Deviant." Her eyes fill with tears. "I want to go back to Haven. I want everything to go back to the way it was. I want to see my parents. I want Scout." Her freckles stand out against her flushed skin.

Cal glances away, and Drake slumps against the wall and puts his head in his hands.

"You should be *grateful* you're a Deviant," I tell Jayma as I try to hold back my anger. "You're safer now. You're less likely to choke to death on the dust."

"That's right," Cal says. "We might be able to survive if we're careful, but the dust can still be lethal for Normals. I heard that just a few weeks before we got to Concord, a dust storm blew in and a woman who couldn't find her mask choked to death."

Jayma's shoulders rise almost to her ears, and she looks like she might be sick. "I don't want to turn into a Shredder."

"Am *I* a Shredder? Is *Drake*?" My fists are tight at my sides. My Deviance sparks to life behind my eyes. I point my lethal gaze down.

"Why don't we take a walk," Cal says to Jayma. "We had a big scare. Exploring will help clear our heads."

Slowly, she nods.

"Can you believe her?" I say to Drake after they leave. His armor has dropped and he doesn't respond, so I nudge his leg. "You okay?"

"Why wouldn't I be?"

"Drake." I sit down beside him. "I know how you feel about Jayma. That must have hurt."

"Which part?"

I put my arm around his shoulders. "Jayma doesn't hate Deviants. Not anymore."

"She sure acts like she does."

"I know, but weren't you shocked when you first found out about your Gift?"

He nods and my stomach sinks. That question is laced with bad memories of the day, three-and-a-half years ago, when Drake discovered his Deviance. It was the worst day of both of our lives.

My memories remain sketchy, but I do know that my Deviance first came out that day, too. If my brother's armor hadn't risen, I would have killed him simply by looking into his eyes. As it was, I damaged his spine, and he didn't regain use of his legs until he was Outside in the dust.

But what happened that day was an accident. I had no idea that I was a Deviant, and I certainly didn't mean to kill our mother.

Chapter Three

"COME SEE THIS," CAL YELLS. "OUT FRONT!"

Drake and I leap to our feet and race to the front of the building where Jayma's crouched in front of a rectangular stone.

"Look." She rubs her hand over the granite.

I crouch beside her. The words *MUSKOKA INN* are carved deep into the rock.

"What do you think it means?" she asks.

"Maybe *INN* means 'big building by a lake.'" I grin.

"Ha!" She puts her hands at either end of the stone and rises, lifting it as if it weighs nothing. "We should put this somewhere more prominent."

I stare at Jayma, not sure if she's registered what she's just done, and not wanting to set her off again if she hasn't.

She shifts the rock in her arms. "Turns out I'm really strong." She looks over to Drake. "I'm sorry I reacted so badly. It's all . . .

It's so strange. But you're right, Glory. At least I don't need to be as stressed about wearing my mask."

"Just don't breathe too much dust," I say. Take in too much and she *could* turn into a Shredder.

Drake steps closer. "How strong *are* you? Do you think you could lift me?"

"Let's try." She tosses the stone and puts her arms around him, but her hands barely meet behind his back. Drake's about four inches taller than Jayma and definitely heavier.

He blushes, and the armor rises on his torso, covering the exposed skin from his fingers to his chin.

"Hey," she says, backing off. "No fair. You've made yourself heavier."

"Sorry."

She bends as if she's about to grab around his thighs, but when she realizes where her face is pointing, she blushes, too. Her eyes meet mine, and I can't help but laugh inwardly at her discomfort. There's no easy place for her to look as she tries to lift my brother.

She moves behind him, and turning her face to the side, she bends her knees, grabs his thighs in a tight hold, and then straightens her legs, lifting Drake.

"Look!" She spins toward Cal. "I did it." She spins to me, and Drake waves his arms to keep his balance. "This is fun." She sets him down, he turns to her, and the pair bashfully gaze into each other's eyes.

Feeling like I've witnessed something private, I head inside the ruins. I'm mostly okay with the idea of Jayma and Drake as a couple, but it's weird.

Walking across the open space behind the old fireplace, my footsteps suddenly sound hollow. I back up and bend down, brushing away dust to reveal metal. I explore further and find a heavy ring attached to what looks like a steel sheet. I continue to brush and scrape.

"What are you doing?" Cal walks over from the fireplace.

"There's something here."

"What is it?" Drake asks, rushing over.

"I'm not sure." I sweep my arm across the surface, then feel for edges. "I think there are hinges at this end. Feel."

Drake bends down and runs his fingers along the ridge I found. He starts brushing along with me, and then Cal puts on his mask and joins us.

"I think this is a handle." Cal pulls up the rusted ring from under the dust. "Get out of the way. I'll try to lift it."

Drake and I step aside and Cal tugs on the ring. Nothing happens.

"We need to find all the edges." I trace my hands along the sides. "It won't open if we're standing on it when we pull."

"Good point." Cal kneels down to help me scrape.

"I see the problem." Drake kicks a huge rock. "This is on top of a corner."

I clean off the edge near the rock. "And that one is, too." I point to another stone sitting at the adjacent corner of what I'm now sure is a metal cover for an opening of some kind.

"Someone put them there on purpose," Jayma says, and I turn to see her standing nearby.

"We don't know that," Cal says.

I step to the center of the metal sheet. "She's right. Look how they're placed." I move to the direct center and judge the angles again. There's no doubt: six rocks were carefully placed along the edges.

"What do you think is down there?" Drake asks.

"I'm more interested in who placed the rocks." Cal tries to move one of them.

"Here, let me." Jayma plants one foot on the rock and pushes it away as if she's flicking a pebble. It slides across the floor and hits a stone wall, which shakes and drops dust to the ground.

I'm still staring at the rock when I hear a crash and spin around. Jayma picked up another rock and threw it, crashing it into a pile of rubble. Stones tumble down from the now unstable pile.

"I could get used to this," Jayma says. I don't recognize the expression in her eyes. It's dark and focused, and she seems like a different person.

Cal grabs the ring again and pulls, straining as the hinges grind and squeal.

"Out of the way." Jayma puts her fingers under the lip of the metal door. The second that Cal moves, Jayma tosses the metal back with a flick of her fingers. The sheet swings over and slams against the ground on the other side. Dust rises around its edges, but my gaze shifts to the hole left behind.

Metal stairs descend into blackness.

I eagerly step onto the top stair, testing it. "They seem safe."

"Don't be reckless, Glory." Cal frowns.

"Does anyone have a torch?" I ask. When I lived inside Haven, I rarely left my home without my crank torch.

"I've got a flint," Drake says. "Now we just need something to burn."

I take another step down the stairs, squinting, willing my eyes to adjust to the darkness below.

"Wait, Glory." Cal grabs my arm. "You don't know what's down there."

"Whatever it is, it's been there a long, long time. Did you see how packed the dust was on the top and around the edges of those rocks? No one's been down here for years. Maybe not since BTD." I take another step and pull my arm from Cal's grasp.

"Do you really think this has been covered since Before the Dust?" Jayma's eyes widen, and her fear fuels my courage. For the moment, she's back to the Jayma I know.

As I continue down the stairs, my shoe nudges something off the next step. It clatters to the bottom. Whatever it was, it didn't take long to hit, so I know I'm not descending into nothingness.

"Here!" Drake yells, and I back up a few steps so he can hand me a burning stick. "It might not stay lit for long."

I lower the flame into the hole ahead of me.

Bones. My shoulders lurch back.

"What?" From behind me, Cal wraps an arm across my collarbone. "What is it?"

"A skeleton," I say, keeping my voice steady.

"Human?" Cal asks, and I nod.

"Don't go down there," Jayma says. "Come up right now."

Drake returns with another makeshift torch, this one burning more brightly. "I wrapped a piece of my shirtsleeve around a bunch of pine needles and some sap." He steps onto the top stair.

"Let me go first." Cal reaches for the fiery torch.

His grip around me loosens, so I take another step down. He keeps one hand on my shoulder and follows. I step to the side to avoid planting my foot on what is clearly a human skeleton. Or a Shredder? I have no idea how to tell.

Passing the skeleton on the stairs, we reach the bottom. Cal walks forward slowly, holding the torch ahead. Mine sputters, little more than an ember now. I swing it and it sparks back to life.

The floor looks like dirt, although it might just be covered in years of grime. The walls are made of stones, much like those that formed the building above us, except that these are less carefully shaped and vary more in size. I put my hand against the wall, and it's cold but dry. Between each stone, there's a binding material that could be concrete.

"What is this place?" Drake asks. He followed Cal and me down the stairs. Jayma's feet are visible near the top.

Wooden and metal shelves line two walls. At the front of one shelf lies a pile of bottles and small metal cylinders. The cylinders are all open at one end, some of them crushed and misshapen.

"Food," Cal says.

"Where?" I ask.

"These metal things are called cans. BTD, people used them to store food to keep it fresh."

"Really?" I kick one of the metal shapes, then pick up one of the cans to check inside. It's rusted and there's no evidence that it once held food. There's a partially attached disk hanging by a tiny bridge of metal, and its edge is sharp. "Looks more like a weapon than a food container."

Cal doesn't respond.

He's standing at the other corner in front of a small area divided from the rest of the room by metal bars—like a cage. The hairs on my arms rise, along with the memory of the cell where Burn and I were held at Fort Huron, a rival settlement of Normals a few days' walk from here. My Deviance sparks, but I force down the fear. While it looks like a cage, it was more likely a storage room used to secure valuable goods. The shelving in there is different, a series of diagonal boxes about four inches square. Some of them hold empty glass bottles on their sides.

The light from my stick fades. I swipe it through the air again, but this time the motion only serves to blow it out. By the light from Cal's torch, I can see the rigid line of his shoulders. Something's wrong. I cross the room.

"There are so many," he says.

A lump rises in my throat. Skeletons are stacked along the back wall and scattered in front. A skeleton that looks to be a child's lies across the thigh bones of another.

"Who were these people?" I ask.

I hear a noise behind me.

"Don't look," I say as I step toward Drake, but he pushes past me.

"They were living down here to escape the dust," Drake says.

"Or the Shredders," I add.

Drake steps closer to the skeletons. "They were hiding down here and someone trapped them."

Cal looks toward the entrance. "I'll bet whoever died on the stairs was trying, right to the end, to get out."

A bell rings in the distance. Two peals, then a pause, in a repeating pattern.

"What's that?" Jayma calls from the top of the stairs.

I turn to my brother, who's lived Outside longer than any of us.

"We need to get back," he says. "Concord is under attack."

• • •

"Who's attacking?" Cal yells to Drake as the four of us run through the forest toward the settlement.

"Shredders." Drake's armor covers his upper body. The bell continues to ring.

Did Dad lie to me when he claimed there weren't Shredders near Concord? With the FA gone, there's barely anyone here to defend the settlement. "Have Shredders attacked before?"

"Not since I've been here." Drake jumps over a tree root.

"Then how do you even know it's Shredders?" Cal asks.

"The alarm pattern," Drake replies.

Jayma's lagging behind. "Come on," I call back. "Hurry!"

She stops.

"What's wrong?" I race back. Her face is pale, her eyes pools of terror.

"We'll catch up to you," I tell Drake and Cal, then turn to my friend. "I know you're scared. But you can't stay out here alone."

"I've never even *seen* a Shredder." Jayma's voice trembles. "Only on the screens in Haven."

I take her hand. "You don't have to fight. We'll find you somewhere safe to hide." With Jayma's strength, she could help, but combat is less about strength and more about technique, bravery—and weapons.

"Okay." Her shoulders slump. "But I-I should . . ."

"Don't worry, Jayma. It's okay. Just hurry."

We run, but we're far behind the guys, and my own fear starts to take over. I'm frightened for Cal but more for my brother. He's too young to die, and he's not trained for this. The boys drop out of view. Jayma's cheeks are red, her breathing heavy, but she's running fast, pushing through her fear.

We slide down a slope and spot Cal and Drake. They're talking to Burn.

My stomach flips. I haven't seen him since the day he brought us here from Haven.

Cal's standing at attention, like he's in the middle of a Comp drill. His shoulders and chest are broad, but next to Burn he looks slight. It's like Cal's made from taut ropes compared to Burn's solid rock. Solid but relaxed—in the same way the large boulder sits by the lake. No tension, just power.

It's hard to remember that Burn's only sixteen. In every important way, he's a man. He picks up a stick and scrapes it along the ground as Cal and Drake watch. I want to see what he's drawing, but I'm finding it hard to breathe. Burn's arm muscles flex with each motion, and his pants hang low on his hips, tied as usual with a slipknotted rope, ready to expand if his body changes. His long coat is on the ground beside him.

"Should we join them?" Jayma asks.

I croak, "Yes." I swallow. "Of course." I'm not sure how long I've been standing here gaping at Burn. And I'm angry with myself for wasting even a moment while Concord's under attack.

I stride toward the guys. "What's going on?"

Burn's head snaps toward me, and he draws a sharp breath. He stands and rakes his chin-length brown hair away from his face. "Shredders were spotted in a clearing on the far side of the path to Concord."

"How many? Are they headed for the pass?"

"About a dozen," Burn says. "Everyone in Concord who can fire a gun headed there."

"What about you?" Drake asks.

"I came to find you." Burn glances at me.

"Is anyone stationed here?" Cal points to the map that Burn scratched in the ground, and he scrapes an arrow at the edge of what must be the lake. "What if they attack from this direction?"

"They won't," Burn says.

"The cliff's too steep everywhere else," I tell Cal. "There's no way to get down. Concord is only accessible through the pass."

"What's to keep someone from crossing the ridge farther down and coming along the beach?" Cal asks.

"We're wasting time." Burn draws a revolver from his coat and hands it to me. It's a weapon from BTD, but I've learned how to use one.

"Thanks," I say. "Give one to Cal."

Burn grunts and picks up another gun for Cal and one for Drake. He eyes Jayma, then looks at me. I shake my head.

Cal checks the safety on his weapon, then tucks it into his waistband. "I still say we could be attacked from this direction." He gestures with the stick along the drawing of the lake where the ridge forms a high cliff as far as the eye can see.

"Go where you want," Burn snaps. "But you're on your own. We can't spread ourselves thin."

"In Comp training," Cal says, "we were trained to attack from at least two flanks."

Burn's eyes narrow under his thick, dark brows. "Do you think Shredders are organized? That they plan attacks or follow rule books like Comps do?" Burn stomps away.

Drake follows him. "Are you coming, Glory?"

"I'll take Jayma somewhere safe first." I touch her arm.

"I should help you fight." Her voice quavers.

"No. You just discovered your Deviance. You need to test its bounds before using it to risk your life."

"I'll take her back into Concord," Cal says. "I'm going to keep watch along the beach."

"All alone?" I ask.

"If I see anyone, I'll sound this signal." He pulls a Comp alarm from under his shirt; he must have taken it when we left Haven.

"Okay." I glance into the forest. Burn and Drake are way ahead now. "See you soon."

Leaving Cal and Jayma behind, I run to join my brother and Burn.

Chapter Four

BURN SLOWS TO LET ME CATCH UP. DRAKE IS AHEAD but not too far.

"When did you get back?" I ask.

"Day before yesterday."

"Oh." He didn't come by to say hello. "I'm glad you're okay."

He turns to me and nods.

I look down. "And I'm glad your FA unit is here to fight off this attack."

"They're not here," he says. "I came back alone. My unit stayed."

"Why did you come back alone?"

"I'm not exactly a fan of Fort Huron."

"We're fighting Fort Huron, too?" Burn and I were held and nearly killed in the prison of that military-run town.

Burn moves a branch out of my way. "No. Rolph's negotiating for their help."

"Their help? Why would the FA deal with those people?"

"Where did you think we got the tanks from?" Burn asks.

"They can't have the *only* big vehicles left from BTD."

"They're the only ones we know of. Plus, they've got weapons—military weapons from BTD—and we have a common enemy."

"That doesn't make them our *friends*. I'll bet they just want the dome for themselves. They don't care about the people inside Haven. They probably see them as meat." One of our captors threatened to eat Burn.

He grunts and shoots me a half grin.

"I'm not joking," I say. "Are they still using Deviants for Shredder bait?"

"They claim no," Burn says. "Things at Fort Huron changed after I killed that general. But they've got twelve more of those tanks that still work and way more fuel to run them than they admitted before."

"So they're just letting us use their stuff?"

"We're working out a trade. We'll have to share our next harvest." He punches his thigh. "Stupid."

"Do we grow enough food for that?"

"Even if we do, we should have just offered seeds. Let them grow their own food."

A rapid series of gunshots reverberate through the air. "That sounded like an Aut," I say. "Only Comps have those. Could it be Management attacking?"

Burn's eyebrows rise. We run.

"Drake, wait for us!" I shout, but my brother's so fast now, as if his legs are making up for all the time they couldn't move.

We race through the trees toward the clearing, hearing shouts and gunshots farther ahead.

I've lost sight of my brother. "Catch up with Drake," I tell Burn. "Don't let him get hurt."

He turns to me, and I can see him weighing the options in his mind. He doesn't want to leave me alone, but he knows how much it will hurt me if Drake's killed. He runs ahead and I lose sight of him, too.

My lungs burn as I run full tilt, and adrenaline pumps through every inch of my body. If I need it, my Deviance will be primed and ready to kill.

I catch sight of Burn as I round an outcropping of rock.

Everything turns quiet.

"Let him go," Burn says.

Who?

A horrible screeching rises, like metal on metal—Shredders laughing.

I skirt the edge of the rock. Downed bodies are scattered across a clearing—some of them Concord residents, some of them Shredders. How many are dead?

A group of six Shredders stands in the center of the field in a vee that looks like a Comp formation. If they're mimicking Comp behavior, did they come from the Shredder-filled hot zone that surrounds the dome of Haven?

Scanning the field, I count barely more than twenty on our side, including me. I don't know everyone in Concord yet. I spot the lookout from the guard station, and the only other person I recognize is Dr. Sanita. She checked us all out when we got here. The others are mostly grandparent-aged adults and kids. The FA left us badly exposed.

Burn's back is to me, and he's about twenty feet away from the group of Shredders.

Then I see Drake. A Shredder has him. Drake's armor is up, but that leaves his legs and neck and head exposed, and the Shredder holding him is huge. Its eyes bulge like white balls in its scab-covered face, and tufts of dark hair jut out from its scalp between sections of raw skin and bare bone.

The arm holding my brother is unusually thick and muscular, out of proportion to the rest of the Shredder's body. Drake's feet kick, but in the grip of that huge arm, he can't move his upper body.

I race forward. "Don't hurt him!"

Burn grabs me, his hand clamped on my arm. I learned techniques in Comp training to break from this hold, but Burn's right: charging forward will make things worse.

The Shredder laughs when it sees me, and its yellowed teeth are pointed, like the teeth of reptiles from BTD.

The monster flicks its tongue and looks at me. "How nice. Something sweet for dessert."

With its smaller arm, it tips Drake's head to the side, and then it plunges its teeth into my brother's neck.

A silent scream rips through me, stealing my breath and my reason, and I realize Burn's holding me tightly.

"Let him go," Burn says calmly. "Take me instead." He's controlling his Gift, and I'm not sure whether to be glad or angry.

The larger, more dangerous version of Burn might prove useful right now.

On second thought, he might tear Drake apart along with the Shredders.

The Shredder smiles and the skin at the corners of its mouth cracks, oozing blood so dark it's nearly black. Blood trails down Drake's neck, bright red against the shiny armor covering his shoulders.

"If you're offering an exchange, I'll take the girl."

Dr. Sanita comes up beside us, carrying a shotgun. "I think I can hit it."

"Don't shoot," I tell her. "That weapon's not accurate enough. You'll hit Drake."

"I'm a good shot." She's a fragile-looking woman, and it's hard to believe she can hold that gun, never mind shoot it with accuracy, but she keeps her gun and her dark eyes trained on the Shredder and Drake.

The Shredder rakes its teeth across Drake's forehead, opening up jagged gashes. Blood rushes down my brother's face, and I feel Burn's hold on me tighten before I realize I'm pulling forward again.

Drake looks at the doctor. "Shoot," he mouths to her.

"No!" I scream.

Everyone on our side is lined up facing the Shredders, but neither side is taking action. My brother's eyes roll back in his head. His armor fades as he goes limp, slumped over the Shredder's arm.

"Let me go." I look into Burn's eyes. "I'll kill the one holding Drake."

Burn's fingers loosen and brush down my forearm as he releases me. I walk forward slowly, my gun still tucked in the waistband of my pants and my knife at my side, out of sight. If this goes well, I won't be needing weapons.

I stop about five feet away.

"Closer," the Shredder says. Its voice grates in my ears.

I step closer. I need it to focus on my eyes.

"Let him go." I allow my voice to tremble. "Take me instead."

The Shredder looks directly at me and flicks its tongue lewdly.

I capture the monster with my gaze. Instantly, I can hear its sluggish heartbeat, its nerves firing, and I can sense adrenaline pounding in its thick blood as it oozes through its body. I'd love to strangle the creature's heart, but instead I choose its brain. I'll make its head explode.

Latched onto its mind, I see black and red flashes, snaps of anger and hate and pain. I shudder as images flash through the Shredder's mind. It's as if the Shredder's thoughts are on a TV screen. I see a lab—one I recognize.

It's from the Hospital in Haven. I see workers in lab coats putting a mask over the Shredder's mouth. I feel how the Shredder felt when the dust hit its lungs. The elation, the rush, the power. And then the creeping madness as it remembers the torture that followed.

I feel the torture, too. Not the pain exactly, but it's like I'm there, experiencing firsthand the horror.

Sucking in a breath, I transfer my focus from its brain to its heart. I'm dizzy. Conflicted. Scared. But I can't let pity stop me from killing this monster. I don't care if someone in Haven tortured this Shredder. It hurt my brother and it's still holding him captive.

Taking hold of the Shredder's heart, I squeeze. Drawing power from inside me, I seize the heart and stop its pumping. The Shredder's eyes swell even bigger. Its mouth twists.

It screams, and the sound slices through my ears like rusty blades. Drake drops to the ground.

Using its oversized arm, the Shredder hits its chest hard enough to break its own ribs. Gunfire and screams fill the air, and the Shredder falls to its knees. Keeping eye contact, I maintain my twisting grip on its heart. I need to be certain it's dead.

Dark blood and guts strike its body as bullets tear into the surrounding Shredders.

A hand grabs my arm. "Enough, Glory."

I break eye contact with the Shredder and turn to face Burn. "Are you hurt?" he asks.

"No. Help the others. I'll get Drake." I used to pass out after using my Deviance, but it's under better control now.

Burn fires his gun at a Shredder that's fleeing to the woods. The bullet strikes the creature's back. The Shredder slows but keeps running. Burn follows.

I crouch down beside Drake and cradle his head in my lap. His eyes are closed. I lean over to put my cheek near his mouth. Feeling a faint exhale, I almost cry with relief. Pressing my hand against the wound on Drake's neck, I look up, scanning the battlefield for Dr. Sanita. The moment I spot the small woman, a Shredder rips open her chest.

The doctor's still standing as her eyes go blank. She collapses. Drake gasps for air, and I look down as he opens his eyes.

"Are you okay?"

"Yes." His voice is weak. "What happened?" He tries to sit, but I push back on his shoulder. If I can keep him out of this battle, I will.

"The Shredder that bit you is dead." I wipe blood from his eyebrows. "Just rest. Stay down."

A gun goes off nearby. Drake winces, and I dive over his body.

His armor rises. "I'm fine." He pushes against me to sit, and this time he's too strong; I can't hold him down.

"We can't just lie here." He reaches into his waistband, but his gun's not there. "We need to help."

"You're too weak to fight." I pull out my gun.

Ignoring me, Drake jumps to his feet. He spots an Aut beside a dead Shredder and rushes to pick it up. It's one of the guns that the Comps use when they're outside the dome.

"Do you know how to use that?" I ask. Drake flicks off the safety, aims it, and fires dozens of bullets in rapid succession. The head of one of the remaining Shredders bursts.

"How's that?" He raises an eyebrow.

At the side of the field, Burn is struggling with a Shredder that throws him to the ground. I race toward them.

Laughing, the Shredder raises its leg to stomp on Burn. But before its foot lands, Burn thrusts up a metal spear that slices through the Shredder's chest. Burn rolls out of the way as the creature falls, then pulls a knife from a sheath on his ankle and slits its throat.

Burn spins back, weapons raised, ready for more.

Drake still has his Aut ready as he walks unsteadily across the open field, but there are no more Shredders. They're all dead.

Burn slides his knife back into his sheath. He wipes dark Shredder blood off his face with the back of his arm and looks into my eyes, which shows a lot of trust given what I've just done.

I want to dive into his arms, to banish the horror around us, but instead I go to my brother. Drake lowers his gun and lets me pull him into a hug. As I hold him, his armor fades, softening to skin under my hands.

"You were nearly killed." I lean back to study him. Most of his face is stained red. So is his shirt.

He grins. "I'm fine." He looks around. "How many did we lose?"

Burn steps up beside us. "The doctor and George. I think that's all."

"Who's George?" I ask.

"A good guy," Burn answers.

Everything that happened is sinking in. If I can trust what I sensed in its mind, that Shredder wasn't simply from the hot zone around Haven, it was once from *inside* Haven. That, plus the Shredders' Comp-like formations, their team discipline, the Auts—all these things raise possibilities I'm not sure I want to consider.

What if these Shredders *are* Comps? Comps that Mrs. Kalin and her so-called scientists turned into Shredders—on purpose. The thought of an army of Shredders under her control is chilling.

"Does anyone else think this was strange?" I ask.

Burn turns toward me. "Very."

A Comp signal sounds from down by the lake.

"It's Cal!" I start to run.

Chapter Five

BURN CATCHES UP WITH ME IN SECONDS. "GET ON." HE stops and bends over. "I'm faster."

Without arguing, I get on his back, holding tight to his shoulders and squeezing his ribs with my legs as he races up through the forest, toward the pass. To my surprise, Drake keeps pace.

"Go find Jayma," I tell him.

Burn and I head through the narrow pass ahead of Drake. Burn's pumping arms brush my thighs, lighting unwanted fires that I wish I knew how to cool. It doesn't help that my body's pressed against his, my face near his neck, and his scent draws out buried memories.

Drake's still behind us as we race down the zigzag path into Concord. The place is virtually deserted, but partway down we reach a group of young villagers about Drake's age. One of them is Tobin, the winged boy I helped get out of Haven. He waves as we go by.

"What's wrong with this place?" I say near Burn's ear. "The FA goes off and leaves the kids unprotected?" Tobin's dad, Gage, is with the FA soldiers fighting in Haven.

"First time we've been attacked." Burn's breath is heavy as he races.

I turn back to see that Drake has stopped to talk to the kids, and I hope he'll stay with them or go find Jayma.

When we reach the bottom of the hill, I strain my neck to focus through the bounce-bounce-bounce of Burn's running. As we head down the beach, I can barely make out the five-foot wall of boulders that runs from the cliff to the water and marks the settlement's boundary.

Cal was right. Concord's not secure from this direction. The people here are naive to assume there's no way to reach the settlement except through the pass.

A large rock sails over the top of the barrier from our side to the other. At first, I can't see where it came from or where it landed, but as we draw closer, I spot Jayma and Cal, crouching, facing us, and partially hidden behind a pile of rocks.

Without standing, or looking, Jayma lobs a rock behind her. Cal rises to see over the wall and shoots his gun before dropping down.

"Jayma!" I yell. "What are you doing?" They're too far away to hear.

I don't know whether to be angry with her or with Cal for not making her stay at the settlement. She lobs another rock, and Cal rises to shoot.

Jayma waves at us, then picks up another boulder and tosses it. Barely taller than the barrier even if she stood, she has no way to aim, but at least she's staying hidden. She hits something this time—based on the roar that rises from the other side of the wall. Cal shoots, and when he drops down, he motions for us to duck.

Shots fire across the barrier. Shots from an Aut.

Burn drops and flattens himself on the stones, me on top of him. I roll to the side. "Were you hit?" I ask.

He shakes his head, rises to a crouch, and moves forward alone. I check behind us to make sure Drake didn't follow. With Burn bending over to run, I've got the speed advantage, and I reach Cal and Jayma alongside him.

"What are we dealing with?" Burn asks.

"You're covered in blood," Cal says to me. "Are you hurt?"

"No."

Jayma tosses another boulder over the wall. We hear a thud and a groan. "Strike!" she says. She and Cal slap their palms together, smiling.

"How many?" Burn asks.

"Assuming Jayma took that one out," Cal says, "there are six, maybe seven, more."

Burn pulls a handmade knife from a sheath and starts to rise.

Cal drags him back down. "They've got Auts." He turns to me. "They must have stolen them from Comps." His voice lowers. "One of the Shredders is actually wearing a Comp uniform. Well, part of one."

It seems pointless to bring up my theory now. I'd only raise questions we don't have time to discuss and can't answer.

"You distract them," Cal says to Burn. "I'll shoot."

Without argument, Burn nods and stands up, running down the edge of the wall toward the lake. The Shredders shout. Cal rises and fires.

A scream fills the air. It sounds like he hit one.

Jayma stands, picks up another boulder, and climbs partway up the rocks before she throws it overhand. A gunshot rings out, and my friend twists as she falls back to the ground.

"Jayma!" I crawl to her side.

"I'm okay." Her shoulder's bleeding.

I feel under her and find a matching wound on her back. "The bullet passed straight through. That's good."

Her face drains of color and she tries to smile.

A loud noise draws my attention. Burn pulls his spear out of the chest of a Shredder that climbed to the top of the wall. It's dead.

"Keep pressure on that if you can," I tell Jayma.

"Look out!" Cal yells as a second Shredder swings a log and strikes Burn in the side. Cal shoots and the Shredder falls behind the barrier.

Cal reaches down for Burn. "You okay?"

Burn nods, takes Cal's hand, and lets Cal pull him to his feet.

I raise my head above the level of the rocks, hoping I'll be able to catch the gaze of one of the Shredders.

"Jayma!" Drake reaches us and drops to his knees.

"You're here," she says. Her eyes widen. "But you're bleeding."

He shakes his head. "Barely. I found some dust. Let me take you to the hospital."

"No." She grabs his arm. "I'm okay. Help them fight."

"Where's everyone else?" I ask Drake.

"Still up on the ridge."

I guess no one here comes at the sound of a Comp whistle. Out of the corner of my eye, I see movement farther along the boulders, close to the cliff.

"Stay with Jayma," I tell him. Keeping low, I run to investigate. When I reach the cliff, I climb up the barrier to peer over the top of the rocks.

Squeezed into a space between the cliff and a large boulder is a Shredder—a female Shredder.

I knew they existed—they must for Shredders still to be here so many years after the dust—but this is the first one I've seen. I wonder why she's hiding. Her skin is dried out and dark red, but it's not as scabbed as most Shredders I've seen. Her matted hair is so filthy it's impossible to tell its color.

She looks terrified. But I can't be fooled by what looks like an emotion, or let it humanize her. Female or not, scared or not, it's a Shredder, a major threat to Concord—and to me.

It needs to die.

I easily lock onto her mind, but I don't kill her right away. Instead, I concentrate.

Her thoughts run together, skipping around rapidly, and I see flashes of the Hospital and other scenes inside Haven. My stomach seizes. She wasn't always a Shredder. She was once a Haven employee, just like me.

Please, no more dust, she thinks. *I'll die. No, I need dust. Need to kill. Can't stop. What's happened to me?*

She's confused, but her thoughts have made my suspicions stronger. Mrs. Kalin and her staff turned innocent Haven employees into Shredders. I need to find out more, but the battle's still raging.

I focus on slowing her thoughts, slowing her heartbeat, her entire nervous system, until she slumps back on the rocks, her eyes closed, her body partially hidden in the crevice.

She's unconscious but still alive. Someone screams. I turn toward the sound.

Cal's gun is pointed at a Shredder that's at the top of the barrier. The Shredder's right arm dangles awkwardly. Cal shot its shoulder. He pulls the trigger again, but nothing happens. He's either out of ammo or the gun jammed.

Burn is at the far end of the wall, battling another Shredder.

As Cal reloads, the Shredder lumbers over the rocks, dragging something heavy with its functional arm.

I spot Drake carrying Jayma away from the action. I'm glad for that, but Cal's alone.

I scramble across the top of the wall. The Shredder's about to swing a huge log, covered in iron spikes, directly at Cal, who's still loading his gun.

"Look out!" I yell. Then I leap, bringing down both fists on the Shredder's damaged arm.

The arm tears off. I fall and my back hits the rocks. The wind's knocked out of me, and now the Shredder's spiked log is aimed straight for my head.

Cal fires. The Shredder's head explodes.

The log drops beside me, and I back up to increase the distance between me and the carcass.

Another Shredder grabs my hair from across the barrier and pulls me, dragging me higher up the rock pile. I try to twist so that I can use my Deviance, but its grip on my hair is low, near my scalp. I can't make eye contact. My scalp screams with pain.

Cal aims but doesn't fire. I must be blocking his shot. "Shoot!" I yell. Being shot is better than being captured by Shredders.

Burn appears near Cal. His face is red and veins pulse at his temple.

Another Shredder reaches the top of the pile and throws a rock. It hits Cal and he's knocked to the ground. The Shredder holding me laughs. It rakes its hand up my body, pulling my shirt up with it.

Its skin is rough and hot against mine, and I want to vomit. I swing my arms back and strike it, but its body's hard, like hitting concrete. Pain radiates along my arms. The Shredder yanks me again, and my hip slams into a sharp rock.

Burn expands before my eyes. His already-large arms double in size, his considerable height grows more than a foot, his chest widens. Anger distorts his face.

Backing away, Cal raises his gun, pointing it back and forth between Burn and the Shredder.

"Shoot the Shredder," I yell at Cal. "Not Burn!"

Burn leaps onto the barrier, landing not far from my head. The Shredder releases my hair and I drop against the rocks. Burn grabs the Shredder and smashes its head on the rock beside me. I roll to the side to avoid looking, but I can't avoid the sound of crunching bones.

When I look up, Burn's looming above me—a mountain of rage.

Cal shot the other Shredder and is once again pointing his gun at Burn. Cal looks confused but determined. He thinks I'm in danger. I'm not sure that he's wrong, but I can't let him kill Burn.

I stand. My head spins. I grab Burn's arm. He raises his fists to strike me but stops. I look into his eyes.

"Get out of my way!" Cal yells. "He'll kill you."

I hold my hand up to silence Cal while maintaining eye contact with Burn.

I calmed him once when he was changed—at least I think I did. Maybe I can do it again. I latch onto Burn's mind. His thoughts are dark and thick, like billowing factory smoke around a broken vent, but the smoke's shot through with fiery red sparks. Anger. Rage.

I force down my fear and think calming thoughts. I think of the lake where Burn taught me to float. I think of the night sky, wind in my hair, ripples on the water. *You don't want to hurt me,* I think.

I have no idea whether he hears my thoughts, but the red sparks in Burn's mind diminish, the black fog dissipates, and the fury in his eyes decreases.

A Shredder shrieks. My concentration breaks, and the image of the Shredder's skull smashing on the rocks replaces my calming thoughts. Immediately, Burn's thoughts darken, sparking with red.

I'm dizzy. Can't focus. I'm making this worse.

I break eye contact. Burn flexes his legs and bounds over the wall.

Pain stabs my head and I raise my hands to my temples. Shouts carry back on the wind, and I duck behind the rocks and peer over, but my vision's blurring. I have to ignore my pain until everyone's safe.

Burn lifts a Shredder and throws its body straight into another. The two fall in a pile and Burn leaps, pulling a metal shard from the sheath on his back and driving it through both of their bodies at the same time.

Burn roars as he pulls the bloodstained shard from their bodies and spears it through them again. Then he heads after another Shredder racing along the pebbled shore.

Holding his gun, Cal scans for more Shredders. I should help him. I should tell someone about the female Shredder hidden at the cliff. But pain and dizziness are winning.

My vision fades.

Chapter Six

I WAKE AND CAL'S FACE IS THE FIRST THING I SEE.

I bolt up and grab my head. It's like someone's slamming rocks on my skull.

"Easy!" Cal holds my shoulders. "Not so fast."

Realizing I'm in my underwear, I pull up the blanket. I'm in the hospital in Concord. "Where's Jayma? Where's Drake?"

"Right here."

I turn to see Jayma sitting on a bed across from me. Drake's on its far side. His neck is bandaged, and there are red lines on his forehead and some bruising. "You look better," I say.

"I heal quickly." He looks down at Jayma and smiles. She's wearing a sling and sitting on top of the bedcovers, leaning against the wall.

"What happened to you out there?" Cal asks me. "You passed out."

"No kidding." My mind's still foggy, but details from the battle break through.

"I thought you didn't black out anymore." Drake leans on Jayma's bed, concern in his eyes.

"So did I." In the early days, I'd pass out every time I used my Deviance, even to kill a rat, and I barely remember anything from the day my Deviance killed our mother. The blackouts stopped months ago—I thought—but this blinding headache is something new.

"Do you want some dust?" Drake asks.

"What? No!" My head pounds again and I close my eyes.

"Whatever happened out there," Cal says, "you're clearly not over it."

I rub my temples. "Thanks for bringing me here."

"Not me." Cal's cheeks flush and he nods toward the corner of the room. "Him."

I lean forward and see Burn standing against the wall, one foot crossed over the other. When we make eye contact, he nods. More of the afternoon's events flood in. Bits of both battles flash in my mind.

"How many people were killed?" I ask.

"Three," Drake says. "It was bad, but I guess it could have been worse."

"I thought you guys told me Shredders never come to Concord," Jayma says.

Burn pushes off the wall. "They haven't. Not for over a decade."

Jayma swings her legs over the side of the bed. "Why *aren't* there more Shredders around here?"

"Not enough dust for them to live on." Burn pulls his hands from his coat pockets. "Something's off." He looks at Cal. "And you were right. They attacked from two flanks."

Cal gives a quick nod to Burn. "I swear those Shredders had a plan. They were using formations and tactics we learned in Comp training." He shifts. "And what about the ones in Comp uniforms? And the weapons?"

"Stolen?" Burn suggests, and I realize it's pretty much the first time I've seen these two talk to each other voluntarily.

"I have a theory about that," I say. Drake crawls over Jayma's bed to sit beside her, and Burn strides to the foot of my bed.

"I heard thoughts," I tell them, "in the mind of the Shredder that had Drake." I don't mention the female Shredder. I'm not sure why, but I want to keep her a secret.

"You can hear thoughts?" Cal rubs his hand over his hair.

"Sometimes." I lean back on my elbows. "I wasn't positive before today, but I am now. If I focus my Gift on a Shredder's mind and listen, if I concentrate without squeezing or blocking, I can see and hear what they're thinking."

"Cool," Drake says. "What did you hear?"

I lick my dry lips, and Cal pours me a glass of water. After taking a drink, I say, "I think Mrs. Kalin *made* those Shredders. They might even be under her mind control."

Cal puts his hand down on my bed, close to my leg. "What? How?"

Burn frowns, but I don't know whether it's because of what I said or because of Cal's hand so close to my thigh.

"She's feeding dust to Haven employees in the Hospital," I say. "Both Deviants and Normals. Cal and I saw her techs doing that. They give different quantities to each subject, and then they study the effects—even hurting them to test their tolerance for pain and healing abilities." I glance at my brother, but he looks away. His paralysis disappeared not long after he first breathed in dust.

"My theory is," I continue, "that when her test subjects turn into Shredders—and some must, given what she's doing—she dumps them outside the dome. It's like she's manufacturing Shredders."

Cal whistles. "No wonder there are so many of them between the dome and that wall."

"The FA calls it the hot zone," I tell him. "Some probably got out when our FA tanks broke through the wall."

"But why would they come here?" Burn asks. "There's barely any dust to live on. And how did they find the way?"

"Maybe they followed the tank we were in?" I suggest.

"We didn't bring the tank anywhere near here."

"Our tracks then?"

Burn frowns. "Hard to track over bare rock even if you know what you're doing."

"Then they found us by luck?" Drake suggests.

I bite my lower lip. We need to figure this out so that we'll know if more are coming. I hope I can learn something from that female Shredder down by the shore, assuming she's still there.

I lower myself to my pillow. "I need more sleep."

"You've got it." Cal leans down and presses a soft kiss on my forehead. He flicks his gaze to Burn, then moves away from my bed.

"I'm starved." Burn approaches Cal. "Let's talk more over some food. You coming, Drake?"

"I'll stay with Jayma." He puts his hand on hers. Both Drake and Jayma seem nearly healed. I'll bet they both breathed some dust, but now's not the time to question him.

"I'm starving." Jayma slides off the bed. "Let's go with them, Drake. If that's okay with you, Glory?"

"Sure," I say. "I just want to sleep and get rid of this headache."

And then I'll go back to find that Shredder.

• • •

I wait until the hospital is quiet. I'm not certain how many other patients are in here and if there are staffers who stay overnight. Concord just lost its only doctor, but someone must be here.

Moonlight comes through the window that's high on the wall, revealing the two beds, a small cabinet, and a wooden bench with my clothes on top and my shoes underneath. As soon as my feet hit the stone floor, I creep over to the door and peek into the hall. It's deserted. At least as far as I can tell in the very dim light.

My head's clear and focused, but I'm glad I decided to stay here overnight. It would be hard to sneak out of our cabin without waking Drake.

I toss on the worn T-shirt and pants, then cover up with my light jacket. I dig my hands into my pockets. My knife's gone. I search the cabinet, but all I find are a crank torch, a few lengths of cloth, and a half-filled water bladder. I stash them in my pockets and then make my escape from the building without notice.

Even though it's the middle of the night, I can't risk going to the armory—someone usually sleeps there—but I need something I can use to defend myself, and also something to contain the Shredder. The cloth bandages won't be strong enough.

The hospital is in the lower part of Concord, near the water. I dash through the streets, keeping to shadows when I can. On the outskirts, I head into the barn that houses dairy cows and goats. The animals remain quiet as I gather what I can find: a coil of rope and a hatchet in a holster that I strap around my waist.

Whoever owns the hatchet is bigger than I am, so I can't fasten the holster using the buckle, but I manage to secure it by tying the straps in a knot. A cow bellows.

I start, still not used to the sound, but I get out of the barn and away from the settlement without running into another person.

The nearly full moon casts a cool light that sparkles off the calm surface of the lake. The pebbles crunch and slide as I run alongside the water toward the wall of boulders where I left the Shredder. It's been more than eight hours, and I expect she's long gone, but I need to check.

When I near the barricade, I slow my pace, trying to lessen the noise of my footsteps; but try as I might, it seems impossible to walk silently on this pebbled surface. The cliff looks even higher in the moonlight, and I understand why Burn and the others didn't think this border was at risk. How in the world did the Shredders get here without going through the pass we use? If we're going to defend this place, someone needs to figure it out. But that's tomorrow's problem.

A shadow moves near the top of the boulders. I stop and listen. Something shuffles.

It has to be her. She's still there, and she's awake.

Before I climb, I unsnap the holster and remove the hatchet. The shuffling sound increases. Nearing the top of the wall, I raise the weapon. If I can't capture her gaze right away, I'll swing. I turn the hatchet so that I'll be striking with the blunt side, not the blade.

I'm shocked to find her in the exact same position, and the noise isn't coming from her but from some kind of animal I've never seen before. It's got a pointed nose and black around its eyes, almost like a mask, and a long tail with rings of gray and white. It reminds me of the rats I used to kill on the rooftops of Haven, but it's much larger than a rat; and although its coat is matted and worn off in places, this creature has much thicker fur.

Sensing me, it rises up on its hind legs and bares its teeth— brown and broken. Its paws almost look like fingers, its eyes are crazed, its lips dark and dry. This large rodent or small bear— whatever it is—has gone mad on dust. Whatever it was at birth, it's now a Shredder-animal. It snarls again and I try to catch its gaze, but it skitters across the boulders toward me.

I swing the hatchet, and the blunt side strikes the side of its head. It falls near the Shredder woman.

One side of its head is crushed but it's still breathing, and from a certain angle it's almost . . . cute. BTD, some humans kept animals as pets—loved them—and I wonder if this strange masked animal was the pet kind.

I can't feel sorry for it.

Avoiding its body, I climb over the rocks and look at the female Shredder. She's halfway on her side, with one leg slightly bent over the other. She's still asleep. Or dead.

When I was in Haven, I managed to awaken a rat that I'd knocked unconscious. That part of my Deviance is as mysterious to me as crushing hearts or lungs used to be.

I shake her. Nothing. I flick her cheek. Still nothing, except that I'm grossed out at the crusty feeling of her skin. Gagging, I push open one of her eyelids. I reach to open the other but realize that if I'm going to wake her I should tie her up first.

I'd prefer to have her hands behind her back, but both of them rest in front, so I pull her hands together. Using the hatchet, I saw off a length of rope and wrap it around her wrists, binding them tight.

I move down to her ankles and tie them, too, leaving just enough rope that she'll be able to take small steps but not run.

I open her other eye and stare, trying to make contact with something inside her, the part that's still alive in her consciousness. Nothing happens. Beside her, the Shredder-animal breathes. Other than its heaving chest, it hasn't moved. I use the top of the hatchet blade to nudge its body farther away.

It twitches.

I jump back.

The animal wakes, snarling and snapping. It lunges and digs its teeth into the ribs of the Shredder woman. She screams. If I ever had doubt that Shredders feel pain, apparently they do—at least while they're being eaten.

She twists and kicks, trying to get the animal off. Her eyes glow, casting eerie light. I've seen that Deviance before.

I swing the hatchet, blunt end first, and slam it into the animal's head.

The creature flies to the side and smashes into the cliff. Yet, a moment later, it rises to its feet and springs toward me, foam dripping from blackened lips. I swing the hatchet.

The blade strikes its neck, and the creature falls onto the rocks in two pieces. Dead at last.

I look at the Shredder woman. Her eyes are glowing with bright-green light. A flash of recognition hits me.

Arabella, the last Deviant kid I saved from Haven, had this same Deviance: green phosphorescent eyes. I've never heard of a parent and child having the exact same Deviance, but I wonder if this is her mother.

The Shredder sucks in a sharp breath and grabs my arm with her bound hands. "You." Her voice is scratchy.

I wrench out of her grasp. She lunges toward me and snaps, her teeth missing my face by less than an inch.

I kick her body as I scramble back and raise the hatchet. I lock onto her eyes, planning to squeeze her heart, but I blink and turn away. If I kill her, I won't learn any more about how she got here.

And if she recognizes me, this *must* be Arabella's mother.

"Dust." She slams her bound hands against her forehead so hard I'm afraid she'll knock herself out. "Now." She leans forward. "Dust." Thick, phosphorescent tears rise in her eyes and trail down her cheeks.

I raise the hatchet again. "I'll get you some dust, but you need to come with me. Quietly."

She looks down at her chest. "Who bit me?" She plasters her back against the rocks and scans around, eyes wide and shining. "Did *she* tell them to? Where am I?"

"Who is *she*?" I ask. "An animal bit you. It's dead now."

She kneels and scrapes the rocks with her fingers. "Dust. Need dust." Her fingers grow raw and leave dark trails on the stone.

"Stop it! You're hurting yourself. There's no dust between these rocks."

She looks up at me. The light in her eyes starts to fade, and I can make out her features better. Although she has the crazed look of a Shredder, her anguish is obvious. But I need to either kill her or leave. If we stay here much longer, someone might come, especially after what happened today.

As if on cue, I hear voices down the shore toward Concord. I pull the cloth from my pocket.

"Calm down," I tell the Shredder. "Be quiet or I'll hurt you."

She's pawing at the gash in her chest and doesn't acknowledge that she's heard me. Moving quickly, I use the cloth to gag her. As she fights against me, her eyes glow again, but at least now she can't scream.

Forcing my knee into her back, I turn her to face the rocks so there's less chance that whoever's coming will see the glow from her eyes. The voices become clearer. I know who they belong to: Cal and Burn.

Chapter Seven

I HOLD DOWN THE SHREDDER WOMAN AS THE GUYS COME closer. Even though we're on the other side of the boulders, they'll see her eyes glow.

I tear a piece of cloth off the bottom of my shirt to blindfold her, then crawl up the boulders to peek over. Burn's long coat flares as he strides, making him even more imposing. As they climb over the rock barrier, I move my body to better block the Shredder.

"Won't you get in trouble for deserting your FA unit?" Cal asks.

"Nah."

Moonlight glints off Cal's hair as he shifts his gun and looks over at Burn. "Because they're afraid of you?"

The Shredder woman struggles, and a small rock rolls down from beneath her feet. I stop breathing.

Burn halts. "Did you hear something?"

Cal shakes his head, but Burn looks straight toward me. *Rat dung!* Burn's wearing his night-vision goggles. The two of them stand still, scanning, listening. Even if Burn didn't see me—which I'm sure he did—they'll hear us breathing.

"It was probably nothing," Burn says.

With my heart thumping against my ribs, I wait. Burn has decided, for whatever reason, not to tell Cal that he's seen me.

Cal turns to face the water. "Look at how the moon shines on the lake. I'm still not used to how beautiful everything is Outside." Cal still says the word "outside" as if it's a specific place, the way we all grew up saying it under the dome.

Burn grunts and crosses his arms over his chest. Staring at the lake, the two remain quiet for so long that I start to wonder if it might be safe to reveal myself, but I can't do that. I'm not sure about Cal, but I have no question what Burn will do. He'll kill the Shredder and my opportunity to learn more.

"So," Cal breaks the silence, "you get big—really big. That's your Deviance?"

Burn shrugs.

"What brings it on?"

"Why? You afraid I'll attack?" Burn's tone is menacing, but I note a hint of humor, too.

"Oh, I can handle you." Cal swings his gun but his words sound mocking.

"If you want to believe that," Burn says. "Go ahead."

Cal laughs. Are they actually kidding around with each other?

"You didn't answer," Cal says. "What brings it on? Is it the same as Glory? Emotions?"

Burn drops his arms to his sides as if all his muscles stopped working at once. "Mine's worse."

"How?"

"Glory can control hers." Burn shoves his hands into his pockets. "She's like a sharpened knife, and I'm more like a sledgehammer. She's a sniper rifle, and I'm the spray from a broken shotgun."

Burn turns slightly toward me—he *knows* I'm here—and I can't decide what's more surprising: that he's talking to Cal like they're friends, or that he's leaving me alone. Has he noticed the Shredder behind me? I feel sure he can't have seen her.

"Glory thinks her Deviance makes her a bad person," Cal says. "She acts like she's defined by the things she's done, even the things she did by accident. But I've known her most of her life. She's not a bad person. She's . . ." Cal runs a hand over his hair. "She's complicated, but she's the best person I know."

My mouth falls open.

"Have you told her that?" Burn asks.

"I've tried, but I think I make her feel worse," Cal sighs. "When I think of all the things I said to her before I knew . . . I bought into the whole Deviants-are-evil line they fed us in Haven. I said some horrible things to her." He shifts and tips his head back. "It's no surprise that she doesn't want to be with me anymore." He turns to Burn. "Well, that and her feelings for you, I guess."

"Don't put it on me," Burn says. "Nothing's happened between me and Glory. Nothing ever will."

His words hit like a hammer.

"Really?" Cal leans away from Burn. "Why?"

"I can't be with her. It's too dangerous. My Deviance comes out when I'm—when I'm around her. She has this crazy idea that I can control it, or that she can control me." Burn laughs harshly. "I can't be controlled."

Cal slaps Burn on the back. "Sorry. That's rough."

They're quiet—too quiet for my comfort—but they seem peaceful. As strange as it may be, I'm glad to see they've found a way to be friends—or whatever this is.

"Let's check along the cliff," Burn says. "The other direction's more secure, because of the gorge, but until today, we thought that this cliff was impossible to come down."

They head away from me. I stay still until I'm sure this isn't some kind of trick on Burn's part—that they aren't turning back. But Burn has led Cal away so that I can leave. I wish I understood why.

I need to move the Shredder. The room Drake found under those ruins would be perfect, but to get there, I'll have to take her through Concord. Do I dare? It's at least three hours before dawn, the settlement is quiet, and I really don't have a choice.

I remove her blindfold, then attach the last piece of rope to her bound hands like a leash.

"Follow me." I raise the hatchet. "If you keep quiet, I won't kill you. And if you cooperate, I'll get you some dust."

• • •

Moving through Concord is easier than I expected. Everyone's asleep and there are no lights, not even a candle in any home we pass.

Nearing the last bend in the road before the top of the ridge, I stop. The second we round this corner, the lookout could see us. We might make it to the top of the trail, given that the guard is likely facing away from the settlement, but if he or she is doing a halfway good job, we'll be spotted the instant we start downhill. The pine forest there isn't thick enough to hide us, especially not in this moonlight. If only there were some way to create a distraction.

The Shredder woman tugs on her ropes, her eyes shining brightly, increasing the probability we'll be seen. There's only one option: I need to reason with the guard.

I pull the Shredder to a tree and tie her to the trunk. It's not perfect—far from it. Her eyes shine like beacons. If she struggles, she might get free, but her legs are still tied. I shorten the slack between her ankles to make sure she won't get too far, too fast.

Now for the hard part.

Racking my brain for a plan, I walk toward the guard tower. Maybe I can convince the guard that I'm leading one of my friends and we're playing a game? Or doing some kind of FA training exercise? From the tower, the floodlight cuts through the darkness and pans the forest below. They use a system that was used in lighthouses in ancient BTD times.

The ladder is pulled up about twenty feet from the ground, so I drop my hatchet and wrap my hands around one of the four wooden bases of the tower. Placing one foot on the wood, I try to climb, but my shoes slip.

There must be a way. I could just yell up, but that might draw the attention of someone other than the guard, and I'd have more than one person to convince.

I stare at a pine tree a few feet away, and a streak on the bark glistens. Sap.

I dash over to the tree, finding the most shadowed side, then take off my shoes and rub the soles on the sticky surface. I rub a little of the stickiness on my hands, too.

I put on my shoes and try again. This time it works. I reach up with one hand, pressing my feet into the wood, and creep up the wooden leg of the tower. My shoes are almost too sticky—it's slow going—but I move up until the bottom of the ladder's in sight. Still, I can't reach it. I'm going to have to jump.

I push into a crouch, both hands gripping the post, and test that my feet aren't completely stuck to the wood. Each of them pulls off with a tacky sound that makes me fear I'll be heard.

Using every ounce of strength, I leap up and back. Midflight, I twist 180 degrees and my arms slam into the ladder's rungs. I slide and my chin bumps something. Pain shoots through my head.

One rung, then a second, slips through my grasp. Then my hands hold. I have the ladder!

I'm on the second-to-last rung, and my legs are dangling. My hands are still slightly tacky with pine sap. I rest for a moment, as much as I can while hanging from a ladder, and then pull myself up. My back muscles strain as my chin rises above the rung. I hook my arm over, then brace my forearm along the rung and press down until I can reach up and grab another rung. Three rungs up, I swing my legs to the bottom one and stand.

I climb the ladder quickly until I realize I have one last complication: there's no opening at the end of the ladder. I push at the hatch at the top, but while I can see hinges at one side, the wood doesn't budge. Doing the only thing I can think of, I knock.

"Who's there?" a female voice asks.

"Glory Solis."

"What are you doing here?"

"Can I come in?"

"Are you alone?"

"Yes."

I hear footsteps, then the sound of a bolt sliding. The door opens above me and a face comes into view. Or rather, a silhouette.

I smile. "Hi. Sorry to bug you. I've always wanted to see the view."

"Now? At night?"

"I couldn't sleep."

"Aren't you one of the kids who fought off those Shredders today?"

"Why do you think I can't sleep?" I shudder, hoping she'll think the experience gave me nightmares.

"I'm Gwen." She kneels down and offers me a hand. "How did you get to the ladder? Did I leave it down?"

I shake my head as, with her help, I pull myself onto the floor of the lookout tower. "I'm a good climber. From living in the Pents—the penthouse slums of Haven."

"Oh." Gwen closes the door after me, and I look straight into her eyes. I don't have much time if I want to get back before sunrise.

Now that I'm up here, I don't have a clue what to say to convince this woman she should let me pass with my prisoner. I'm thinking I should have taken my chances and snuck past. My anxiety fuels my Deviance, and I don't fight against it as the familiar tingling rises in the backs of my eyes. I focus in on her mind and listen.

What's with this kid? she thinks. *She must've had a reason to come out here in the middle of the night. But she seems harmless, and I could use the company.*

She doesn't suspect anything devious, but then again, why should she? She doesn't know me.

"Just over two hours until shift change," Gwen says, rubbing her temples. "You can stay if you like. Help me with the light." She grins and doesn't seem to notice that she hasn't blinked and can't look away. She'll notice soon.

Gently squeezing the blood vessels flowing into her brain, I concentrate on her thoughts, the waves of brain activity, and carefully, I slow them.

Her eyes remain wide as the waves and sparks in her mind slow. Then her body crumples, and I catch her under her arms to help her lie down.

What have I done? I don't have time to think about it now.

I open the hatch and scramble down the ladder, releasing the catch that lowers the final twenty feet.

The Shredder is where I left her, mercifully alone. My hands shake as I release her from the tree and get us ready to move.

We need to be fast.

Chapter Eight

THE PINE FOREST'S PUNGENT SCENT INVIGORATES ME, and I'm almost tempted to remove the rope between the Shredder's ankles so we can move more quickly.

She trips over a root and falls to her knees. She scrambles over the ground, probably searching for dust in the pine needles. I tug on the rope. "Get up."

She looks up at me with hate in her eyes, and it helps remind me which one of us is the monster. Yes, I might be a killer, but I only kill when I need to. Only in self-defense or to protect those I love. And I don't enjoy it, like Shredders do. If I were a true monster, this Shredder would already be dead.

I tug again. "It's not much farther. Cooperate and I'll give you some dust." The promise gets her to her feet. She strains and snarls against her gag, but she follows.

We pass the boulder where Drake was showing off for Jayma, and then we follow the marked trees until the woods clear, and I see the stone walls of the ruins rising before us. The moon is lower now, and although the stars are fading with the hint of dawn, the night seems darker, and the building looks like a mass of creatures reaching out from the rock.

I lead the Shredder to the secret room we found, and I realize that I'm going to need both hands to open the door.

Not far from us, I discover a stone impaled in the ground outside the structure. It might once have formed the base of a window. I kick it to test its sturdiness. On my third kick, I conclude it's dug in enough to hold the Shredder. I loop the rope around it and tie several tight knots.

"Wait here," I tell her. She rushes after me, but when she hits the end of the rope, she tugs without budging the stone.

I set down the hatchet beside the metal door and tug on the ring. With a loud creak the door opens. The Shredder groans behind her gag, and I can't help it—I'm feeling a bit sorry for her. Not long ago, she was a Haven employee, the mother of a young girl who needed safe passage out of the dome. *What happened to you?* I wonder. I hope I can find out.

When I turn back, she's fumbling with the knots. "Hey!" I shout, and she backs away from the stone.

I untie the rope and lead her to the stairs. "Go down."

She shakes her head.

"Now." I pick up the hatchet.

She eyes me for a few moments as if weighing her options, then starts down the stairs. Halfway down, she stumbles, and I'm yanked forward.

I lose my footing. The hatchet's head swings down, missing her back by inches and clanging as it strikes the metal stairs.

My heart thuds as I regain my grip and imagine the damage the blade could have done.

Taking advantage of my vulnerability, she jerks the rope out of my hands and jumps down the final few stairs. The glow from her eyes lights the small room as she spins, looking for a way out. But I'm on the stairs, blocking the exit and wielding the hatchet.

She's clearly as freaked out by this tiny underground space as I was yesterday—as I still am now. I creep forward slowly until I'm a few feet from the end of the rope. I reach for it.

She sees the pile of skeletons and shrieks. She spins and the rope flies away before it's in my grasp.

Enough.

I lunge, plant my foot on the rope, and then grab it.

She tugs but I wrap the rope around my hand, refusing to let go even as the rope burns my skin. I drag her until I've got her inside the metal cage. Something crunches underfoot. I look down. A skull.

I jump to the side. The Shredder's eyes glow bright as she pulls on the rope and it pinches my fingers. Looking into her eyes, I concentrate and latch onto her gaze. I knock her unconscious. She slumps to the ground, landing on the rib cage of one of the skeletons.

Grasping her under the arms, I drag her to the side of the cage and lean her against the bars. After spotting a series of heavy pegs sticking out of the wall nearby, I toss the end of the rope through the bars, run to the outside of the cage, and bind the rope around two pegs. She's still got about four feet of slack. I don't think she can reach the door of the cage, but just in case, I need something to secure the latch.

I pull out my crank torch and creep over to the shelves beside the stack of tin cylinders. Covering my nose and mouth with a dust mask, I sort through the items on the shelves.

A moldy book falls apart in my hands. Then I pry the lid off a tin box with the word *Photographs* written on top. Gasping, I sort through the contents, looking at faded images of people. People who are smiling and laughing in a world I barely recognize as our own.

The Shredder stirs and I turn. The patch of sky visible through the hatch is getting brighter. I quickly check the other shelves and spot what I need: an ancient locking device I recognize from the time that Burn and I spent trapped in Fort Huron.

A key sticks out from a hole in the main part of the device, and holding my breath, I turn it.

It clicks, and I tug on the arch at the top, and one side lifts from its hole. Perfect.

I hurry back to the cage door, secure the locking device, and then stash the key in my pocket. But I can't afford to lose it, so instead, I place the key on the highest shelf I can reach, right in the center. The Shredder moans.

She needs dust. I need information. The first chance I get, I'll be back.

· · ·

The morning light urges me to run faster, and as I climb back to the ridge, my legs and lungs burn. The searchlight's still pointing down to the side, so I assume Gwen's still unconscious.

I sprint the last few hundred yards, then leap onto the ladder and climb. I'm panting, and my heart rate's through the roof by the time I pull myself onto the floor of the tower. Gwen is still lying where I left her, eyes open.

I cringe. The least I could have done was close her eyes. They're going to be dry and sore when I wake her. Assuming I *can* wake her.

Lying down next to her, I focus on her eyes, but it's hard to concentrate. My pulse is too rapid, my breathing too fast, my anxiety too high. I put my hand on her shoulder to steady myself, and I try again.

This time my power builds easily, and I lock onto her slow-moving brain waves. She's dreaming.

Dreaming of swimming and holding on to a small child with curly blond hair. She tosses the child, a three-year-old boy, into the air. The boy laughs as his mother catches him and holds him close.

Gwen is a mother. What have I done? I *am* a monster.

Wake up! I think, and I concentrate on increasing the blood flow, loosening all the holds I put on her mind. Experimenting this way—with someone's mind, someone's life—I'm no better than Mrs. Kalin.

Gwen blinks. Then she closes her eyes tightly for a few seconds before opening them again.

I touch her hand. "Wake up."

"What happened?" She brings her other hand up to her head. "Did I fall?"

I nod. It's the truth, but it feels like a lie.

She pushes up on one elbow. "It's already light? How long was I out?" Her eyes fill with worry. "You won't tell anyone, will you?"

"No, I won't tell." I do my best to look calm as I help the guard to her feet.

"Thank you." She squeezes her eyes shut again. "And thanks for keeping watch." She puts her hands on her belly. "I've been light headed lately, but I'd like to stay working as far into this pregnancy as I can. I have a feeling it's another boy."

"You're pregnant?" I blurt the words way too loudly and feel rude and ashamed all at once. I could have hurt her. I could have killed Gwen and her baby. Something inside me trembles.

She pats my back. "What's wrong?" She looks at me knowingly. "Oh. You lost your mother in Haven, didn't you?"

I close my eyes, and she sweeps her palm down my cheek. "If you ever need anything, you let me know, okay?"

I try to smile, but I'm drowning in guilt, and her words are too much like Mrs. Kalin's offer, when she tried to adopt me.

"If you ever have any questions," Gwen says, "or problems that, you know, you'd rather not discuss with your dad—"

"Thanks," I cut in and force another quivering smile. "I'd better get home."

"Okay." She sits with her hands on her belly again.

I wince. "Are you really okay?"

She stretches. "I actually feel better after getting some sleep. Thank you so much for helping me out and for keeping my secret." She winks. "Tonight, I'll remember to bring more food so I won't get so weak. It's not like me to pass out. This pregnancy..."

I open the door to the ladder.

"You're a good kid, Glory," she says. "And remember. Stop by to visit me anytime. I live in one of the cottages down by the cornfields."

"Thanks," I call back as I scramble down the ladder, feeling like I'm descending into shame.

Chapter Nine

As I'm rushing from the tower, a dried branch cracks under my foot, and the sound seems a hundred times louder than it probably is.

I stop and crouch. But there's no indication anyone heard. I continue.

"For someone sneaking around," a deep voice says, "you're making a lot of noise."

It's Burn, but where is he?

He steps from behind a thick pine bough. "What are you doing out here?" he asks.

Although his clothes are dark and they blend into the surroundings, I can't believe I didn't see him standing there. I glance around, wondering what else I might have missed. Did anyone see me going up to the guard tower? Did Burn?

I hold the hatchet in both hands. "Are you following me?"

"You didn't answer my question."

"Neither did you."

His voice is gruff, but as he steps into the light, I can see that his dark eyes are teasing.

"I snuck past the guard tower twice," I say. "This place is defenseless without the army. When is your FA unit due back from Fort Huron?"

"It depends on whether they stick to just talking."

"I thought you said they were negotiating? Do you think there might be a battle?"

Burn's thick eyebrows draw closer together. "Hard to say. That place was a military base BTD. Fighting is in their blood."

I nod. Those Fort Huron people are brutal. "My dad's not with that unit, is he?"

"Hector's not there."

Holding on to the ax head, I let the handle swing down to my side.

"Why were you down on the beach?" Burn asks.

"Why were *you* there?" I shoot back.

"Cal and I figured out how the Shredders came down the cliff."

I step forward. "Really? How?"

"Someone drove spikes into the rock and strung chains between them. It takes some upper body strength, but both Cal and I scaled the cliff easily once we found the route."

"Wow." It's amazing to me that the two of them worked together on this—on anything. "Shredders did that?"

"Or someone did it for them." He scratches his head. "Are you positive those Shredders came from Haven?"

"I saw flashes of the Hospital in that Shredder's mind. Images of people doing experiments."

"What kind of experiments?"

"Mrs. Kalin's trying to find the limits of the dust. She claims she's searching for a cure so that Normals can live safely Outside."

"You don't believe her."

"I don't think that's *all* she's doing. Especially if she's making Shredders." I rub the goose bumps on my arms. "What if she can plant thoughts in Shredders' minds? What if she sent them to find us?"

"That seems unlikely. No one knows where we are."

"With so many FA soldiers in Haven right now, she could have easily convinced someone to tell her where we are."

Burn's jaw tenses. "Then more Shredders could come. Or Comps."

"And with the FA gone, we're in trouble." My stomach churns. "I should have killed Mrs. Kalin when I had the chance."

"You couldn't have known what she'd do."

I wish he were right, but I knew Mrs. Kalin was capable of this. I knew she had to die; I just couldn't bring myself to do it. Not after what I did to my mother. I slump, shaking my head.

Burn pulls me to his chest. Engulfed in his embrace, I can no longer think clearly. I no longer want to. My ear presses against the thud-thud-thud of his heart, and I grab on to the collar of his coat as if letting go would mean drowning.

But instead, I'm drowning in the scent of Burn, in the heat, in the feelings I've tried so hard to suppress. It's been so long since I've been in his arms, and the memories tug inside me, waking pieces of myself that I've worked hard to ignore.

Burn draws a ragged breath, then pushes me back.

The cold air snakes between us, and I raise my gaze to join his. His expression's pained, almost angry. He drops his hands to his sides and puts more distance between us.

"It's okay, Burn, we can—"

"No. We can't. I won't. Never again."

I swallow hard, but my mouth is so dry I'm not sure I can respond. I wish I could believe that this is someone impersonating Burn again. Zina, a Deviant with that ability, fooled me once by pretending to be Burn. But I know it's not her now. I recognized his smell, the beat of his heart.

I know he doesn't want to hurt me, but does he realize that his pushing me away hurts, too?

Burn's quiet for a long time, looking down, avoiding my gaze. Unable to bear the silence, I part my lips but discover I have no words.

He drags a boot along the ground. "When you locked onto me with your Gift"—his voice is hoarse—"when I was the monster . . ." His words fade out and his face reddens. "You heard that Shredder's thoughts . . . Did you hear mine?"

I don't want to answer. I *didn't* hear his thoughts, but the things I *sensed* in his mind were angry, ugly, terrifying. I can't tell him that.

"When I'm locked onto you," I reply, "can you hear *my* thoughts? Because yesterday, during that battle, it felt like you understood me."

His eyes widen. "I *felt* you. You calmed me down." He squeezes his forehead. "And that day when we got out of Haven. Up on that balcony—"

"You felt me then, too?"

He nods. I suspected as much, but suddenly my heart's too big for my chest. Looking into his eyes, I don't think I've ever felt so understood, so connected to someone, so much *a part* of someone. I step toward him.

He steps back and looks down. "Do you know what I'm thinking right now?" He's clearly horrified at the thought.

"No." I grab his arm. "No. It's only when I'm using my Deviance, and even then I don't really *hear* you."

"But you heard those Shredders."

"It's not the same with you. I don't know why."

"Can you plant thoughts in my mind?"

"No!" I shudder. "I am *not* like Mrs. Kalin. I can't make you *think* anything. I only tried to calm you down."

He frowns.

"Burn, I—"

A bell sounds from the lookout tower. Three rings followed by a pause. The pattern repeats.

"More Shredders?" I ask.

A grin spreads on his face. "No. My FA unit is back."

Chapter Ten

STANDING AT THE HEAD OF THE RIDGE, I SCAN THE crowds as the FA unit files by. Burn took off to find Rolph, the FA Commander, and tell him about the Shredder attack. Awakened by the bell, others have rushed up the hill from Concord, and each reunion amps up my urge to see my father.

When I'm sure that the last of the unit has passed, I slump against a tree trunk. Burn already told me that Dad wasn't with his unit, but I hoped somehow he was wrong. Drake insists that he doesn't know which FA unit our dad is with, either, but I'm starting to suspect he's lying to me—again.

I stomp down the hill, looking for Drake. My little brother is going to tell me the truth if I have to latch onto his mind to hear it.

If Dad's with the units fighting in Haven, I can no longer keep to the sidelines. I have no idea what's happened inside the dome in the two weeks since the FA invaded. No one has come back. I wish I had some way to know—

I stop short, then turn to run back up the hill. I *do* know someone who might have been inside Haven since the FA invasion, and I need to get into that Shredder's mind to find out what else she knows.

• • •

As soon as I lift the door, I see the glow cast by the Shredder's eyes.

"Let me out!" she shrieks. I almost stumble on the stairs as I cover my ears. "You can't keep me trapped here."

I jump down the last steps and shine my torch in her direction. She covers her face and cowers in the corner, stretching to the far end of her rope. She's huddled on top of the pile of skeletons as if they don't bother her at all.

I direct the light downward. She's too far away for me to make eye contact, so I retrieve the key from the shelf and then slowly open the cage door. The metal bars are cold and the hinges creak. She doesn't move.

As I step into the cage, I try to calculate the exact length of her rope. I need to get close, but not too close.

She leaps up and rushes toward me, wielding a leg bone.

I stumble and fall, my hands slamming on the stone floor.

She stops before reaching the end of her rope. I scramble back on all fours, fighting to catch my breath. She could have attacked me with that bone. Broken it and stabbed me. Bitten me. Hurt me in countless horrible ways. Yet she didn't.

She extends the bone toward me like some kind of macabre offering. I recoil, then realize she's offering to help me stand.

I grab the bone and she pulls, stepping back as I rise to my feet.

"Thank—"

She charges forward again. "Dust. Need dust." I back out of her reach and press against the metal bars.

I forgot. The one thing she asked for. The thing I know she needs to survive, and I *forgot*. I will my heart to slow down. "You need to earn it. Tell me what you know."

Her eyes glow and her shoulders drop as the bone falls to the floor with a clatter.

I look into her eyes and we're connected in seconds. Her mind is like a tangled web. She's confused, upset, in pain.

"Who turned you into a Shredder?" I ask.

"Hospital," she says, then raises her hands to her temples. *Hurts. No. Stop*, I hear her think.

In her mind, I see flashes of rooms, of lab coats, of a mask filled with dust being strapped to her face. I sense a knife cutting her arm, a flame burning her foot, sandpaper being scraped over her skin. I tremble.

"Why did you come here?" I ask. "How did you find the settlement?"

President Kalin, she thinks. *Find the girl. Bring the girl. The President needs the girl.*

I gasp and blink, breaking the bond. *Am I the girl?* The Shredder cries out and crouches, cradling her head and rocking, moaning. Is that why she recognized me? Maybe she's not Arabella's mother.

"What does she want from me?" I ask.

She scrambles away. "Don't hurt me. Need dust. Please." Phosphorescent tears stream over her cheeks, and my chest tightens. It seems like it hurts them, when I listen to a Shredder's thoughts.

"Who told you where to find me?"

She bangs her head against the floor.

"Stop that!" I pull on her shoulder.

She swings one of the bones and strikes my leg. Throbbing pain shoots through me, and I back away.

I'm not going to get more out of her now. Not until I bring her some dust.

Her breaths are quick and loud, and her moan is rough, nearly rasping. Does she need water? No, Shredders don't drink. That's why their flesh resembles dried rat meat. That, and they revel in smearing their victims' blood on their own skin.

At least that's what we were taught in GT, but who knows if that's true, given all the lies.

I find a metal bowl on the shelves and wipe out the grime and rust with the hem of my shirt. I pour in most of the water I have left, then put the bowl on the floor inside the cage. Using a bone, I push the dish until I'm sure it's within her reach. The bowl scrapes on the stone, but she doesn't seem to notice. I close the cage door and replace the lock.

If she does drink the water, will she need something for waste? I find a plastic bucket, ignore the grime at the bottom, and set it inside the cage.

Scanning the shelves again, I spot something wrapped in thick plastic on the very top shelf. I reach up on my toes to take it down. It's a book.

I tuck it into my jacket, then head up the stairs.

• • •

"What's that?" Drake asks, and I snap the book shut.

I slide it under my blanket. I took a long nap when I got back, and since then I've been sitting on my bed reading.

"Are you feeling better?" Jayma asks, and I nod.

Drake's eyes open wide. "Is that from the ruins? Did you go back there without me?"

He looks hurt. I pull out the book. "It's a journal kept by a boy who was trapped down there. One of those who died."

"A boy?" Jayma gasps and sits on the bed next to me. "Who?"

"His name was Jason and he was our age."

"What happened to those people? How long were they there? Who trapped them?"

Her cheeks drain of color and she grabs my hand, waiting expectantly. Drake, on the other hand, stands with his legs wide, arms crossed, eyes accusing.

"You were going to show us the journal, right?" Jayma looks at my brother. "She wasn't going to keep it a secret."

I keep a firm hold on the book. "You're the one keeping secrets, Drake."

"What?" He tips up his chin.

"Where's Dad?"

His shoulders snap back. "I told you. I don't know."

I narrow my eyes. "I don't believe you. And it's not like you've never lied to me before."

He looks down and his shoulders slump slightly. That was a low blow. I pat the bed on my other side. "Sit. We can read the rest together." Later, when Jayma's not here, I'll press him more about Dad.

He sits beside me, and I open the book not far from the end. The writing is messy and hard to make out in spots.

"A: 4, D: 17," I read aloud. "I think that means four alive and seventeen dead. And these markings"—I point to the corner of the page—"I'm pretty sure they mean that he wrote this 94 days after they ran out of food and 417 days after the cellar door was blocked."

"Cellar?" Drake asks.

"That's what the room in the ground is called," I tell him.

Jayma slides closer to me, and I can feel her tremble as I continue to read: "Sarah died in her sleep last night. We put her with the others and the smell . . ."

"Can you imagine?" Drake cringes.

I nod, then continue: "I sit at the top of the stairs most of the time now, pushing, yelling, fighting for a breath of fresh air, but the cracks are too small. When the wind blows, or there's an earthquake, dust comes in and Kevin tries to pull me down off the stairs. But what's worse? Breathing a little of the dust, or the stench of our dead families and friends?"

I turn to Jayma and she's even whiter now. "Are you okay?"

She nods and rubs her shoulder where she was shot.

Drake grabs for the book. "Who locked them in? Who put the rocks on the door?"

"It's probably faster if I tell you instead of reading. Okay?"

He nods, and Jayma's grip on my hand tightens.

"Ouch." My fingers are nearly crushed.

"Sorry." She releases my hand. "I forgot my strength."

"No worries." I shake out my fingers. "Nothing's broken."

I back up on the bed, lean against the wall, and cross my legs. Jayma and Drake turn sideways to face me.

"There were five families in there at first," I tell them. "When the dust clouds came, they didn't know what was going on and could only guess, because none of their communication devices worked anymore. They were called cell phones. A lot of other people headed for what they called 'the city' to get news, but these five families decided it would be safer to stay where they were. So they went to the cellar to wait out the dust storms. The adults took turns guarding the door from the outside: two at a time.

"Above ground, the air was clogged with dust, and all they had were paper masks. The first to die was one of the dads." My guts twist. "His mask tore. Jason was down in the cellar, so he could only describe what he heard: the shouting and screaming, the sounds of a fight, and what little his dad told him afterward. But it's clear that the first man to die choked on the dust and almost killed Jason's dad, trying to take his mask."

"That's terrible," Jayma says. "But at least he didn't turn into a Shredder."

I go on. "When Jason's dad came down that day, he was different. He was sullen and would barely talk about what had happened to his friend. In one journal entry, Jason says he saw his father dragging a knife over his arms, like he was trying to cut himself. Jason figured the knife was dull, but when he checked the next day, it was razor sharp. It was like his dad couldn't be cut."

"A Deviant," Drake says, and I nod.

"Jason was interested in science, and he guessed that something in the dust flipped a switch in his dad's DNA. Something had activated a dormant gene that gave him this strange new ability. But his dad wouldn't talk about it."

My voice is hoarse, and Drake hands me the water from the shelf near my bed.

"Jason's theory's not that different from what we learned in GT," he says.

As I gulp, the cool liquid spreads through me. I hand the cup back to Drake. "There are pages and pages of entries—I haven't read them all yet—but at some point, one of the moms got dust madness. One day, when she was on guard duty with her husband, she nearly killed him. She would have except that Jason's dad shot her."

"Jason saw that with his own eyes," I tell them. "And then the man attacked Jason's dad for killing his wife, but when he tried to stab Jason's dad, they all learned the truth about his super-tough skin."

"What did they do?" Jayma whispers. Drake reaches across me to take her hand.

"Sounds like they fought about it. A lot. Trying to figure out what it meant."

"Who put the rocks on the door?" Drake asks.

"Jason's dad."

"Really?" Jayma gasps. "He trapped them? All those people? His own son?"

I shift on the bed. "He figured that, since he'd already been changed by the dust, he was the safest outside. But no one trusted him anymore—not even his wife—so he decided to live above ground from then on."

"All by himself?" Jayma asks, and I nod.

"But why the stones?" Drake presses.

"He didn't do it at first. In fact, he stayed away and was rarely spotted. Then one day, between guard shifts, when there was no one else up top, he moved the rocks onto the door. Everyone screamed and tried to push up, but he called down to them that he was doing it to keep them safe. That he'd take all the guard shifts from then on and would let them know when the danger passed. Jason talked to his dad through the door every day for weeks. But over time, his dad's voice changed. And then one day, he never came back."

"Dust madness," Jayma says.

"Sounds like it. They banged on the door. They shouted. But the door never opened again."

"Not until we opened it," Drake says.

"Why did his dad leave?" Jayma asks.

"He was afraid that he'd kill them," Drake replies.

"Why do you think that?" I ask.

"Jason's dad was the one who saw the other man go crazy, right?" Drake clears his throat. "And if he was up top a lot, I'll bet he saw Shredders. He was afraid that he'd change. He was afraid that if he didn't leave, he'd move the rocks and attack his friends and family."

Realization hits me. "He trapped them. He killed them. But he did it hoping to save them."

The cabin door opens. "Here you are!" Cal's cheery voice is so out of place, it's like he arrived from another planet. "Come on! We're going to be late." His bruises are the only evidence, on the four of us, of yesterday's battle.

I slide forward to stand, and my legs feel shaky. I really need some sleep. "Late for what?"

"For the banquet," Cal says. "There's a feast planned. To celebrate the return of the FA unit and the treaty with Fort Huron."

Still sitting on the bed, Jayma leans forward, her head in her hands. Drake gets up and crouches in front of her. "A party sounds like fun."

She lets him pull her to her feet, and they walk toward the door.

"Come with us, Glory," Drake says.

I sit back down on the bed. "You guys go ahead." I feel compelled to read the rest. I want to read every word Jason wrote.

Drake comes back to sit next to me. "If you don't go, neither will I."

"No." I pat his leg. "You go. Have fun. I'll talk to you later."

He puts his arm around my shoulders. "You're my sister. We're family. And we need to stick together. I see that more than ever now."

My brother looks so serious, and my love for him floods through me. He's right. Nothing good will come of my sitting here alone.

"Okay, let's go."

Chapter Eleven

"LET'S DANCE!" JAYMA GRABS MY HAND. ALL AROUND us, people are dancing and shouting and laughing. A few of the women are wearing dresses dyed cheerful colors, and a small part of me wishes I still had that dress that Mrs. Kalin bought me—the only pretty thing I've ever owned.

Music fills the Assembly Hall from the players gathered on a raised platform. It's not like we never heard music inside Haven, but it was always quiet, slow, gentle, not this raucous sound coming from violins they call fiddles, and guitars, and drums fashioned from barrels and metal pots.

"With everything going on, why is everyone so happy?" I ask.

"It's a celebration." Jayma smiles as if no other explanation is necessary.

An alliance with Fort Huron doesn't sound worth celebrating to me. Then again, I've never told Jayma what Burn and I went through in that place.

"But what if a whole army of Shredders or Comps comes tonight?" I say.

"Why would *Comps* come?" Jayma's brow furrows. "If Management takes over Concord, will they expunge the Deviants?"

"No. That won't happen. And no one's going to kick us out of Concord." I feel bad. There's no reason to ruin her night. "And now that some of the FA is back, they can defend us. I'm worrying for no reason. Tonight is a party."

"That's more like it." She grins. "And don't forget—I'm super strong now." She gives me a stern look. "If you don't cooperate, I can *make* you dance."

"Yes, ma'am." I let her drag me a few feet toward Drake and Cal, who are deep in conversation.

Cal misses his younger brother, and with Dad away, it's nice to think that Cal might provide a big-brother figure. Drake needs that, especially after being so isolated for those years when his legs didn't work.

They see us coming. My brother bounds over and takes Jayma's hand.

"Drake, can I talk to you for a sec?" I ask him.

"Now?" He flits his eyes toward Jayma and then stares at me, like I can't take a hint.

I can, but this is more important than his crush on my friend. Sighing, he walks with me to an empty corner.

"You never answered before." I step closer. "Do you know where Dad is?"

Drake's body stiffens. "I told you. He's on a mission."

"In Haven?"

He shakes his head.

"Then where?"

"I'm not sure." He looks away.

"You know more than you're saying." I'm glad my dad's not in Haven, but he could be lost or hurt. "What if he's captured by Shredders?"

"You worry too much." Drake squeezes my arm. He looks at me as if he's the older sibling, not the other way around. "Dad can take care of himself."

"Where do you think he might be?"

"I don't know, okay?" Drake snaps. "He goes off sometimes. He could be anywhere. But he always comes back."

"He's done this before?"

Drake walks away and pulls Jayma out onto the dance floor. I follow. "Why did you let Dad leave?"

Drake ignores me. Copying the other couples, he clasps Jayma's hand and holds it high, placing his other hand at her waist.

"I don't know how to dance," she says, her cheeks pink.

"Don't worry." Drake grins. "I'll teach you. It's easy." Like he knows any more than we do. He pulls her closer, and she laughs as he spins her around to the beat of the music.

Cal steps up beside me and leans in. "Mademoiselle, may I have this dance?" His blue eyes catch the light from the lanterns hung in the room's center.

"You don't know how to dance," I say, but his smile is infectious.

"How do you know?" he asks. "Maybe you're not the only one who's been keeping secrets."

I look down.

"That was a joke." He rubs my arm. "I shouldn't have said that. I get why you couldn't tell me you were a Deviant. Really."

I raise my gaze to meet his. "When did you learn to dance?"

"It doesn't look that hard. Come on." He grabs my hand and tugs me forward, holding me the same way Drake's holding Jayma. He watches the others for a moment. "Ready?"

"As I'll ever be."

He steps forward—onto my foot. "Sorry." He steps back and looks down at me sheepishly. "Are you okay?"

I nod and grin so he won't feel bad.

"Maybe this won't be quite as easy as I thought." One of his eyebrows rises.

"Let's try again." I slide my fingers across his shoulder. "Dancing can't be more complicated than our hand-to-hand combat classes in COT."

"Good point. And this looks like more fun." Looking down, he steps forward again. I step forward at the same time and our heads knock together.

"Ouch." He takes his hand from my waist and strokes my cheek. "I'm sorry. I'm not very good at this." He looks so disappointed in himself.

"You're doing great. We'll get the hang of it." We look over at an adult couple who are nearly galloping around the room in tandem, weaving in and out of the others.

"How do they *do* that?" Cal grips my waist more tightly, then tips his head to the side. "This way first, okay? Step-hop-step. Then the other way."

He studies the other dancers, obviously counting in his head, memorizing the moves. The festive lanterns cast highlights in his blond hair, and I look up at the face that starred in all my best dreams—until I met Burn.

I look down again.

I wish this could be easier. I wish that I felt nothing around Cal or nothing around Burn, so that my way forward would be clear. But when I think about either of them, all I ever feel is confused.

Without my old stack of secrets between us, there's nothing left keeping Cal and me apart. Nothing keeping me from being his girlfriend again. And without the formality of Haven's Human Resources Department stamping our union as valid, the idea of committing to Cal feels more real, more substantial.

Being around Cal is so comfortable. But I can't be with him just because it's easy. Or worse, because Burn doesn't want me.

I need a sign to tell me what to do.

"This way!" Cal leans toward our clasped hands. "Step-hop-step."

As he repeats the words, we do them in one direction, then awkwardly in the other.

Eventually, we fall into a rhythm. Back and forth, back and forth. Cal has a serious, concentrated expression, and I try to hide my smile as he repeatedly mouths, "Step-hop-step," over and over.

The dance starts to feel more natural, and we vary our steps. Relaxing, I let his strength guide me, and my stress and anxiety flow away. He looks into my eyes. Is this a sign that I'm meant to be with Cal?

All our obstacles are gone. We work well together. Why am I looking for trouble?

We bump into another couple. All four of us say sorry at once and laugh.

I realize that Cal and I have moved around the hall to the far side. The music stops, but Cal doesn't let me go. The band plays another song, this one slower. Many of the couples move closer together, their bodies touching as they dance. Cal pulls me toward him until our hips nearly touch, then he lowers his head toward mine.

He's going to kiss me.

I turn my head and rest my cheek on his shoulder.

He begins to sway, taking small steps, and his hand brushes over my back. He spins us and pulls me even closer. "Oh, Glory." His lips are close to my ear. "I've missed this."

"Missed it?" I raise my head and laugh. "We've never danced before." But I know what he means. I look past Cal.

And see Burn.

He's leaning against the wall near the door, one leg bent, arms across his chest.

Watching me.

Our eyes meet and it's like the electric jolt from a Shocker tag.

The air vanishes from my lungs, and the rest of the people in the room fade into the background. Even Cal's arms around me feel fuzzy, not quite real. The only thing in focus, the only thing solid, is Burn. The only thing real and alive in the room is the connection between us. The only thing tangible is the heat in his eyes.

Burn might deny that it's there. He might claim to feel nothing. But I see the truth in his eyes.

He looks down, but I know what I saw, what I felt. My heart and lungs expand to fill my chest. What Burn and I have isn't easy or comfortable, but we can't give up—not without trying. There's got to be a way.

I finally have a sign. A sign from myself. And that sign is so clear.

Here I am, relaxed, having fun in Cal's arms, and I know what I want, who I want, who I need.

I've always loved Cal. I probably always will. But I want Burn.

Cal spins me. Another couple gets in the way, and I lose sight of Burn. I push away from Cal.

"What's wrong," he asks.

"The song's over." My voice is raspy.

"No it's not." He looks at me quizzically.

I glance around, hoping to see where Burn went.

I spot him talking to a man with very short hair and dressed in the military garb of Fort Huron. Burn's frowning and I can't see the man's face, but the conversation doesn't look friendly.

"Can you hear me?" Cal rests his hands on my shoulders. "What's going on?"

I snap my gaze back to him with no idea what he just asked.

I hear a shout and look past Cal again. He turns to see what drew my attention.

"Oh." His shoulders slump.

The man pushes Burn, hard. Burn doesn't fight back. The music changes to a faster tune. Couples dance around the room, smiling, seemingly oblivious to what's going on in the shadows.

Burn walks out the door and the man follows. This does not look good.

I run forward, but Cal grabs my arm. "You should stay out of this."

I pull away and race out of the building, vaguely aware that Cal's following. Outside, Burn is scowling at the other man, whose back is to us.

"You're a monster!" the man yells. "No one is safe around you. We'll be better off once you're dead." He shoves Burn.

Burn doesn't react. The man shoves him again, and anger builds on Burn's face.

"Hey!" I shout. "Leave him alone!" Burn's eyes rise to meet mine and he shakes his head, signaling me to stop.

The man spins. "And you! You little slut. I saw you with that blond kid on the dance floor." He looks back to Burn as if hoping to get a reaction.

"Listen now." Cal walks toward the man with his hands held up in surrender. "Let's calm down and talk like civilized—"

"Civilized?" the man shouts. "How can any of you here claim to be civilized when monsters like him run free?" He slams the heel of his hand into Burn's collarbone.

Burn's jaw line is rigid, his eyes narrowed, and I can tell he's fighting to contain his anger. If he lets it loose, he'll prove this man's point.

Cal leans down close to my ear. "Let's go for help."

Keeping my eyes on Burn and the man, I shake my head. Cal's jaw twitches. "Okay, but stay back. Don't get involved." I don't answer, but I stay still as Cal goes inside.

The man's gaze darts between Burn and me. He's full of hate, but he's also panicking, and that's never a good combination.

Then, in an instant, the man transforms. Into Zina. She smirks as the moonlight bounces off her silver hair.

I charge forward. "Murderer! Because of you, Cal's brother is dead!"

Burn puts up an arm, and I stop a few feet from them. "She's not worth it," he says.

"Who are *you*, either of you, to call *me* a murderer?" Zina asks.

She waits for a reaction. I don't give her one.

"Sabotaging that scaffolding in the Hub got Management's attention," Zina goes on. "That was my mission. Disruption. Killing your little friend was inconsequential."

"Inconsequential?" Fists form at my sides.

"What I did helped our cause," Zina says. "I was completely under control. I knew what I was doing. My actions were strategic and helped the FA. Whereas he"—she points at Burn—"went into a rage and killed Andreas, my *brother*, in cold blood. Then to make it worse, everyone let it slide." She's talking about events that happened more than three years ago—the day my dad was expunged.

"Burn was a kid then," I say. "You're an adult. And you're a coward. If you're so proud about causing the accident that killed Scout, why did you do it disguised as Burn?" *Where is Cal?* I wonder. I hope he brings Rolph. I still don't believe Rolph ever condoned Zina's actions. I want to hear him say it.

"Get lost, little girl." Zina transforms into my father, her silver hair shortening and turning dark brown, her curvy feminine body converting into Dad's lean, ropey one, her caramel skin becoming leathered. The shadow of a beard muddies her chin, and she even mimics his mannerisms, drumming her fingers on her thigh.

I stagger back.

She turns back into herself. "Scat. Monster boy and I have a score to settle."

"*You and I* have a score to settle!" I step up to join Burn.

"You'd best put a leash on her," Zina snarls at Burn. "Or maybe you don't have any influence on her anymore. I saw her rubbing up against that other kid. Looks to me like you've been replaced."

Neither of us respond, but I can see the vein over Burn's temple pulsing.

"Come on, monster boy. Come at me like you did Andreas. Show me what you've got."

"You're seeing it." Burn's voice is calm.

"What's it going to take for you to show your true colors?" Zina taunts. "Once everyone sees what you *really* are, they'll give me a medal for putting a bullet in your head." She pats a pistol at her side.

Burn turns to leave, and I'm so proud of him. Proud that he stayed in control.

I start to follow, but Zina grabs me and pushes me up against the wall.

"Maybe I took the wrong approach," she says. She transforms into Thor, the bully from my COT class. Her body expands to his wide girth and her breath is putrid. I almost choke as I bring up my knee to connect between her legs. She doubles over.

"I knew one of you would attack me," Zina croaks as she transforms back. "But I expected the other one." She falls to the ground just as Cal arrives with three other men.

Burn takes off, running so fast he's out of sight within seconds.

"Are you hurt?" Cal slides his arm over my shoulders as the other men head toward Zina.

"No." I look toward the lake. "I need to go check on—"

"Burn," Cal finishes for me. "Yes. Of course. Go. Find him." The hurt on his face is obvious, but I can't worry about that right now.

I need to make sure Burn doesn't hurt anyone—or himself.

Chapter Twelve

I RUN DOWN TO THE BOULDER WHERE I KNOW BURN sometimes sits to look out at the lake. It's my favorite place in Concord, too. It's where we first kissed.

He's not there.

The moon reflects off the quiet ripples that lap against the rocks. The iridescent highlights on the lake make me think of the Shredder I've got captive. I planned to wait until tomorrow morning to visit her again, but maybe Burn's leaving the dance was a blessing in disguise. If I go now, I won't be missed. Everyone will assume I'm with Burn.

Can I get there without going past the lookout towers? I head down the beach, climb over the rock wall, then walk along the base of the cliff until I find the chains that the Shredders used to come down. If I'm right, this should cut the distance to the ruins in half.

Bracing my feet on the rock face, I climb hand over hand until I reach the top of the cliff. The way looks clear, so I head for the shelter of the trees and descend the other side of the ridge. The slope is steep and the going tricky, but once I reach the bottom, it doesn't take long to find one of Drake's marked trees, and I speed toward my destination.

Halfway there, I stop. *Dust.* I promised.

I search along the cracks and crevices of the rocky landscape, hoping for a place where some dust from the last windstorm might have settled. Finally, my fingers discover a mini-cave of sorts in between two rocks. It's full of dust. Cupfuls. I wrap as much as I can in a piece of cloth and stash it in my pocket.

The forest is dark and quiet, and the pine trees reach high, punctuating the landscape like guards.

A twig snaps.

I stop and spin around but don't see anyone. I wait, but there's nothing. The sound must have been my imagination or maybe an animal. I think of that creature I killed last night. There might be other Shredder-animals around. I need to be careful.

At the edge of the woods, the ruins rise in the distance, dark and ominous. The moon glows through the clouds, but it only makes me feel more exposed.

Clouds frightened me the first time I saw them. After living my first sixteen years under a dome, the only reference I had for clouds was that they spread the dust. But when I first got out of Haven, Dad told me that the clouds sometimes bring rain, although they haven't for years. Apparently rain is water that falls from the sky. When it comes, it's good because we don't need to use water from the lake to irrigate the crops.

I open the cellar door. On the third step, I retrieve the crank torch I've had stashed in my pocket since I took the Shredder. After winding it, I shine it around the space before going farther.

The light strikes the Shredder. Scrambling back in the cage, she wails. I want to cover my ears.

"Calm down," I tell her. "It's just me. I'm not going to hurt you."

Her eyes glow and her wails turn to whimpers. She rushes to the end of her rope and strains against it. "Dust. Please. I need dust." Her voice is so hoarse.

"What's your name?" I ask.

"Dust."

"Did you drink any of the water I left?"

"Water?" she asks as if she's trying to remember the word.

"It's right here." I reach through the bars and pick up the bowl. It's still full. "Take a sip. You'll feel better."

With her bound hands outstretched, she approaches, and I resist the urge to drop the water and back away. My hand trembles as her fingers brush mine. It's like she's on fire—both softer and warmer than I expected.

I remind myself that—if I'm right—not long ago I talked to this woman about saving her daughter. Her humanity might still be inside her.

Waiting, I watch as she stares at the bowl, sloshing the water back and forth. A few drops spill and strike her fingers. She jumps. Then slowly, she draws the bowl toward her face until it's right at her lips. She tips some liquid into her mouth—and chokes. I leap to the side as she spits it out.

She smacks her tongue against her lips and sucks on the sides of her cheeks. Lifting the bowl again, she tips it more carefully and takes a smaller sip. Relief and delight flash across her face. "Good."

"Drink more." I grab on to the bars separating us. "But slowly."

She takes another sip and the phosphorescence in her eyes fades, a sign that she's calming down, perhaps even starting to trust me.

"What's your name?" I ask again. The more I can remind her of her life, before she became a Shredder, the greater my chances of getting through to her. I hope.

Her eyes narrow, then widen as something like a smile spreads on her cracked lips. "Caroline."

My heart lifts. "Caroline. That's your name? How do you feel? Do you remember what happened to you? Do you remember being in the Hospital?"

Wailing again, she drops the bowl and backs away from me. "No. No. No." Her head shakes from side to side so violently I'm afraid she'll break her neck. Her eyes glow.

I raise my hands toward her. "Don't worry. I'm not from the Hospital. I'll never let them hurt you again. I'm here to help you. Do you remember when I helped Arabella?"

"Arabella's dead. My beautiful baby is dead." Phosphorescent tears spill over her red cheeks. She tucks down into a ball and turns to face the back corner of the cage. "Need dust." She slams her forehead repeatedly against the stone wall.

"Stop it!" I shake the bars. "Don't hurt yourself. *Please.*"

"Hurts." She slumps down onto her side, and I wonder if she's knocked herself unconscious.

After a few moments, I open the lock. Caroline's still breathing—her rib cage rising and falling—but she's injured. I've confirmed her identity and know she was fully human not much more than a month ago.

Like it or not, it's time to make good on my promise. She needs dust.

I crouch down beside her and rest my hand on her shoulder, shocked again by the heat. "Caroline?"

She doesn't move or open her eyes. Her forehead shines where it struck the wall. There's a gash but little blood, confirming that, in spite of everything, she's still a Shredder, still so dehydrated by the dust that her blood is thick like tar.

I pull out the cloth, place a tiny amount of the dust in my cupped palm—just a few grains—and hold it near her mouth. Her wheezing breaths pull the dust from my hand.

She bolts upright.

I fall back, the dust-filled cloth still in my other hand. I quickly stash it in my pocket.

"Better." Her eyes glow, then fade. "Thank you," she says. "More. I need more."

She looks up at me with pleading eyes that are clearer and more focused than I've yet seen them. It might be wishful thinking, but she seems more like the woman I met back in Haven.

"You've had enough." I keep my distance, moving outside the metal cage.

"What do you know about it?" Her tone isn't angry. She's asking an honest question.

"Too much dust is dangerous," I answer with more authority than I feel. "You've haven't had any for nearly two days." Maybe longer. "You need to take it slow."

She slumps down to sit.

"Can you tell me why you came here?" I ask. "How did you find the way?"

She rubs the back of her hand on her forehead and winces as the rope scrapes over the gash there. "I was picked," she says. "Chosen."

I stiffen. "Who told you that you were chosen?"

"She did. The President. She chose us for this mission."

I grab the bars of the cage. "What was the mission?"

"To find you." Her eyes glow. "To bring you back."

My muscles tense, but I don't move away. "Why?"

Caroline's eyebrows draw together. "I don't know." She pulls her arms forward. The rope pulls taut, and she rubs the binding. "The rope's cutting me." Her speech is more coherent now, gentler, less like a Shredder's.

"Can you remember your life before—before she changed you?"

Caroline looks up at me and nods slowly. "I had a daughter, a husband, a work placement in Haven."

"What was your placement?"

"Pre-GT child care."

This woman took care of babies and toddlers, the kids too young for General Training. Just months ago, she was kind and patient and loving—she'd *have* to be in that job. Is it possible that version of her still exists somewhere inside?

And, if Mrs. Kalin is turning Deviants into Shredders, is it possible they can change back?

"What happened?" I ask her. "Why did Mrs. Kalin choose you?"

"I went to the Compliance Department," she says, "to report my daughter missing." She rakes her fingers through her matted hair. "You said you'd take my Arabella to safety, but I worried what might happen to my husband and me if we didn't report her missing."

"That was smart."

Her head snaps up toward me. "Stupidest thing I've ever done. Compliance told me she was dead. They showed me footage of my Arabella and a man being torn apart by Shredders." She gags. "It was horrible. I screamed. They grabbed me. I fought back and my eyes started to glow." She looks straight at me. "That's when *she* came into the room."

"Mrs. Kalin?"

Caroline steps away from me, her eyes widening. "President Kalin! You're her daughter!"

"No I'm not. She says that I am, but it's not true. My mother's dead." My chest tightens. "I know who Mrs. Kalin really is. She's evil. She's a Deviant, like us, but she thinks she's better than everyone else—Chosen." *And she thinks I am, too.* "Mrs. Kalin can plant thoughts in other people's minds."

"Really?" Caroline struggles to her feet and pulls forward as I move out of reach. Hitting the end of the rope, she yelps in pain.

Right now, it's hard to believe Caroline's a Shredder. She's coherent and sane and doesn't seem bloodthirsty or cruel. In fact, she's showing almost no signs of dust madness. Can I trust her enough to loosen her bindings?

She sits again. I step toward her, trying not to show fear. When I reach her, she still hasn't moved, and I crouch down and stare into her eyes. I'd like to hear her thoughts again. I blink. I don't want to hurt her. Not if I don't have to.

"I'm sorry for keeping you captive." I touch her hands. "But I need to know more about what Mrs. Kalin is doing."

"I didn't ask for this." She shakes her head. "I'm not a killer, but Kalin forced dust on me. She made me *want* to kill. She made me *enjoy* hurting others." She pounds her fists on her lap.

"You're safe now. And I'm sorry about Arabella. I really did try to save her."

She nods, and her shoulders rise and fall as she takes deep breaths.

"Here." I reach for her hands. "I'll loosen your ropes."

"Thank you." Her voice is clearer, less scratchy.

The knots are tight, and it takes several minutes to get her hands free. I'd been hoping only to loosen them to decrease the chafing, but she's so patient as I work, and it seems beyond cruel to leave her tied up. I untie her legs, too.

After reading that journal and knowing how and why people died here, it's no comfort to claim that I'm holding her captive for her own good. And if I'm holding her prisoner, who am I to be disgusted by Shredders, or horrified by Mrs. Kalin trapping people in the Hospital?

I carefully pull the last of the rope from her ankles. "Are you hungry?"

"No."

"Are you sure? The water made you feel better, right? And with less dust in your system, you might get hunger pangs again. You need food."

She stares at my pocket and rubs her raw wrists. "Can I have more?"

I put my hand on the bundle in my pocket. "I thought you hated Mrs. Kalin for making you take it."

"I just want one tiny breathful." Her voice breaks. "It hurts so much." She rubs her wrists again. "Please."

I pull out the cloth and instantly wish I were sitting farther away. But I don't want to crush whatever trust we've forged, so I tip a small amount of the dust into my palm. Closing the cloth as best I can with one hand, I stuff it back into my pocket.

Rising up onto my knees, I reach my palm toward her. She leans and inhales through her mouth, pulling the dust in a cloud from my hand.

Her eyes flash with light and she slams back against the bars, breathing too heavily, too quickly. "More," she rasps.

"No." Standing, I put my hand in my pocket to protect the bundle of dust as I back toward the door of the cage. "That's enough. I'll come again. I promise."

She leaps to her feet and tackles me.

My head smashes against the floor and pain radiates through my skull. My vision goes fuzzy. I can barely breathe.

Caroline claws at my arm, my hand, her nails digging in deeply. I let go of the cloth so I can use both hands to trap her neck in a choke hold, but it's like the fresh lungful of dust turned her from a weakling to a powerhouse. She's not much bigger than I am, but it doesn't matter. She has the better of me. And she's grabbed the dust from my pocket.

She buries her face in the cloth and draws long breaths.

"Caroline! Stop!" I grab the rope and try to figure out a way to tie her again. If only she'd look me in the eyes I could subdue her, but she doesn't look up. Not until she's emptied the cloth. Her shriek fills the room and my head.

She lunges.

I spin and kick her, landing a blow to her midsection, but it doesn't faze her. Her ragged fingernails reach forward. I duck, hoping to flip her over me, but one of her hands catches my face and rakes down my cheek. I falter and miss the chance to take advantage.

She wraps her arms around my waist, lifts me up, and throws me sideways against the bars. I drop to the floor. My wrists scream in pain as they take the weight of my fall, but I stand, ready to attack.

Her eyes glowing, she stares at something behind me.

I look over my shoulder—and see Burn.

Chapter Thirteen

BURN GRABS CAROLINE, TRAPPING HER ARMS AGAINST her body.

"Don't kill her," I say.

He frowns. "Get the rope."

I secure her ankles. She kicks, but I dodge, and she misses my face by an inch.

Burn leans toward her ear. "Try that again, I'll break your neck."

I quickly wrap the rope around her lower legs, tying off the knot, and Burn forces her hands forward so I can bind her wrists. She's snarling, snapping, and shows no hint of the sane woman I was speaking to earlier. Once her hands are tied, he drops her feet.

She tries to walk but topples forward. I grab her to keep her from crashing. She rewards me by biting my shoulder.

Burn grabs her, forces her to sit against the bars of the cage, and binds her there, wrapping the end of the rope around her chest and through the bars. She twists and turns but can't move.

Veins pop out on Burn's forehead. I put my hand on his arm, and he spins toward me sharply.

"Calm down," I say. "It's okay."

"I am calm," he says gruffly. "You don't need to be frightened. Not of me. Not right now."

"I'm not afraid of you." I draw my hand up to the bite on my shoulder. It's going to bruise, but I don't think she broke the skin.

"What's going on here?" he asks.

"I—she had too much dust. It's my fault. We were having a perfectly normal conversation just minutes ago."

"I heard." He steps out from the metal cage and clangs the door shut. "How do you keep her from getting out?"

I hand him the lock.

"That's it?" He looks at the device as if it's easy to break.

"She's tied up." I lift my chin. "And I store the key over there." I nod to the shelves.

He grunts. "It wasn't tied up when I got here."

"I . . . That was a mistake."

"No kidding." He glances back at Caroline who's still wailing and straining against her bindings, her eyes casting an eerie glow, illuminating the skeletons.

"Let's get out of here." He gestures toward the stairs. "This place gives me the creeps."

Tied the way she is, Caroline can't get to what's left of her water, but she's so mad on dust that I doubt she'll be wanting any soon. I'll come back tomorrow night or the next day, once she's less dangerous. Once she's back to the way she was when I got here today.

After storing the key, I start up the stairs. Burn follows, and I'm acutely aware of his presence behind me as we climb.

The sky's dotted with stars, but the ground's dry, so I assume the clouds blew away without dropping any water. In the shadows, Burn's an imposing silhouette, and I step forward, hoping to see his eyes, but he turns and strides toward one of the walls.

"What were you thinking?" His voice is low but booming.

I open my mouth to respond but don't get the opportunity.

"You're holding a Shredder prisoner?" He raises his hands to his head, then drops them. "Do you know how stupid that is?"

"It's not stupid. I have questions, and—"

"You think that *thing* has answers?" He looks at me. "Even if you get it to talk coherently, Shredders can't be trusted."

"*It* is a *she*," I say, "and she already *has* talked to me coherently. When she was off the dust, she was different."

"Different?" The word drips with skepticism. He steps forward, and the moonlight catches his face as he rolls his eyes. "Once a Shredder, always a Shredder. There's no 'different' for Shredders."

"How do you know?" I ask. "How does anyone know? Mrs. Kalin turned that woman—her name is Caroline, by the way—Mrs. Kalin made her into a Shredder. By force. She forced her to breathe dust through a mask in a lab. How can you possibly know what will happen if I can get her to stop breathing dust? If Shredders can be made, how do we know they can't be un-made?"

Burn folds his arms over his chest. "And what do you expect to learn from her?"

"What Mrs. Kalin is doing. How the Shredders found us. Whether more will come. Why they came in the first place."

To bring you back, is what she said, but I can't tell Burn that. Not if I want Caroline to live.

"You think she knows any of that?" He raises an eyebrow. "Even if she's coherent, she's just a pawn. She doesn't know anything useful."

"But what if I can help her? What if I can cure her?"

"*Cure* her?"

"How can you be sure it's not possible? I'd think you of all people—"

"Why me?" He frowns.

"Because you want better control over your Deviance. Because you don't want to hurt people. And because . . ." I chew on my lip.

"Yes? What else?"

"Because of where you were born." I put my hand on his arm, softly, like touching him might trip a wire. "You told me that you were born in a Shredder camp."

He doesn't respond, doesn't move. I'm not sure if he's breathing.

"This is about what Zina said, isn't it?" he whispers. "She told you I was a Shredder."

"Zina said a lot of crazy things when she was pretending to be you. Not to mention tonight. Burn, I know you're not a Shredder." *He* told me about the Shredder camp. Has he forgotten?

He looks toward the sky.

Suddenly cold, I wrap my arms around myself. I stare up at him for what feels like ages, but he doesn't say a thing and won't look me in the eyes. As uncomfortable as the subject is, I need him to understand the potential I see in Caroline. "Burn, if you were born in a Shredder camp, then your parents—"

He holds up his hand to stop me. He breathes like he's been holding his breath for days and his lungs are making up for lost time. It's clear that he doesn't want to talk about this, and I get that. I've got my fair share of parental issues.

"Burn." I rest my hand on his arm again. "The fact that you're *not* a Shredder, that you're *not* addicted to the dust . . . doesn't that prove that it's possible to recover from dust madness?"

He stands very still, and the heat from his arm spreads from my hand through my whole body. His face is hard and impenetrable, his emotions shrouded. I want to know what he's thinking, what he's feeling.

I wish I could help him.

I was thirteen when I killed my mom, and I lost my memories of that day. Burn was just a baby when he was in the Shredder camp. He probably doesn't remember his parents.

He leans against the wall, and unless it's a trick of the moonlight, his eyes are glassy. My eyes fill with tears, too, and I move a few inches closer, feeling the pull between our bodies, the magnetic connection I always feel around him.

But then he bolts away, leaping over a six-foot wall to leave the ruins. By the time I'm outside, he's at the edge of the woods.

"Burn, wait!" I race after him.

He stops but doesn't turn back.

"Please." I slow down as I approach.

His shoulders slump. "I don't have parents. And I was *never* a Shredder."

My fingers ache to make contact. I slide my hand onto his back and his muscles react. "I never said that *you* were a Shredder." I walk around to face him. "Talk to me." I reach for him, but he puts his hands in his pockets.

"My parents weren't Shredders, either. They escaped from Shredders and then ditched me when they figured out what I was."

"You never told me that. What else do you remember?"

"Nothing." He kicks a rock. "I don't really know what happened, okay? But that's the way it *must* have been. I know *they* weren't Shredders, because *I'm* not a Shredder."

"How do you know they abandoned you? How do you know they weren't killed? How do you know they didn't choke on dust, only leaving you alone because they died?"

"No one wants a kid like me."

"But Burn." I touch his coat sleeve. "The first time your Gift kicked in you were thirteen or fourteen." That's what he told me. It was the day he killed Zina's brother.

"That was the first time I *know* of," he says. "You used your Deviance without remembering."

I swallow the prickles that rise in my throat. I have no interest in playing the who's-done-worse-things game with Burn. Especially not now.

I take a tiny step forward. "Let's change the subject."

"To what?"

"The dance."

"Zina?" He shakes his head. "Rolph will take care of it."

"No," I say. "Before that. When you were watching me dance with Cal."

He raises his hands, palms toward me. "No need. Not a problem. I get it. I'll stay out of your way."

He turns and sets off at a run. I yell after him, but this time he doesn't stop.

Chapter Fourteen

HOW DID YOU GET THOSE SCRATCHES ON YOUR FACE?"
Drake asks as we take our seats in the Assembly Hall the next
day.

"I ran into a tree." I touch the marks Caroline left. They're
tender.

"You should take some dust," Drake says. "They'll heal
faster." The cuts on his face and neck from that Shredder are
almost gone. And seeing Jayma, you'd never know she was shot.

"Quiet," I say. "Rolph's starting."

The FA Commander takes a wide stance on the platform
and the room falls silent. He looks older than he did when we
met, not four months ago. Lines are prominent on his freckled
forehead, and his reddish hair is flecked with gray.

"As most of you know," he says, "because of our alliance with
Fort Huron, we have enough soldiers and weapons to mount

another mission to Haven. But we can still use more volunteers. Anyone here who would like to join us, please stay after the meeting to receive your training schedules."

"When will we leave?" a man dressed in one of the Fort Huron uniforms asks.

"As soon as we train the new recruits," Rolph replies. "Current target is four days. Maybe five. We can't leave it longer than that. Our people inside need our help. All the employees of Haven need our help."

Cal stands a few rows ahead of me. I haven't seen him since the dance. "What are the reports from inside?"

The lines on Rolph's forehead deepen. "We haven't had any reports for nearly two weeks. The Comps must have compromised our communication equipment."

Gwen stands. "With even more people going on this mission, who's going to protect Concord?"

"You will," Rolph answers. "You, Terry, Alastair, and Greggor. The four of you will do twelve-hour shifts on the guard towers until further notice."

He's not leaving anyone else? Those are the same ones who were here while he was in Fort Huron.

"And if more Shredders come?" she asks.

"Let's worry about known risks, not remote ones," he says. "Let's worry about freeing all those people in Haven."

I stand. "You can't leave Concord undefended again. The Shredders who attacked came here from Haven."

"So you claim." Rolph shakes his head. "But even if you can hear Shredder thoughts—"

"I can!"

He holds up a hand. "Even if I accept that you can, and even if I accept that the Shredder you killed was once in the Haven Hospital, it doesn't mean more will come."

"But they had Comp uniforms and weapons. They used combat strategy we learned in COT. They were *sent* here."

Rolph frowns. "We can't leave an FA unit behind on the off chance you're right. You have no evidence to back up your claim."

"I agree," Burn says. I glare at him, but he looks away quickly as if he doesn't want to make eye contact.

I bite my lip. I don't want to tell anyone about Caroline. Not yet. I'll talk to Rolph in private after the meeting and figure out a way to convince him. Once she's recovered from the dust I gave her, I'll get her to tell him what she told me.

"Will someone shut up that girl?"

Who said that?

Scanning the room, I spot Zina standing on the far side. "Rolph, there aren't any Shredders within twenty miles of here. If there were, they'd be spotted. A few wandering in the other day was a fluke. And they must have been weak and starved for dust, considering they were taken down by a bunch of kids."

"You can't know that there aren't more," I say. "You can't be sure more won't come."

"And you can't be sure they came from Haven." Zina smirks.

"Sit down!" Rolph commands. "Both of you." He pauses for a moment as Zina and I take our seats. The entire room's so quiet I'm not certain anyone's breathing. At least Burn stayed calm. He's wrong about which of us has more control.

"Zina"—Rolph strides across the platform—"you've proved once again that you're incapable of being a team player. I'm giving you a separate mission. I'll brief you later."

My nerves stay on edge for the rest of the meeting. At the end, I rush up to be the first one to speak to Rolph.

"You need to be careful about Mrs. Kalin," I remind him. "She can get into people's heads."

"You already told me. Thank you. Are you planning to join us?" he asks.

"I . . . I'm not sure. Where's my dad?"

"Hector?" He shakes his head. "I have no idea. He's AWOL."

"What does that mean?"

"It means I wouldn't worry about him if I were you." Rolph drops a hand onto my shoulder. "If anyone can take care of himself, it's your dad. I'm sure he'll be back soon."

"I should be here when he gets back."

"That's fine," Rolph says. "I understand. And given Kalin's special interest in you, I think it's best if you sit this mission out. You've already done so much for the FA cause. You saved dozens of lives."

Someone scoffs behind me, and I turn to see Zina.

"Are you *done*?" she asks. "The real soldiers need to talk."

I look at Rolph. "You won't let Zina hurt more innocent Haven employees will you? Did you know she killed Cal's brother? Did you know she framed me for the murder of the VP of the Compliance Department by poisoning his food while pretending to be me?" Back when I was in Haven and undercover for the FA, Zina did horrible things in the army's name, all of which she claimed were under Rolph's orders, but I doubt he knows the details of how she carried our her missions.

"Glory"—Rolph's voice is stern—"I need more than accusations. If you have proof that Zina did these things, bring it to me. Meanwhile, Zina's next mission is none of your business, and I need to brief her."

Zina's expression is so condescending that I have the urge to punch her. She maneuvers herself between me and Rolph, and her silver hair flies into my face.

I reach for her, but Drake's hand lands on my shoulder.

"Leave it," he whispers.

I scan the room, hoping to find Burn—he'll back up my claims—but he's already gone. I need to talk to him about last night, if I can find him.

Chapter Fifteen

IT'S BEEN THREE DAYS SINCE THE FA UNIT CAME BACK. Three days since the dance. Three days since Burn and I argued. And I've barely seen or talked to either Burn or Cal. Both of them have been busy with training, I've been avoiding Cal, and Burn's been avoiding me. If I'm honest, I've been avoiding everyone.

Telling everyone that I need time alone, I've been spending most of my time helping Caroline. Today, she didn't even ask me for dust. And she was fine. Calm. We talked about Arabella.

I don't want to get into another fight with Burn about Caroline. When I left today, I didn't retie her. I left a bowl of water and a loaf of bread in the cage.

She lived in the Haven's Pents, like I did, so I'd guess she's never seen or smelled bread before—only Management got luxuries like that—but as I went up the stairs, I saw her taking a bite. Her appetite returning is a good sign.

Shielding my eyes from the sun, I scan the field that the FA is using to train volunteers. This is the first day I've gathered the courage to watch. I feel guilty not going with them, and watching just makes it worse.

Cal is demonstrating techniques we learned in COT to some of the men from Fort Huron. He looks so strong and assured, so much a man, and I realize that I missed his birthday. He's turned nineteen.

I spent years hoping Cal would like me, then a short time as his girlfriend, and now . . . now I'm not sure how to act around him. Before the dance, it was easier just to be Cal's friend. Like we were on neutral territory. But now that I'm sure who I want . . . Now everything feels strange. I'm not with either of them, but I'm no longer neutral.

Cal side kicks a fake Shocker gun from the hand of another man who's playing the part of a Comp. That disarming technique works, but the Comps know that method. They were trained by the same people who trained me and Cal. The FA should think of some new ideas.

Burn strides onto the field, heading straight toward Cal. They talk for a few minutes, with their heads close together. I squirm. Of all the ways I thought things would turn out, their being friends was not on the list.

I spot Jayma and head toward her. "What are you doing here?"

"Training for the mission. What else?" She strikes a pose with a staff in her hands.

"You're joining the FA?" I wait for her to start laughing, but my tiny friend just stands there, trying to look fierce. It's not working.

"You'll get killed," I tell her. "What if you're attacked by Shredders before you even reach Haven?"

"You're forgetting how strong I am." She flexes her arm. It's still so thin. "You were the one who said I should embrace my Gift."

"But Jayma—" I regret neglecting my friends these past few days.

"Out of my way. I'm training." She sounds determined. She swings the staff, and I have to back up or be hit.

I stride to the end of the field and plop down on the ground.

Jayma shifts her staff quickly, and the force of movement pulls her off balance. She falls. Her strength is working against her. I hope she'll soon realize she's out of her depth. She's not ready, and I can't bear the thought of losing another person I love.

Drake runs over and offers her a hand up. He demonstrates how Jayma should plant her feet. She tries again, but it's no use; the force of her swing sets her off balance each time. If she won't listen to me, perhaps Drake can convince her not to go. I'm hoping that's why he's here.

He stands a few feet ahead of her, braces himself, and encourages her to swing at him.

I leap up. "No!" The wind swallows my words so I run toward them.

Jayma's shaking her head, too—she's not going to strike him—but Drake seems to be insisting. He slaps his arms and nods.

She swings. A fraction of a second before the staff strikes Drake, the armor on his torso appears. The weapon strikes. My brother flies in the air, landing several feet away.

Jayma drops her weapon and runs to him, but he's on his feet before she gets there. And grinning. They hug, apparently pleased with their little exercise.

Jayma needed a real target to absorb the force of her swing, and my brother—once his armor was up—could take it.

Drake notices me and looks down.

"That was a big risk," I say. "You know how strong she is. What if your armor didn't come up in time?"

"I was testing *my* Deviance, too," he says. "I've got to be ready."

"For what?"

"For the mission." He raises his chin.

"You're not going."

"Yes I am."

"No, Drake. You can't." I grab his hand. "How could you possibly leave our family now that we're finally together?"

"That's what *you* did when you went back to Haven."

I can feel my heartbeat inside my ears. "That was different. I wasn't going into a battle. And we didn't know about Mrs. Kalin then and what she could do. Plus, you and Dad were together. You can't leave me here alone. I won't let you."

He rolls his eyes. I want to smack him, but I'd break my hand on his armor.

"Please, Drake. At least wait until Dad gets back. Then we can all go to Haven together."

"Can we talk about this later?" Drake motions toward Rolph, who's staring at us. "We're supposed to be training. Either take part or get out of the way."

There's no sense in talking to him now—he won't lose face in front of Jayma—so I return to the end of the field and watch. I've given up trying to reason with Rolph, and I'm not sure even meeting Caroline would convince him to leave Concord more protected. Yesterday he said that, even if I was right and the Shredders *were* sent here from Haven, that's all the more reason to hit Management with everything we've got. It was hard to argue.

Burn strides over to Jayma and Drake. Burn lunges and grabs Jayma, trapping her arms at her sides. She struggles, and I can tell from Burn's face, he's struggling, too.

Twisting her body, she frees her arms and raises them, pushing Burn off her. He flies backward, landing hard on the dirt.

My breath catches, but Burn raises a hand to say he's okay. Drake claps and then runs to hug Jayma.

Burn comes at Jayma again. This time she ducks down and he misses her. She grabs him around the knees, straightens her legs, and tosses him. Burn's arms flap as he flies twenty feet across the field. He lands and rolls, before jumping up.

Maybe Jayma *will* be able to handle herself.

It doesn't matter. I don't want her to.

"She's good, isn't she?" Cal says as he approaches. "I didn't think she could take on Burn, but they both insisted."

Sweat beads on Cal's forehead, and he swipes it off with the back of his hand. "I've barely seen you since the dance. Do you have time to talk?"

"Sure." My mouth is suddenly dry.

"Hot day," he says. "The real sun beats the sun lights inside Haven, doesn't it? Feel like a walk by the lake?"

I look back over at the others and nod.

• • •

Cal offers me a hand as we climb up onto the boulder at the side of the lake. I accept it, only realizing my mistake once we make contact. I pull my hand away before we sit.

"Fresh air suits you," he says. "Your skin almost glows."

He's looking at me the way he used to, the way I once desperately wanted him to. "Thanks. You too. And your hair's lighter from the sun."

"A lot of things have changed."

I shift over on the rock. "What day does the FA unit leave?"

"Either tomorrow or the next day."

My stomach tightens. "I wish I were going to Haven with you, but I need to stay here for my dad."

"I get that." His shoulders hitch.

"I'm sorry. You must be missing your parents."

"Yeah." He tips his face to the sun. "I feel bad for them, having me disappear so soon after we lost Scout." His gaze meets mine. "But the FA isn't what I want to talk about."

I look out at the water. "I know."

Cal bends one leg and leans onto his knee. "Before I leave on the mission, I want to talk—about us."

"Let me go first, okay?"

He shifts on the rock, straightening and bending his leg, as if he can't get comfortable.

"Cal"—my mouth feels full of sand—"first, I want you to know that I really appreciate how patient you've been with me. And . . ." His expression falls and I can tell that he knows what's coming.

"But you don't love me," he says.

"I *do* love you," I blurt without thinking. My cheeks feel hot. "I think I'll always love you."

His face brightens. I'm blowing this. I'm making it harder, not easier.

"But . . ." he says.

"But—it's not *that* kind of love. I don't love you the same way you . . ."

He clears his throat. "You don't love me in the way I love you."

I see the hurt in his eyes. The pain. It slices into me. And now I'm the one squirming on the rock. I want to throw my arms around him, to hug him, to comfort him, but I know doing any of those things will only make this worse.

"I don't have a name for how I feel about you." I chew on my lower lip. "I feel different about you than I do for Drake or Jayma or my dad, but it's not—"

"It's not what you feel for Burn." Cal says this quietly, without hate, without the accusation I deserve.

I lick my lips—so dry—and he wipes his forehead.

We sit for a few moments, both staring out at the lake. Then he breaks the silence. "I'm glad you told me. I only wish you'd done it sooner." His cheeks redden. "I feel like an idiot. The way I waited for you, the way I held you last week at the dance . . ." His jaw shifts. "I knew you had a crush on me since, well, since you were way too young for a dating license. And I didn't think—I took you for granted."

"Cal." I lay my hand on his shoulder. It twitches under my touch, so I drop my hand to the rock. "You have every right to be angry. I'm so sorry. I've been confused."

"How long have you known?" he asks.

"For sure? Since the dance."

He turns toward me quickly, surprise in his eyes. "I hope you and Burn will be happy together. He's a good guy. Not at all what I first thought. I misjudged him."

I drag my palm along the rock. "Burn and I aren't together."

He glances at the water. "I'm sure you'll work it out."

My chest starts to ache—a deep, heavy pain that crushes my lungs, making it hard to breathe. "I don't think we can work it out. Burn—" I hesitate. "It doesn't matter."

"Of course it matters." Cal faces me. "You deserve to be happy. You both do."

"Thanks." I stare at the water, thinking how wrong he is—at least about me.

We sit in silence again as the waves lap against the rock, creating what should be a soothing lullaby but sounds like a dirge.

I'm toxic. I've hurt Cal. Burn won't even talk to me. And look what I did to my parents, my brother.

People who care about me get hurt.

Cal jumps to his feet. "Let's go for a swim." He grins, and his eyes flash with kindness and forgiveness that break my heart. "Come on. I'll race you."

He slides off the rock, throws his shirt onto the pebbles, and runs into the water, jumping over the waves. I follow, catching up when the water reaches his waist. He picks me up and throws me, and when I rise from under the surface he's laughing.

"You snake!" I splash him and he dives under.

As he paddles about, I lie back, floating on the undulating surface, and I wonder if maybe, after all that's happened, Cal and I *can* stay friends.

I close my eyes and my lids glow red. I think of poor Caroline under those ruins. *It's time.*

It's time to trust her. Tonight, I'll bring her aboveground, but I doubt anyone at Concord would accept her. Or that, even with her help, I could convince Rolph not to head to Haven. He's right. The FA has to hit Management hard.

I could lead Caroline far away from Concord and set her free, but I'm not sure how she'd survive.

"Hey," Cal says to someone on shore. "Come join us!"

I stand and blink against the bright light.

Burn turns his back to us and walks away.

Chapter Sixteen

BURN! COME ON IN!" CAL YELLS.

I run toward shore, slogging against the water. "Wait!" I'm not sure why I want Burn to wait, or what I'll say when I reach him, but I know that I don't want him to walk away from here thinking that Cal and I were sharing a romantic moment. It would be a cruel mockery of the first time Burn and I almost kissed. It's bad enough that he has the wrong idea about the dance.

Cal's longer legs move faster than mine and he passes me. "Come in," he calls to Burn. "The water's great!"

"Don't want to interrupt," Burn replies.

"You're not!" Cal and I yell at the same time.

In a single, almost violent movement, Burn pulls off his shirt.

I've seen his chest before, but my breath hitches at the contrasts between smooth skin and scars, tanned muscles and dark hair, hard planes and curves. Cheeks aflame, I duck down below the water to cool off.

When I reemerge, Cal and Burn are talking nearby, and I remain crouched, my chin just above the surface.

"See you later," Cal says to me.

"Bye," I manage to respond.

"No," Burn says. "You go with Cal. No need for this to be awkward."

Still mostly underwater, I step toward them. "Burn, I think you have the wrong idea."

He claps Cal on the arm. "You two fit together."

"It's not like that," Cal says.

"No need to deny it." Burn frowns. "It's not like I'll turn into a huge, jealous monster."

"Very funny," I say.

"Oh, I get it. Funny." Cal laughs, but it sounds forced.

Burn heads toward deeper water.

Cal looks at me and raises his eyebrows. "You're okay if I leave, right?"

"No," Burn says just as I say, "Yes."

"Ha!" Cal says. "You two really are perfect together." He strides out of the water and uses his shirt to dry off as he walks away.

I rise as I turn back toward Burn. My lips and brain can't coordinate. It's like they've forgotten the teamwork required for speech.

"You're shaking." Burn's deep voice fills the space between us.

"The water's cold."

"Go back under. It'll feel warmer than the air."

I slip down and the water's like a warm blanket. "You're right."

"It's the breeze," he says. "Chills your wet skin and makes the water feel warmer in comparison."

Keeping the water below my chin, I step forward. A wave rises to lick the ridges of his abdomen.

"Your lips are blue."

I rub the back of my finger across them, but all I see are *his* lips, imagining how they'd warm mine. He pulls his arms forward, creating small waves. I creep closer, like I'm stalking prey.

A few feet from him now, I slowly rise up and reach to squeeze the water out of my hair.

Burn draws in an audible breath. I glance down. My shirt clings to me like paint, and I tug at the fabric to loosen its tight hold. Self-conscious, I cross my arms over my chest.

"You and Cal," he says. "I'm sorry if I messed that up."

"You didn't."

"Oh." He rakes his hair back. "Good."

"Cal and I are just friends." I step closer. "I don't love him."

"He loves you."

"I don't care."

He shifts back. "You don't care?"

I slap the water. "Of course I *care*. Cal's my friend. I care about his feelings, but that doesn't mean . . ." My mouth's dry again. "That doesn't mean I *love* him. Not the way I love you."

The words are out before I can think. Heat singes my entire body as if the water between us is boiling. Burn looks down like he's discovered something fascinating below the water's surface.

Am I wrong about how he feels? "Burn?"

He raises his gaze, and in his eyes I see nothing but pain.

I reach toward him but he shifts away, and I drop my hand back into the water with a splash. "I'm sorry."

"For what?"

"For saying . . . for saying that I love you."

"I'm the one who's sorry. I don't—" He stops.

His meaning's obvious.

I force a smile, but I can't look him in the eyes anymore. Instead, I focus on his left shoulder, on the scar that's the shape of a pine cone, a remnant of battle during our first trip out of Haven together. "Don't feel bad," I say. "It's okay if you don't feel the same way."

A thousand gallons of adrenaline slam into my chest, and suddenly I'm giddy. My hands stroke back and forth under the water, and I dig my toes into the sandy bottom. "It's kind of funny when you think about it. Well, not funny. More like ironic or tragic." It's so much easier to talk to his shoulder than his face.

"Glory."

My cheeks are on fire again and I look up to the sky. "I'm not kidding. It really *is* funny." I raise my hands, then drop them, splashing us both. "Cal wants me, but I don't want him. I want you, but you don't want me. And now you and Cal are friends. Ha! I guess your friendship with Cal is easier this way. That's a good thing, right? And when you think about it, this is all good.

I mean great. I mean there's so much going on right now. None of us needs extra complications like . . ."

Gulping for air, I push off with my legs and float, dropping my head back. I rise and look down at the water. "I got the wrong idea. Crazy when you think—"

Burn strides through the water and takes my face in his hands.

His large fingers dig into my hair and his palms cover my cheeks. His eyes seem to darken, and I can't catch my breath. With so many emotions coursing through me, looking him straight in the eyes is dangerous—I could hurt him—but I can't look away.

He leans down, closer and closer, until our foreheads touch.

"Glory." The sound is so deep that I feel it as much as I hear it: the heat of his breath, the vibrations from the pitch and timbre of his voice.

I've run out of words. My lips part but nothing comes out.

His mouth hovers so close, there's barely a molecule of air separating our lips. His nose slides against mine as our mouths draw even closer, as we breathe the same air, and I don't want this perfect moment to end. I want to stay here forever, lost in time with my lips aching to taste his, my wet skin yearning for his touch.

His thumbs brush my cheekbones, and he exhales so loudly it's more like a groan. I raise my hand to the scar on his shoulder, and the space between our mouths is erased. His lips crush mine in a hungry kiss.

My fingers dive into his hair, grip his neck, slide over his back. He lifts me against him, and his body's hard and hot against my cold, wet skin.

As we kiss, Burn cuts through the water toward the shore, and I grip the sides of his chest with my knees.

The stones crunch under his feet, and he sets me gently down on the same sloped boulder where we first kissed. He balances above me, our bodies close but not touching. His breaths come heavy and fast; his eyes stay focused on mine.

Fear eats into my joy. This is too much like last time when he changed and almost hurt me. I can't stop shaking. He'd never hurt me on purpose—I know that—but that doesn't mean it won't happen.

As if sensing my thoughts, he rolls to the side to lie next to me on the boulder.

"Burn, I know you won't hurt me."

He doesn't respond. He puts on his shirt, then lies back beside me and shifts to put his arm under my shoulders. As the sun bakes our skin and dries our clothes, I cuddle against him, and our breathing synchronizes.

I don't think I've ever felt so calm, so content. This—lying like this in his arms—is enough.

But as time passes and the sun sets, reality creeps in.

"Are you going to Haven with the invasion team?" I ask.

"Yes. Are you?"

I turn toward him. "I don't want to leave until my dad gets back. I'm terrified that I'll never see him again."

Burn shifts onto his side to face me. "He'll be back."

I want to ask him how he knows, but now that we're lying face-to-face, body-to-body, I can no longer talk. My senses heightened, I can almost feel the air flowing between us—heating, pulling us closer together, even though neither one of us is moving.

Looking into his eyes, I concentrate on suppressing my Deviance. I want to see Burn, really see him, and not in the way my Gift allows. I don't care about his inner workings, the organs, the blood, the synapses in his mind. I want to see the truth of him—what people BTD called the soul.

He draws his hand down my arm. "Are you cold?"

I shake my head.

"Are you comfortable?"

"I'm fine. I'm great. I'm perfect."

He takes a breath. My shirt brushes his and it's like the cloth is part of our bodies. He closes his eyes. "Maybe . . . We can . . . One more kiss."

"You're trembling."

"I'm—"

"It's okay." I cup his face. His chin stubble rubs against my thumb, lighting sparks inside me. I feel like we're connected, joined as one person. He'd never hurt me.

Minutes ago, I was content just to lie in his arms, but now— now, now—I feel like if he doesn't kiss me, I'll die.

I slide on the boulder until our faces are close together, our lips inches apart, his breath, heavy and hot, mingling with mine. I tip my chin up to press my lips softly to his.

"Just one," he says against my lips.

"Mmm," I say, not wanting to break the bond. I'm not frightened, not really, but his fingers are stiff, frozen in place on my back.

"Relax," I murmur, as my hands roam over his shirt.

His muscles are like rock—hot, rippled rock—and when I slide my hand up, his shirt comes up, too. My fingertips brush his skin, and a sound—almost a growl—vibrates against my hand.

He cups my head in his palm and deepens our kiss.

I can't think, I can't hear, I can't reason—the only sensations I can process are the heat and texture and movement of our exploring mouths and hands. His tongue grazes mine, and a new feeling, urgent and sharp, flashes through me. It's like the world has vanished. I can't sense anything but him—his skin, his breath, his heartbeat. My own.

Rolling me onto my back, his body presses me down. I'm drowning in his lips, engulfed in his scent, willingly captive to his muscles and weight.

Then he flies off me so quickly I gasp. The air over my body is cold but still charged.

I sit up. "What's wrong?" I don't want to stop. We said just one kiss and have already gone past that limit, but my whole body vibrates, and all I can think about is having his lips on mine again and again and again.

"You won't hurt me." I reach toward him. "It's okay. I trust you."

He lunges forward, and I have no choice but to lie back down on the rock as he hovers above. His huge arms bend, his forearms flat against the boulder on either side of my head. He lifts one arm and remains above me, leaning on one hand, his other tracing through my hair, over my face, my neck, my shoulder as we gaze into each other's eyes.

When he finally kisses me again, I realize he's changing. Under my touch, his body expands—muscles stretch his skin, veins pulse on his forehead, and his lips become larger, harder.

Pushing down my fear, I run my hands up the sides of his torso, testing the changing surface, exploring the hard disks and ridges, the heat of his skin through his shirt. I arch, and our bodies brush.

He pulls back to hover over me again, and I look deep into his eyes. His face has changed, but he's still there, I think—I hope. As long as I can see into his eyes, I'll be safe.

Yet I'm aware that, at any moment, he might push against me too hard, he might crush me, or his body might demand things mine's not ready to give. And when we're kissing, I can't see his eyes.

I try to force down my doubt. I want the heat from Burn's body to melt the snaking tendrils of fear that have chilled the delicious fire inside me.

But my fear doesn't melt. Instead, my Gift kicks in.

Trembling, I connect to him until I can sense the sparks in his mind. They flash from green to red, as he struggles to stop the transformation.

You won't hurt me. I think calming thoughts as I look into his eyes. *It's okay. Don't be frightened.*

I don't know whether I'm trying to reassure him or myself, and I have no idea whether he even senses what I'm thinking, but the sparks change from black and red to blue and green.

Then, drawing ragged breaths, he slowly changes back to his normal self.

I blink to break our connection, and he rolls onto the rock beside me.

A screaming pain grabs my head. I raise my hands to my temples.

"What's wrong?" Burn sits and pulls me up with him.

It's as if someone drove a spike through my head. The pain's too intense. I can't fight the darkness as Burn gathers me into his arms.

Chapter Seventeen

MY EYES OPEN. WHERE AM I? COVERED BY SOMETHING soft and heavy, I run my hands over its surface. Fur. From a big animal, based on the size of the pelt.

Through the remnants of my headache, memories flash, but I can't form a full picture of what happened, where I am, or why.

Across from me, sunlight paints stone walls as it streaks through the wooden shutters. A wooden table, like the ones they have in the Concord pub, sits in the center of the room with two chairs built from branches. A cupboard is next to a fireplace on my right.

Burn must have brought me here.

The door opens, bringing a rush of light and fresh air. I shield my eyes against the brightness and see Burn's silhouette filling the doorway as he ducks through.

"You're awake."

"Is this where you live?"

"Yup." A wonderful smell wafts through the room as he strides over to the table and sets down a cast-iron pan. He goes to the cupboard and retrieves metal plates, forks, and two cups that he fills with water from a jug. "Hungry?"

"My stomach's been growling since you brought in that pan. What's in it?" I lower my feet and they land on a small gray rug. Under it, the floor is formed by hundreds of interlocking flat rocks, fit together like a puzzle. Someone spent a long time creating it. Burn?

"Eggs and bacon." He scoops the food onto the plates. "The only way to cook in my house is over the fire"—he tips his head toward the fireplace—"and it's too hot today, so I used the stove at the Assembly Hall."

"What's bacon?"

"It's salted and smoked pig meat. Really good."

Stretching, I walk over to one of the chairs. "What happened last night?"

His head snaps up, but he doesn't answer.

"How did I get here?"

He leans onto the table, his knuckles turning white. "I hurt you again."

"No. You didn't hurt me." I rub my temples. My memories are drifting back. "But I have a headache."

"Eat." He pushes a plate toward me. "The food's getting cold."

I dig my fork into the scrambled eggs and close my eyes at the first bite. "So good."

Burn picks up a piece of the bacon with his fingers. Following his lead, I eat with my fingers, too. The fried meat is crunchy in places, soft in others, salty everywhere—and so, so good. I barely breathe as I gobble up everything on my plate.

Popping the last piece of bacon into my mouth, I look up.

Burn's smiling. Unable to waste even a drop of the fat and salt, I lick my fingers, and the intensity in Burn's eyes deepens.

"Thank you. That was so good," I tell him. "It cured both my hunger and my headache."

He nods and piles my empty plate on top of his.

Full of happiness and food, I run one of my hands across the wooden table toward Burn's. He stares at the decreasing space between our fingers. I let my fear take over last night, but it turned out okay in the end. Next time I'll trust him fully. Next time will be better.

"Last night was encouraging, don't you think?"

His brow furrows. "Encouraging?"

"We kissed, and you didn't hurt me." I reach for him, but he pulls his hand back.

"Only because you used your Gift."

"And it worked. Everything was okay."

He stands, and the legs of the chair scrape along the floor. "You got a blinding headache. You passed out. How is that okay?"

"I haven't passed out for ages." I rub my temples. "I can't figure out why that's started again. I'm sure I'll get over it."

"It's because of me. When you're in my head, it hurts you."

"No." But as soon as he says it, I realize he might be right. A lump rises in my throat. I didn't get a headache when I used my Gift on Caroline. It didn't happen when I knocked out Gwen, and it didn't happen when I killed that Shredder. The only other time was when I calmed Burn.

He puts our plates into the empty pan and moves it to the cupboard. "I can't put you through that again."

I walk slowly toward him. "But we don't know for sure why it happened."

He gives me a look.

"Okay. But it might stop. I used to pass out killing rats. That changed when I learned to control it better. This side effect will go away, too."

He shakes his head, but I realize something else.

"Back in Haven, the day of the President's Birthday"—hope bubbles inside me—"you said I calmed you that day, and I didn't get a headache." Sadly, I didn't calm him until *after* he killed the former President, leaving the door open for Mrs. Kalin. But I feel sure that I kept him from killing others.

He leans back against the cupboard. "Did you use your Gift on me that day?"

"No, but don't you see? I didn't need to. You recognized me. You didn't hurt me, even though you were . . . bigger."

"I don't remember." His voice is low and sad.

I take another step toward him. "It proves that you can control it." I reach my hand toward his.

He shifts out of reach. "No. Both times we've gone past a short kiss, I've lost it. If you hadn't stopped me—" He raises his hands to his head, then drops them. "I'm too dangerous."

"Burn." I touch his arm. "You can't get rid of me that easily. We'll figure this out."

He pauses, and I think for a moment that he's going to agree, but he nods toward the door. "You should go find your brother. You were out all night. He'll be worried."

• • •

On the way from Burn's house to mine, the sun brightens the cottages and has the same effect on my mood. Not far from our house, two young boys are throwing a rock back and forth. I smile and wave as I pass, then tilt my chin up to the sky.

Burn loves me. He's never said it, but I can tell how he feels. We'll figure out the rest.

I reach our cottage and push with my shoulder to open the door. It sticks when it's warm. The cottage is empty. I hope Drake is training. What if he goes to the ruins and discovers Caroline? It's past time to get her out of there.

A piece of slate sits on the table, and I cross over to take a look. It's a note written with a soft, chalky rock.

Glory,

I'm going to get Dad. I'm pretty sure he's at a Shredder camp. Sounds bad, I know. But don't worry. I know where to look. Jayma's coming. We're hoping to be back before the invasion team leaves.

See you soon,

Drake

• • •

I sprint back to Burn's, run into him halfway there, and quickly explain the note.

"Please, help me find them. What if they get captured by Shredders?" I can't stop my heart from racing. My muscles are twitching, like everything inside me is already running after

Jayma and Drake, but I have no idea where to look or which direction to go.

Burn frowns. "I could kill Hector for this."

"Do you know where this Shredder camp is?"

"I've got a pretty good idea."

"How far away is it?"

"For Jayma? I'd say an eight-hour walk. When did they leave?"

"I don't know. Were they still training when you came down to the lake yesterday?"

Burn shakes his head. "We were done for the day."

My heart sinks. "They could have left any time after that. Let's go!" I tug on his coat sleeve. "Now. Please. Maybe we can catch up before they get there."

He puts his hands on my shoulders as if he wants to hold me in place. "Drake's a smart kid, and Jayma's strong. They'll come back."

"No." Fear rises, making it hard to control my Deviance. "I've already lost too much. My family has been separated too many times. I will not let them be captured by Shredders."

"We don't know where they are, or if they're in danger," he says, but his eyes tell another story.

"If you know where they are and don't help me . . ."

Burn's jaw is tight, but he nods. "I know one place we can check."

I pull him up the hill. "First, I need to check on Caroline."

• • •

Burn stops just as we reach the ruins. "Wait."

"We need to hurry."

He crosses his arms over his chest. "Before we go down, I need you to agree to something."

"What?"

"I get to decide if the Shredder lives." He thumps his chest. "Me."

I back up a step. "Who said anything about killing her?"

"I did. I said it. Just now."

I grab his sleeve. "I came to bring Caroline food and water"— *and maybe release her*—"and you want to kill her?"

He frowns. "She's a waste of food and a danger to Concord."

"She's getting better."

"She attacked you."

"That was five days ago. She didn't even ask me for dust the last time I saw her."

Burn clears his throat. "I've agreed to everything you've asked. I've kept your secret. But I've got more experience with Shredders than you do. You have to leave this decision to me."

I nod. "Okay." Once he sees Caroline's improvement, he'll agree.

Nerves twitch in my stomach as we walk the remaining distance. But no matter what Burn does, in the long list of my current problems, Caroline falls to the bottom.

Besides, after reading that journal, it seems kinder to kill her than to leave her locked down there forever. What if I'm killed at the camp? What if no one opens that cellar door for another eighty or ninety years?

Burn pulls up the door.

"Caroline?" I call. There's no answer. I start down the stairs, but Burn pulls me back up.

"Me first."

I hand him the crank torch and he descends, each step clanging on the metal stairs.

"Go away," Caroline yells. "Go away!" The second time it comes out like a screech.

I push past Burn. She's standing in the corner of the cage, her eyes glowing brightly.

I raise my hands. "It's okay, Caroline. This is my friend Burn. Remember? We've come to bring you some food and water."

Burn holds me back. "She got out of her bindings."

"I untied her," I tell him. "She's better. You'll see."

Caroline steps forward, shaking, and I pass her one of the water bladders from my pack. Her eyes, trained on Burn, only close slightly when she takes a long drink.

"She's thirsty," I say to Burn. "For water. Is that enough proof for you? She's not a Shredder anymore."

He grunts. I drop my pack and dig out the food I brought for her. "I'm sorry I didn't come to see you yesterday."

The brightness of her eyes decreases and I can see her better. She rubs her dry lips. "I need to get out."

Burn shines the light around the cage. The bones have been moved.

I grab the torch from him and shine it toward the pile of skeletons. "What did you do?"

Caroline moves over to the pile, picks up some bones, and cradles them protectively, like a baby. Gasping, I recognize what she's done. She's made dolls. Using scraps of clothes, and maybe some soot from the ground, she fashioned figurines.

"This is my—" She looks down. "I'm taking care of them."

Burn's face is shrouded in shadows.

I open the cage and she steps toward me.

Burn rushes to my side, but I hold up my hand. "I'm fine." Guilt clogs my throat. "Caroline, I have to take a short trip. I might not be able to visit tomorrow."

"Take me with you. Please." Her voice breaks. "I need to be in the light. I need fresh air."

Burn moves out of the shadows. "If you're from Haven, what do you know of fresh air?"

"I had a taste." She points above. "And I can feel it every time you open that hatch. It's so dark down here." She coughs.

I touch Burn's arm, and his muscles are flexed, like he's ready to attack. "She's not lying about being from Haven. I met her in there. Her daughter—" I see the sadness in Caroline's eyes, but she nods, so I continue. "When Clay died, he was saving Caroline's daughter." Clay, my former contact with the FA, begged me to go with them that night. If I had, would they still be alive? Or would I be dead, too?

Burn stares at me.

"Please," Caroline says, "at least let me go out for a walk."

"There's no time," Burn says. "We've got to go."

"Where?" Caroline asks.

"We're going to a Shredder camp." I nod at Burn. "She might be able to help. We should bring her."

"No!" Caroline yells and backs away. "Don't take me to a Shredder camp."

"Then you need to stay here," I tell her. "You should have enough food and water for a few days."

Caroline trembles. I feel terrible but also relieved that she seems resigned to her fate. While I'm away I'll have to come up with a long-term plan.

I take Burn's hand. "We should go."

Caroline bolts past me toward the stairs. She's on the third step before Burn grabs her around the waist and lifts her.

Her legs kick; her arms flail. "Please! If you won't let me out, just kill me. *Please.*"

Carrying her, Burn strides toward the cage.

"Don't hurt her!" I yell.

He adjusts his hold, freeing one of his arms, then bends to pick up a length of rope. She swings back, trying to hit him, but she doesn't have a chance against Burn.

He places her face down on the floor, more gently than I expect. Putting his knee on her upper thighs, he pins her with his weight.

"Burn, don't," I whisper. Is he going to crush her? Strangle her?

"Help me," he says.

"I won't. I won't help you kill her."

"I'm not asking you to." He looks up at me. "You were right. We'll take her with us."

Chapter Eighteen

THE THREE OF US WALK FOR HOURS. BURN KEEPS HOLD of the rope that's bound tightly around Caroline's waist, and she keeps up in spite of our blistering pace. For the past hour we've been going steadily uphill and the route has grown rockier, trickier. We haven't seen a forested area for the past few miles, and we just traversed a rocky ridge to avoid what looked like a vast pool of dust in a valley. Burn seems to know the route well.

"Will this camp be like the one we saw in the hot zone around Haven?" I ask Burn.

"No," he says. "Not the same."

"Better or worse?" *Please say better.*

"Better in some ways, worse in others."

"What do you mean?"

"You'll see soon enough."

"That's no answer." I wait, but it's the only answer I get, so I ask, "Why have you been to the camp? Did the FA send you?"

"No."

"Then why?"

"Exploring." He leaps onto a boulder that's nearly five feet up, then offers me a hand.

I nod toward Caroline, then start to climb up on my own. Burn takes the hint and reaches to help her, and I don't know whether I'm more surprised that he does it, or that she accepts his assistance.

"So, do you believe me now?" I ask Burn a little while later.

"About what?"

"That Shredders can recover."

"Recover?" He looks over his shoulder. "You think that's what this is?"

"What would you call it?"

"Forced starvation. You've kept her from getting what she wants."

"I gave her a little bit of dust. It made her better." I glance back, and Caroline's trudging along, her head down. "You've got to admit that dust helps people heal."

"Stay away from it," Burn says.

"I do."

We scramble over loose rocks and boulders. Caroline falls, landing hard on her hands and knees. Burn stops to help her. The blood on her scraped knees is still thick and dark, still more Shredder-like than human.

"Look." Burn points down to the space between two rocks. "Dust."

Caroline's eyes open wide and she stares down at it, not moving.

"Go on," Burn says, "you know you want it."

She shakes her head and backs away.

"Burn, don't." I move between them. "Is that why you brought her? To test her?"

"Once a Shredder, always a Shredder."

Caroline's shoulders drop, but she doesn't turn away from the dust.

I touch Burn's hand. "Give her a chance."

His jaw hardens, but he checks to make sure that Caroline is ready before he starts walking again.

• • •

On our way up a steep slope, Burn stops. "We're nearly there."

I climb the final section ahead of Burn and Caroline, and when I reach the top, I see the camp. I duck down. I was hoping we'd run into Drake and Jayma on the trail, or even better, on their way back with my dad. But at least we're here.

Burn comes up beside me, flattens himself against a boulder, and then stretches slowly to see over the edge. Just behind us, Caroline leans against a rock and closes her eyes, clearly exhausted and not wanting or caring to see what's ahead.

I slide up the boulder to peek over the edge.

Ahead, the ground is flat compared to what we've climbed, and in the distance there's a large concrete-block building that's about three stories high. Its only windows are high up, in a single line like a row of teeth.

Burn whispers to me, "What spooked you before? Why did you duck?"

"Isn't that the camp? It's right there."

"You didn't see anyone?"

"No, but they must have lookouts or guards or something." He rises. I reach up to grab his hand. "What if they see you?"

He looks down at me. "I come here all the time."

"All the time? Why?" What else don't I know about Burn? I climb over the rocks. Caroline follows, but her shoe slips and she slides back down. I kneel, planning to go down to help her, but Burn grasps her under the arms and hoists her up.

As we stride forward, the smaller rocks crunch underfoot, and my shoulders tense. Between us and the building stretches a wire mesh fence, sharpened coils at its top.

"Is that some special kind of wire?" I ask.

"It's called razor wire," Burn says. "It's from BTD."

I shiver. If there were no Shredders BTD, then why did they need something like razor wire?

There's a gate in the fence, and a row of long dark objects hangs from the razor wire at intervals. I squint to focus, then nearly gag.

They're dead bodies—dangling from the fence like decoration. The deep maroon of what little flesh remains makes me think they were Shredders. Most of the bodies are hanging by the neck on loops, and the wire has cut all the way through to one Shredder's spine. It looks like the body might separate from the head at any moment.

"Do you think Jayma and Drake are in there?" I stand beside Burn, willing my legs to stop shaking.

"I'm not sure."

"What's inside the building?"

"No idea. I've never been past the fence." He tugs on Caroline's rope. "Come on."

She looks at me nervously.

"I need to find my family," I tell her. "But we won't leave you here, I promise." I've yet to see any sign of life beyond the fence—only death all over it.

"Where are the Shredders?" I ask Burn.

"Inside the building or around the back."

"I thought you hadn't been past the fence," Caroline says, and Burn grunts.

I smile inwardly. It's the first time she's spoken on the entire trip.

"I've walked the perimeter," Burn says. "If we keep our distance, the Shredders won't bother us."

"That doesn't sound like Shredders," I say just as a door in the back of the building opens and someone comes out.

Burn raises an arm to stop me, but I stop on my own. I hold my chin high and plant my feet firmly as the Shredder—or man?—approaches the gate in the fence.

His skin is deeply tanned and lined from the sun, and his gray hair is shorn close to his head. The day's worth of stubble on Burn's chin seems longer. A sleeveless shirt made from a coarse fabric hangs loose over his torso, and his pants are leather, sewn together with large stitches and belted at the waist with a woven rope. Scars snake up his muscled arms, and I realize some of the lines on his face are scars, too.

He's not carrying a weapon, but there's a band of leather across his chest and the handle of what must be a sword thrusting up over his left shoulder. The handle is a deep ivory color and might be made from antler or bone.

He looks more human than Shredder, but I'm no longer sure I fully understand the difference. His expression is stern but not threatening—exactly. As we approach, the man steps up to the gate. "Welcome to Simcoe," he says. "I'm Houston. Who are you?"

Welcome? "I'm Glory Solis. This is Caroline and Burn."

"Burn." Houston repeats the name as if he's expecting a reaction, but he doesn't get one. Do they know each other?

"If you're dropping her off"—Houston nods toward Caroline—"intake is around back."

Whimpering, Caroline moves as far away as her rope allows.

"No." I give her a reassuring glance. "We're not leaving her here."

"Come closer." Houston leans onto the fence. "So we don't have to yell."

I slip past Burn's arm.

"Careful," he whispers, but he follows with Caroline.

"How long has she been off the dust?" Houston asks.

"About a week." Not counting her slip up, which I decide to ignore.

He raises his eyebrows. "I would have guessed longer."

"How can you tell?"

"It's what we do here." He sheathes his weapon. "We help folks get off the dust. No one on dust is allowed to live in Simcoe."

"Are you a recovered Shredder?" I ask.

"That's an interesting way to put it."

I grab Burn's sleeve. It *is* possible to recover. I'm almost vibrating with excitement. I want to learn more. My gut says to trust Houston, but as he unlocks the gate, one of the bodies moves.

"Are you looking for Hector?" Houston asks.

My breath catches. I draw my knife. "Where is he? Do you have him? Let him go!"

Houston laughs and raises his hands. "Whoa, there. No one means you harm."

"But my dad—is he here in this Shredder camp?"

"Nope. Wish I could help you," Houston says. "And by the way, Simcoe's not a Shredder camp."

I'm about to argue—they have bodies hanging from the fence—but Burn steps in front of me. "How did you know we were looking for Hector?"

"Her name," Houston says. "And she looks like him."

"We're looking for someone else, too. A boy about this tall"—I hold my hand up several inches higher than my head—"and a girl. My age, red hair, a few inches shorter than me."

He steps through the gate. "I did hear about a couple of kids coming through. Might be inside." He gestures behind himself. "Come in and look around."

"No." Burn stays between Houston and me. "We'll wait out here."

"Your choice," Houston says. "But you look tired. We've got food and water. And you don't want to be out here past night-fall."

"Why do you have bodies hanging from the fence?" I blurt.

"Ah." He shakes the fence and the bodies move. "Camou-flage."

"What does that mean?"

"Disguise, subterfuge," Houston answers. "They help ward off unwanted guests."

"Like us?" Burn asks.

Houston frowns. "I invited you in. If you don't want to . . ." He starts to close the gate.

I tug on Burn's sleeve. "What if they're inside?"

"It might be a trap," he responds. I know he's right, but finding my family is worth the risk.

"Are you coming?" Houston asks. "You can bring her." He nods at Caroline. "Just don't let her out of your sight."

Caroline's eyes glow.

"Don't worry," I tell her. "I won't let anyone hurt you." Comforting her makes me feel braver as we walk through the gate.

Chapter Nineteen

BURN TAKES MY HAND AS WE WALK DOWN THE PATH toward the building. A woman with long, dark hair and brown eyes steps outside the door and watches us intently. There's something oddly familiar about her. Perhaps she came from Haven, too.

In the building, it's almost as bright as it was outside. The high windows let in more of the late-afternoon light than seems possible given their size and height. I stop and look up in awe. The ceiling is covered in shiny metal or painted with some kind of reflective coating. I suspect they've done something with mirrors or panels to direct and maximize the light.

The center of the space is open, the air is fresh, and there are carts and tables set up where people are offering food. I smell cooking meat. People are all around us. Most of them have thick, leathery skin and bear scars that make them look like Shredders. But no one is acting like a Shredder.

"This is the market," Houston says. "And up there"—he points to the three levels above, all with railings along the edges—"are the residences."

At the camp in the hot zone, the Shredders were screaming, torturing one another. I'm so amazed by this place that I almost forget to scan the faces for Dad, Drake, and Jayma. We pass an open door and I stop short. Children. Playing. And they don't look like Shredders at all.

Houston steps up beside me. "That's our school."

"Were the kids all born here?"

"Most of them. A few we rescued."

I look toward Burn, but his gaze is focused down as if he doesn't want to acknowledge what he's seeing.

"I'll head up to my office," Houston says, "and make an announcement to ask if anyone's seen your friends." Houston touches my back.

"Don't touch her." Burn says.

"Relax," Houston says. "You can let go of your friend's rope if you like. She doesn't look like a runner."

I take Burn's hand and pull him a few feet away. "Is this really your first time past the fence?"

He nods.

"It's not what I expected. You?"

He shrugs.

I lean in close. "I get that you're wary. So am I. But I think we should give Houston the benefit of the doubt—at least until he gives us a reason not to. So far, he's been helpful."

"Morag," Houston says to the woman who followed us, "will you take over the tour while I make the announcement?"

"Yes." She's been trailing us like a fog, but now her shoulders straighten and she lifts her chin. "Come." She gestures to us. "It'll be dark soon."

"Thanks." I look at Burn, but his face is a mask. I turn back to Morag. Then back to Burn. She's staring at him, and it might be my imagination, but the more I see them together, the more they look alike.

We follow Morag through the rest of the enormous building, and at the other end, large doors stand open, creating a space that's nearly a story high and wide. Outside, various smaller buildings are scattered around a massive fenced-in space. In the distance lie fields, much like the ones we have around Concord, and rows of windmills. No one I know inside Haven or at Concord would believe that Shredders could be this organized, this civilized. Civilized if it weren't for the bodies hanging from the fence.

"Attention, citizens of Simcoe." Houston's voice comes over a loudspeaker. "If anyone has seen Hector Solis, or a teenage boy and girl who arrived last night or earlier today, please report the information to the Mayor's office immediately."

I'm shocked to hear that my dad's so well known here that Houston uses his name. "What's a Mayor?" I ask Morag.

"Houston is the Mayor."

"Is that like a President?"

"Not like in that dome," she replies. "We hold elections." Morag looks over at Burn, but he's standing silent, like he's ignoring our conversation.

A group of children rushes by, jumping and shouting, and it makes me smile. One of them, a boy of about four or five, slams into Morag's legs. "Mommy!"

She rubs his head. "Go play, poppet. Mommy's busy right now."

I turn back to Burn. In spite of his claims, he might still have family—somewhere. He's given me contradicting stories about his past. Is that why Morag's staring at him? Is she why he comes here? I can hardly think it—*Is Morag his mother?* If so, is this little boy Burn's brother? Half brother? I want to ask him, but I should wait until we're alone.

"What's an election?" I ask.

"An election"—she pats the boy on his bottom, and he skips off to follow the other kids—"is when we choose Simcoe's leaders."

"Who gets to choose?"

"Everyone over thirteen," she answers. "Elections are held every five years. That way, if someone's not doing a good job—"

"They're replaced," I finish. "That's an *amazing* system. Don't you think so, Burn?" He raises his eyebrow a fraction of an inch.

"We should do that in Concord," I go on. "I mean, how was Rolph chosen to head the FA? And why does the army run things, anyway?"

Burn shakes his head, either unsure or unwilling to discuss it further. He won't even look at Morag, fueling my suspicions.

"Mommy! Catch!" The little boy runs back and throws a ball, but not nearly hard enough, and it's too far to the right.

Morag holds out her arm and the ball veers, changing direction and altitude until it lands in her hand.

"How did you do that?" I ask.

She rolls it toward her son. "It's my Gift. I can draw objects toward me."

"Anything? Can you pick that up from here?" I point to a stool not far from us.

"No." She tucks her hair behind her ears. "I can only alter the trajectory of something already in motion."

"That's cool, don't you think, Burn?"

He looks the other way.

Morag glances behind me, and I turn to see Houston striding down the path toward us.

"Did you find them?" I ask.

Houston shakes his head. "If anyone's seen them, we'll find out soon."

Burn glowers. I wonder if he knows or detects something I don't. I'm certain that no one's messing with my judgment. After my experience with Mrs. Kalin, I can detect that kind of interference in my thoughts, and my gut still says that this place is safe.

"What's behind that fence?" Burn points to a solid fence— more like a wall—that I assumed formed the end of the settlement.

Houston frowns. "You know very well what's behind there."

"Tell her what you're hiding." Burn leans forward. "It's not all smiles and laughing kids here."

I remember the bodies on the fence as Houston raises his hands, palms facing us. "We have nothing to hide." He turns to me. "But speaking of hiding, do you know how often Burn comes here? He thinks we don't see him watching us, but we do, don't we, Morag?"

Morag's hand trembles as she tucks her hair behind her ear, again. "Yes, I've seen him." She moves toward Burn.

Burn shoves his hands into his pockets.

Morag's skin looks flushed. "I've wanted to talk to you. To apologize—"

"Apologize?" The word bursts from Burn like a gun blast, and he drops Caroline's rope.

I touch Burn's arm. "Calm down."

He shrugs off my hand. The telltale vein pulses on his temple.

I gently turn his face so his gaze meets mine. "Take a deep breath," I say. "Calm. Down. Now."

Rage twists his features as he looks into my eyes. But he doesn't change.

He turns to Houston. "Show Glory what's behind that fence."

Chapter Twenty

WE FOLLOW HOUSTON AND MORAG, AND AS WE get closer to the fence, I can hear noises—screams and shrieks, the pitch and tone of metal on metal. The sound of Shredders. As badly as I want to find my family, I hope I won't find them behind this fence.

We reach a set of stairs. "Best to leave her down here." Houston nods to Caroline.

Morag reaches for the rope joining Burn to Caroline. "I'll watch her for you."

Caroline's eyes glow, but she says, "Okay."

Following Houston, we climb the stairs and find a series of catwalks. The space below is divided into three large sections, each about one hundred yards wide and maybe double that in length. It's hard to judge the sizes from this distance. We can't see inside any section except the area right below us. The walls between each segment are solid.

We slowly walk along the railing of the catwalk. Below us, people mill around in groups. Most look like Shredders; some are obviously Deviants; some are constrained—hobbled or shackled—but none are fighting against their restraints. The shrieks are coming from farther away.

"Is this a detention center?" I ask. "What did these people do?"

"People?" Burn says. "They aren't people."

"This is Stage Three of our renewal center," Houston says. "Most of the people you're seeing below have been fully off the dust for at least three weeks. They undergo daily interviews, and a committee decides when they're ready to enter Simcoe again."

"Again?" I turn toward him.

"Some for the first time," he says, "but some are former residents who slipped."

"What do you mean?"

"They inhaled too much dust and needed help."

"Holding people captive isn't *help*." Burn's voice is full of scorn.

I tug on Burn's coat sleeve. "You can't have it both ways. One minute you're claiming they aren't even people, and the next you accuse Houston of holding them against their will."

"Show us the rest," he says to Houston.

"You know what's there," Houston replies. "You've been spotted climbing up to look in more than once."

Burn doesn't respond. He pushes off the railing and strides down the catwalk.

He stops halfway along the second pen and I join him.

"This is Stage Two," Houston announces.

This pen's smaller, and all of the Shredders inside are restrained—some are shackled to the sides, others trapped in cages, and still others are facedown in the dirt. Most of them are shrieking and moaning, writhing in obvious pain.

I flash back to the rooms in the Hospital inside Haven and Mrs. Kalin's barbaric experiments. Is this any better? And what about my own treatment of Caroline?

"Admittance to Stage Two is voluntary," Houston tells us. "Many of the addicts in the farthest section"—he tips his head toward the final barrier—"were put there against their will—captured by our recruiting team, or at the request of a family member or friend who's already recovered."

"How exactly do they volunteer to get into this part?" I ask.

"See that door?" He gestures to the wall that divides this area from the pen we have yet to see. There's a dented and rusting steel door.

"To get to that door," he says, "the applicants crawl through a tunnel, then submit to our guards, lying facedown, arms behind their backs, before they're constrained and brought through."

"What if they want to leave here once they're in?" If I've learned anything over the past months, it's that the line dividing right from wrong can be fuzzy. Before I decide about this place, I need to know all I can.

Houston puts a hand on the fence in front of us. "Once they enter Stage Two, they have to stay for at least a week. After that, they're given a choice: either leave Simcoe or remain in captivity until they're ready to be interviewed for admittance to Stage Three, the final stage."

"And can we see what's in Stage One?" Past the next wall, the catwalk itself is fully enclosed like a cage, and it's covered in razor wire.

"Are you sure you want to?" Houston asks. "It isn't pretty."

"I already saw the bodies strung up around your gate. Where do they come from?"

Houston shifts. "They're Shredders who never made it out of Stage One."

"I thought you said they could leave renewal if they wanted."

"I said that entering Stage Two was voluntary. We need to keep Simcoe safe." He motions for me to follow.

The ethics of this place bother me, but I've seen Shredders in action. It could be a disaster if Shredders who left here led others back to attack.

Once we cross onto the caged portion of the catwalk, the noise level increases, and as I step up to the edge, Burn slides his arm over my shoulders. Below, a gangly male Shredder charges the wall, his bulging eyes focused on me. He jumps and his hands tear on the razor wire. He drops to the ground.

Something slams into the fencing above me. I jump. Another Shredder has landed on our cage. Blood as thick as oil drips down. I wipe some off my cheek and move out of the way. Bracing myself, I look up, ready to kill the Shredder—but he's already dead.

Burn squeezes my shoulders.

"Are you okay?" he asks, and I nod.

"We need extra security for the Stage One viewing area." Houston points to the cage above us. "In addition to the razor wire, there are spring-loaded spikes."

I creep back to the edge of the fencing and scan the throng below. What if my dad's down there? When I first saw him, after three years of thinking he was dead, his skin was darker and thicker. I shudder. *No.* My dad was never a Shredder. I can't think that. His skin was just darker and wrinkled from the sun.

This last pen is smaller and more crowded. A few Shredders are at the far side, keeping quietly to themselves, and I can see the opening to the wire-covered tunnel system that Houston told us about. A female Shredder is crawling very slowly over—

"Is that razor wire?"

Houston's jaw tenses. "Yes. Razor wire and glass shards."

"Why?" The word comes out as a high-pitched breath. I wanted to believe that the people of Simcoe were good, that it was possible to recover fully from being a Shredder, but it looks as if Houston and the others have set up a torture course as the price for so-called renewal. Crawl over glass or get strung up on the fence.

"We need to be sure that those in Stage Two *want* to recover. That they aren't coming in to attack those already in renewal."

Bile burns my throat as I watch a Shredder cut long slices along the bare chest of another who's being held by more Shredders. Screams rise, and I cover my ears. "Why do you let them have weapons?"

"We confiscate everything we find," Houston says, "but they always have ways."

"That knife's made from an arm bone," Burn says.

"Exactly," Houston says. "They make knives by sharpening bones against the rocks."

Another snarling Shredder leaps up to try to reach us. Hooks—that must be part of his Deviance—protrude from his wrists. If he can jump as high as the Shredder who landed above us, those hooks could easily snag on to the fencing right in front of our faces.

He tries again and again, and on his fourth attempt, I hear breaking bones when he lands. He walks away, dragging one leg at an awkward angle behind him.

Another Shredder with scalelike skin jumps on the wounded one, knocking him down. The scaled Shredder steps on the broken leg and laughs at the screams of pain.

I've had enough.

Chapter Twenty-One

I RUN BACK ALONG THE CATWALKS, NOT LOOKING DOWN, even when I reach the Stage Three area.

I take the stairs two at a time. At the bottom, I squeeze my eyes shut and bend over, wishing I could erase the images from my mind.

"Which one of you is responsible for her?" Houston gestures toward Caroline, who's standing very close to Morag, her rope on the ground.

"I am," Burn says loudly before I can respond.

"Don't agree to anything without talking to me first," I tell him. The thought of Caroline being tossed into the Stage One pen makes me ill. Even Stage Two. And I promised we wouldn't leave her here.

"You said I could decide," he replies, but his voice is soft. "Trust me."

"Let's talk. The three of us," Houston says, and he leads Burn and Caroline to the side of one of the buildings.

Morag starts after them, but I stop her. "Can I ask you something?"

"Okay." We sit side by side against the wall of a wooden building.

I'm not sure where to begin. I don't want to blurt out my real question without first talking to Burn. "How long have you lived in Simcoe?"

"About thirteen years—on and off."

"How did you end up here?"

"The first time"—she shifts on the ground—"I escaped from a camp. Me and my—"

"You and Burn?" I can't help myself.

She turns away from me, and I draw a long breath. "Morag, is Burn your son?"

She nods.

"Are you sure?"

Tears are running over her dark, wizened cheeks. "I knew the moment I saw him."

"He's sixteen—he thinks." I rest my hand on her back. "He must have changed a lot."

"He turned seventeen last month." Her eyes well. "But I've seen him over the years. The first time when he was eight."

"How? And how did you first lose him? And . . . if you live *here*, how and why did Burn end up where he did?"

"I didn't live here when I gave him up." Her voice trembles. "I escaped the Shredder camp and took Burn to the settlement when he was three. I left him at the bottom of the ridge."

She draws a ragged breath. "I grew up at the settlement. I took him to the only place I knew he'd be safe. After I left him there, I expected to die. But I stumbled on this place instead. They saved me."

"What about Burn's dad?"

"Killed, trying to keep the Shredders from taking me. When I was captured, I was already pregnant with Burn."

"That's terrible." I squeeze her hand.

"I don't like to think of those times." She runs a hand over her long hair. "After I found my way here and finished renewal, all I could think about was my son and whether I dared to try to see him again."

"So you went to find him when he was eight?" I ask.

"No." She closes her eyes for a moment. "I would have been shot by the tower guards if I tried to get anywhere near. A group from the settlement came here. Burn was with them. I think he followed in secret. He was such a brave boy, even then." She pauses, and I bite my tongue to keep from interrupting.

"I recognized him right away. I thought"—she twists her hands in her lap—"I thought he came to find me." She blinks and tears trail down her cheeks. "I ran out to talk to him, but he didn't remember me."

She looks into my eyes. "I tried to tell him who I was. I tried to tell him that I loved him, that I only gave him up so that he'd have a chance of a real life—a life away from Shredders—but he didn't let me explain."

"What happened?"

"He pelted me with rocks." She tugs at the neck of her shirt. "He nearly killed me."

"But you deflected the rocks with your Deviance?"

She rubs a scar on her head.

"You let the rocks *hit* you?"

She nods. "The commotion drew attention. A fight erupted between Simcoe and your people. The talks broke down."

"Is that why no one from Concord comes here? Why no one talks about it?"

"Probably. That was the worst day of my life. Still, that was no excuse . . ." She bites her lower lip so hard it draws blood, which I'm glad to see looks human.

"Excuse for what?" I whisper.

"I left here. I went back on the dust. For more than three years I was back in a camp, tortured daily, raped . . . But I got out. I did it for my baby."

"The little boy we saw?"

She nods. "I didn't know I was pregnant when I escaped the camp. Not for sure. But Duncan was born when I was in Stage Three of renewal."

I gasp.

Her eyes well up again. "He was so tiny. He almost died. So did I."

I squeeze her arm. I don't want to ask about Duncan's father. Not if he was conceived in a Shredder camp. "You saved both of your boys. You made sure they didn't grow up to be Shredders. That was brave."

She stares at the ground. "Burn probably still wants to kill me. Or would if he figures out who I am."

As my mind is reeling and I'm unsure what to say to make her feel better, I glance over to the others. Burn's watching Houston talk to Caroline, and she seems more relaxed than she has since we left Concord. Houston looks directly at Caroline and asks her something. After Caroline responds, Houston smiles and so does Burn.

A woman walks over to them and talks to Houston. Then Burn strides toward me, and the other two follow.

I jump up and we meet halfway. "What is it? Does someone know where they are?"

"No one's seen Hector," Houston says. "But your friends came through here about five hours ahead of you."

"Came through? They left? Where did they go?"

"That woman"—Burn nods toward the person he and Hector were talking with—"thinks they were headed for the closest Shredder camp."

"Where is it? We have to go. Now."

"The sun's going down," Houston says. "It's too dangerous. Shredders are mostly nocturnal."

"We need to go after them!" I step in front of Houston. "Where is the camp? Tell me!"

"Going to that camp is suicide," Houston replies.

"We're going," Burn says, and I'm flooded with relief. I'd rather die than not find my family.

"Which direction?" he asks Houston.

"I'll take you," Morag says.

"Thank you," I tell her. "Let's go."

Burn shifts awkwardly. "Tell us which way to go. It can't be that hard to find."

"Actually it *is* hard to find," Morag says. "And if you approach from the wrong direction, they'll see you coming and you'll be captured or dead before you even get close."

"We'll figure it out," Burn says.

"Fine for you." Morag's tone is sharp. "What about the girl?" She tips her head toward me. "Do you need me to tell you what they'd do to her in that camp?"

Burn flinches, then narrows his eyes. "Glory can handle herself. Better than you could possibly know."

"Burn." I squeeze his arm. "She wants to help us. Why not let her?"

"Fine." He won't look at her. Does he know who she is?

"At least wait until morning," Houston says. "I hate to say it, but if your friends went there, they're already captured or dead."

"We can't wait."

"I'm ready," Caroline says, and I realize that Burn—or Houston—took off her ropes.

"No," Burn says. "You should stay here. Houston will take care of you."

Houston steps forward. "I agree. Caroline, it's too risky for you to be near Shredders. You're ready for Stage Three. Going to that camp would set you back. Assuming any of you get out."

"I promised I wouldn't leave you," I tell Caroline.

"It's okay." Her hand trembles through her wispy hair. "I don't want to go to a Shredder camp"—she turns to Houston—"and Houston says they can help me."

I draw her into a hug. Holding her frail body, I can't believe how far she's come in a week.

Thinking of the Shredders I've killed, a chill traces through me; but even if I'd known at the time that recovery was possible, I only killed to survive.

Chapter Twenty-Two

THE SUNLIGHT DISAPPEARS NOT LONG AFTER WE LEAVE, and the sliver of a moon casts a faint glow through the hazy sky. Morag walks ahead, and Burn and I follow in silence, the air between us like a living, breathing thing.

After not getting a full night's sleep and walking for a good chunk of today, adrenaline's my only fuel. But there's no chance that I'll slow down. I keep hoping that we'll come upon Drake and Jayma behind the next boulder, around the next corner, within the next grove of trees.

Please, I think. *Please don't let them be at the Shredder camp yet.*

The ground becomes softer, with a layer of dirt—or dust?—over the rock. "Should we wear our masks?" I ask Burn.

"We'll be fine as long as we don't kick up too much dust."

Morag stops, a silhouette in the darkness. She draws a swordlike weapon off her back. We join her.

"Why did you stop?" Burn asks.

"We should keep close from here on out."

I blink to adjust my eyes to the inky blackness, then follow behind Morag, who walks slowly. We choose each step carefully as we weave through a sparse pine forest scattered with boulders.

Morag stops just past the edge of the forest. In the distance, it looks like the world drops away to nothing. There must be a cliff.

Pointing behind an outcropping of rock, Morag says, "We'll wait here until it's light."

"Why wait?" I ask. In spite of my fatigue—or maybe because of it—my nerves are firing so fast I can't stand still.

"Glory's right," Burn says. "Let's go."

Morag steps tentatively toward Burn. "The Shredders are most active at night—especially the males. Now is the worst time to go in."

"What would you know about it?" he asks.

"I used to live there."

Burn turns away.

"Sunrise is in three hours," Morag says. "I need some rest." She sits behind the rocks and leans back.

"We should rest, too," Burn says to me. "Over there." He points to a dark shadow that might be a cave. He drapes his arm around me and we walk in sync, the side of my body curving against his.

The shadow turns out to be more like an indentation than a cave—the space goes back only a couple of feet—but it's sheltered, relatively dust free, and we'll be able to keep watch.

I face toward the cliff, imagining my family below, and Burn steps behind me.

He gently rubs my shoulders, and I nearly groan. No other parts of our bodies are touching, but still I'm buzzing. His thumbs press into my neck, and his fingers span my shoulders, reaching to the tops of my arms.

I've been waiting for a chance to talk to him about Morag, but I'm no longer able to speak.

He brushes some stray dust off the ground, then we sit side by side. "Comfortable?" he asks.

"Yup." I shift forward to keep a sharp edge of rock from digging into my shoulder blade.

He slips his arm around me, and I lean into his chest.

"You should sleep." His voice vibrates through me.

"Later." I reach across him to place a hand lightly on his chest.

He looks into my eyes, then shakes his head and looks away.

I know what he's thinking. He can't kiss me. Not without consequences that neither of us can afford. Not tonight. And even more than I want to kiss him, I want to talk. I'm just not sure how to start.

"How often have you visited Simcoe?" I ask softly.

"That was my first time past the fence."

"But you've been there several times?"

He stiffens. "Yeah. Scouting. Keeping an eye on them. Keeping Concord safe."

"Morag's seen you."

He bends one leg and rubs his shin. "So she said."

"Burn, do you remember going to Simcoe when you were a child? Morag said she saw you when you were about eight."

He stays very still, but I can feel the thump of his heart on my cheek.

"I tried to kill her." His voice is a raspy whisper.

"What?" I lift my head. *He remembers.*

"She told me she was my mother, and I tried to kill her."

"Why?"

He doesn't respond.

"Burn, don't beat yourself up. It makes sense that you didn't believe her. And your reaction makes sense, too. You were a kid. All alone. She probably looked like a Shredder, and you thought you were in danger."

"I knew she wouldn't hurt me. I knew who she was."

"Then why?"

"I was angry," he growls. "I wanted my mother dead. You of all people should understand that."

The air presses out of my lungs. My stomach clenches, as do my chest, my heart, the insides of my ears. The pain moves down to tighten my throat.

"Glory, I'm sorry." He touches my back. "I didn't mean that. What you did to your mom, it's nothing like what I did."

He slides closer to me again, enveloping me with his body. "What happened with your mom was an accident," he whispers. "You didn't mean to."

"Neither did you." I twist to look at him through blurry eyes. "You were a kid. You were scared."

"I wasn't scared. I was angry." His voice is deep against my ear. "She left me to die. She never wanted me."

"But she *did* want you. She still does." I wipe tears from my eyes. "She only wanted you to be safe."

"You're wrong." His hand forms a fist. "She's got another kid now. One she wants."

"Burn."

"Even when I was a baby, she knew I was a monster." He punches his thigh. "And by trying to kill her, I proved she was right."

"Burn," I whisper, and he draws a jagged breath. "You are not a monster, and you're wrong about why Morag left you. Ask her."

His body slumps and his hair falls forward to hide his face.

"She took you to the settlement to save you. Talk to her. Ask her to tell you what happened. I know you care. That's why you watch Simcoe. You go there wanting to see her." I push his hair back and my thumbs brush over his cheeks.

If I can't soothe him with words, maybe I can *show* him the truth and prove he's no monster. I scatter light kisses over his eyebrows, his cheekbones, the bridge of his nose. His skin tastes of salt and what seems like sadness.

He hasn't moved, so I press a light kiss to his lips. He tenses but doesn't stop me, so I wind my fingers through his hair and kiss him again, harder. I want to kiss away his pain—and my fear.

As the kiss builds, my body heats, and I can't tell whether the fire comes from me or from him. It doesn't matter.

"Break it up." Another voice invades.

"Drake?" I pull away from Burn's lips.

My brother and Jayma are standing nearby with Morag.

I leap to my feet and into Drake's arms. "You're okay!" I stretch an arm toward Jayma and pull her into our embrace. "How did you find us?"

"We were looking for a safe place to sleep and found her." Drake points to Morag.

"I introduced myself," she says matter of factly.

"Where's Dad?"

"Down in the camp," Drake answers.

"Have you seen him?"

"We didn't get here until sunset." Drake's expression turns grim. "I know better than to go down there at night."

"Dad can teleport," I say. "Why didn't he leave after he was captured?"

"I'm not sure he was captured," Drake says, looking down.

"Of course he was. Someone must be holding him, making it impossible for him to use his Deviance." Dad can't teleport if someone's touching him.

Drake shakes his head. "It's not that simple."

Simple or not, we need to act. "What did you see down there? How many are there? What's the layout?"

"It's horrible." Jayma shivers. "We reached the edge just as the sun was going down. They're cutting and torturing each other. Then laughing about it."

"I don't get why Dad would risk coming anywhere near here alone." I look at Drake. "Or why you let him."

Drake drags one foot along the ground. "There's something you should know."

"*More* secrets?"

"Let's go over there." He points back toward the forest. "I'll tell you everything."

I check over my shoulder. Burn's standing a good distance away and staring at us. For the moment, he seems okay and I need to talk to my brother. As I follow Drake toward the woods, Morag and Jayma sit under the overhang. Morag doesn't face Burn, but I can tell that she's watching him.

I hope they'll talk. He needs to hear what she told me, and he needs to hear it from her.

As we walk, Drake says, "You should have stayed in Concord. I've got this covered."

"Me?" I grab his arm and his armor rises. "What in the world were you thinking, coming here? How did you even *know* about this place?" Morag was right about one thing—it was hard to find.

"I've been here before—with Dad."

"Dad took you to a Shredder camp? Tell me what's going on!"

"I will." He sits on a bed of pine needles. "Remember when Dad told us he has a twin sister?"

I sit, too, and lean back against a tree. "*Had* one. Yeah. She was a Deviant. Management expunged her from Haven when they were teens."

"Well, she lives in this camp."

"You're kidding me." My insides feel pulled in opposite directions. I can't blame Dad for wanting to reunite with his sister, but if she's lived down there for twenty years . . . "She's a Shredder?"

"I should have told you as soon as you got back to Concord." Drake rubs his arms and his armor recedes. "I'm sorry, but I knew you'd run off after him. He said he'd be back ages ago."

"And now they've got him captive."

Drake grimaces. "Maybe not."

"Why do you keep saying that?"

"Dad's been breathing too much dust." His fingers trace through the pine needles.

"You've seen him do it? Why didn't you stop him?"

"It's easier for him to get into the camp if he takes some dust first. It cuts down the chance he'll be attacked."

"Dad pretends to be a Shredder?"

Drake shifts. "Kind of."

"But Shredders attack other Shredders," I say. "I've seen it."

"Yeah, but not if there are non-Shredders around." Drake leans back.

"How could he take such a huge risk?" I slam my fist down, and a small cloud of dust rises, glittering in a stream of moonlight. I'm mesmerized for a moment, but I make myself look away from it. Drake's raising a handful of dust toward his face.

I yank his arm and the dust flies around him. His armor rises again.

"What are you doing?"

He clasps his hands in his lap. "I don't breathe it often, but a little bit helps. It makes me stronger, braver. You saw how it fixed my legs and healed me after that battle."

"Have you been doing that since we got out of Haven?" I take his hands. "Do you want to turn into a Shredder?"

"You don't know anything about it," he says.

"What do *you* know about it?" I ask harshly. "I've seen the renewal pens at Simcoe, I've been attacked by and killed Shredders—and I've seen what goes on in the Hospital in Haven."

Drake tugs his hands from mine.

"Is our aunt really down there?" I ask more gently.

He nods.

"How can Dad be sure it's her? He hasn't seen her in so long."

"He knows. He recognized her Deviance."

"What is it? How does Dad know she's the only one with that particular Gift?"

"It's our aunt," he says. "I've met her."

I pound the ground. "He took you *down there*?"

"We went once, when the males were sleeping. It wasn't so bad." Drake shrugs. "Dad tried to get her to come with us, but she wouldn't leave. He took me back to Concord and came to try again." He stands. "But he should have left by now."

I rise and pull Drake into a hug. "We'll get him out."

• • •

Moving quietly in a tight group led by Morag, we head to the camp before sunrise. The sky is pale purple, and all but the brightest stars have faded. Cold air fills every last corner of my lungs.

Morag bends over and whispers, "From here, we have to be extra careful, or we'll be spotted."

We all follow her lead and bend at the waist as we continue to creep forward. As we draw nearer, the size and depth of the hole become apparent. When Morag nears the edge, she drops to a crawl, then flattens to her belly. We lie on our stomachs along the edge.

Below, the cliff goes straight down, like the pale stone was cut with a knife. It must be man made, although why people BTD, or after, would have dug such a big hole is beyond my comprehension.

The pit is rectangular, and we're near the corner on one of the short sides. It drops down at least four stories, but most of the space is taken up by a higher plateau that's only about two stories down. I wiggle forward on my belly. A sloping ledge, about fifteen feet below, looks like a path except that it doesn't lead anywhere.

On the other side of the pit, I spot what looks to be a road down—long, steep switchbacks that traverse the whole width of the rectangle.

Almost diagonally opposite us, there's a cluster of buildings, and more structures stand at the far end of the deeper pit. A partial wall that looks like it's built of stones and tree trunks separates that smaller square from the rest of the area.

In the main space, Shredders sleep on the ground in groups, some around smoldering fires. I can't spot my father. The buildings obstruct parts of our view.

"Where is he?" I ask Drake.

He shakes his head. "I'm not sure."

"They're probably holding him on the other side of those." Morag points to the cluster of buildings. "Or, if he's smart, he's hiding with the women and kids."

"Where are they?" That makes sense if he's looking for his sister.

Morag points straight ahead to the area beyond the deep pit, the part that's partially cordoned off by the makeshift wall.

"What is this place?" I ask. "I mean, what was it before?"

"BTD," Morag says, "this place was called a quarry. This rock is called limestone." She pats the ground. "The stones they cut out of this hole were used to make buildings."

"Let's head for the road." I start to rise.

She puts her hand on my shoulder. "If we go down the main road, we'll be spotted. It's suicide."

"Then how?"

She points down.

"To that ledge? Even if we can jump down there without falling off, where do we go from there?"

"There are ladders carved into the rocks, connecting a series of paths you can't see from this angle. The route's steep and the ledges are narrow, but it's the best way. I'll head to the women's camp. If I find Hector, I'll bring him back."

"That's your plan?" Burn says with more than a hint of disdain. "There are five of us and you're going down alone?"

"I know some of them," she says. "I'll be fine."

"I could care less about you," Burn says.

Morag's shoulders twitch, and I touch her arm.

Burn's scowling. If he and Morag talked last night, apparently it didn't go well. But Burn has a point.

"He's right, Morag. You shouldn't go alone. We've all got Gifts to protect us."

Morag nods slowly.

"I think we should all go down and head toward the women's camp," I say. "As soon as we know where my father is, we'll plan from there."

"Ready?" Morag rises to a crouch.

With a yelp, she backs up quickly, falling over. A head rises from the edge of the pit.

"Cal!"

Chapter Twenty-Three

WHAT ARE YOU DOING HERE?" MY VOICE SHAKES, but I'm not sure whether it's from happiness or confusion or fear.

"You know this guy?" Morag asks, and we all nod. "Okay. We should get moving while they're sleeping most soundly."

Cal grins at me as his head drops below the edge. I lean out and see that he's descending steps carved into the stone. I follow. The jutting stones serve as both hand- and footholds, and I go down quickly to the narrow ledge that's about three feet wide and slopes sharply.

As soon as my feet hit the ledge, Cal hugs me. The hug feels awkward and goes on too long. I push back on his shoulders. "Why aren't you with the FA?"

"Aren't you glad to see me?" He bends to kiss me.

I dodge his lips and back away. *What's going on with him?*

Burn reaches his hand toward Cal. "Hey. Good to see you. Did you come with Drake and Jayma?"

Cal pauses before shaking Burn's hand. "I followed them. To make sure they were safe. Why are you guys here?"

"My dad's down there," I tell Cal.

"I'm sorry." He reaches to hug me again.

I sidestep out of his way, and he stumbles toward the edge of the narrow path. His arms windmill.

I lunge, but Burn is faster. He grabs Cal's belt and yanks, throwing Cal back toward the stone wall.

I look down. If he'd gone over, nothing would have stopped him before the bottom of the pit.

Drake jumps off the ladder. "That was a close one."

"No kidding." Cal brushes dust off his pants.

I overreacted to the hug. Cal and I are friends. He knows I'm with Burn and was just being friendly. I don't know how to be around him right now.

Jayma jumps off the ladder and waves hello to Cal.

"Let's get moving," I say.

In single file, the six of us head down the steep path, keeping close to the wall. Even though it's shadowed, I feel exposed.

At the end of each stretch of path, there's another ladder leading down to the next section. When we reach the bottom, we keep tight along the wall, then turn to our right and follow along the edge of the deeper pit. One misstep and we'll plummet to our deaths, but if we walk too far from the drop, we'll wade through Shredders.

They're spread over the dust and rocks, sleeping—I hope— and their weapons litter the ground. Not far ahead, a spear stands straight up, and when we get closer, I realize it's stuck through someone. Dark blood stains the ground beneath the impaled body.

It looks like these Shredders don't compost their dead, or even burn them, although I'm not sure why this surprises me.

Suddenly, the head on the body turns. He opens his eyes.

I jump and clamp my palm over my mouth.

"What's wrong?" Burn's hand is on my shoulder instantly.

"I thought that Shredder was dead."

Burn raises his spear and drives it straight through the Shredder's head. He turns to me. "Seemed best to put him out of his misery."

I cringe, but now the Shredder can't yell out to raise the alarm.

In front of us, Jayma is walking alongside Drake, her head turned into his chest. I don't blame her. And I'm glad she didn't see what Burn just did. Morag's in front of them, and Cal's trailing behind us.

I step on something soft and nearly lose my balance. A severed hand.

I cannot let fear take over.

Morag stops beside a building and we all join her. From here, we're shielded from the main part of the camp, but we can see the women and a few children.

"When do the women and children sleep?" I ask.

"They take turns," Morag answers.

In the women's camp, a small group is gathered around a fire, and it looks as if they're heating something in a pot. That simple sign of civilization gives me hope. I creep forward a few feet to look past the building to the main camp.

I see Dad.

His wrists are tied to two tall poles in the ground. He's slumped, head down and knees bent, and his entire weight seems to be borne by his straining shoulders.

I stop myself from heading straight for him. My barreling in would not only be futile, it would get all of us captured. Killed, if we're lucky. I beckon to the others so they see him, too.

"I think I see someone I know." Morag points toward the women's camp. "I'll ask her for help. We might be able to distract the guards long enough to get him free."

"Those are chains." I turn toward Burn. "Are you strong enough to break them?"

"Maybe."

"I can break them," Jayma says. "If I can reach high enough."

"I can lift her," Burn says.

Jayma looks pale, and Drake pulls her in closer.

"That sounds like a plan." I drag my teeth along my dry lower lip. "As long as the guards stay asleep."

About five feet behind Dad, a Shredder shifts a sword from one hand to the other. Not asleep. There's another rock that's closer, and a foot sticks out from behind it. That guard might be sleeping, but we can't count on it.

"Just the two guards?" I ask the group.

"Hard to be sure." Morag nods toward the camp. "I'll go get help."

"No." Drake steps forward. "Let me go. I see my aunt."

"Which one is she?" I crane my neck, scanning the faces.

"Bad idea," Morag says. "They won't like a male stepping into their area. It'll spook them."

"She knows me," Drake says.

"I'll go with him," I say. "It'll be less threatening if he's with a female."

Cal grunts. He's got a sour look on his face, and he hasn't contributed to the planning at all. I wish he'd stayed up top. He's not safe down here without a Deviance to protect him.

"Be careful," Burn says and squeezes my hand. I look up into his dark eyes and feel braver.

I love you, I think, but I hold the words inside.

Chapter Twenty-Four

DRAKE AND I WALK TOWARD THE FEMALE SHREDDERS. They seem calm, but they are filthy, covered in scabs, their hair matted. One Shredder, crouching behind the fire, stands and kicks dust toward the others to draw their attention.

Drake's armor rises to cover his torso and arms. I glance back. Dad and his captors are blocked from my view now by a building that Burn and Jayma are creeping toward. Morag and Cal watch them intently.

I scan the female camp again. "Which one is our aunt?" One of the females draws a metal spike from the fire and charges toward us. The metal glows red, and I resist the urge to duck behind my armor-skinned brother. But another Shredder, with ragged black hair, stops the one wielding the weapon.

"That's her," Drake says. "Aunt Olivia."

She stares at us and I gasp. Her skin is scarred and dark red, like it's one giant scab, but she has my father's cheekbones and—I note as she strides toward us—his gait.

Drake waves and his armor retracts. She has a wild-eyed look, and aunt or not, I'm ready to defend my brother—and myself.

"Drake," she says, "you changed your mind." Her voice is scratchy. "And you brought a mate. Good luck keeping her to yourself." She looks over to the men.

"We're here to get Dad," Drake says.

"Hector's still here?" She glances again toward the male compound, and I see a flash of concern in her eyes. It quickly vanishes, and she kicks dust toward me. "Who's your girl?"

"This is my sister. Glory, this is Aunt Olivia."

"Hi." I slowly extend my hand.

Laughing, she reaches to shake. Drake's armor rises, and he slams my arm down.

"Drake!" Rubbing my throbbing arm, I stare at Olivia's hand. Her palm is covered with hundreds of thin blades that glint in the sunlight.

"What's wrong?" She holds both of her blade-covered palms to face me. "Don't even want to shake hands with your dear auntie?"

My father risked his life to save *her*? My jaw tightens and I focus on controlling my Deviance. I know that life out here must have been tough on her, but that doesn't excuse trying to hurt me—as some kind of joke?

"Will you help us get Dad?" Drake asks.

"Hector can leave if he wants."

Drake takes a step forward and I fight the urge to pull him back. "I don't think so," he says. "He was supposed to be home weeks ago. They've got him chained over there, behind that building. He can't teleport for some reason. I don't get it. Metal shouldn't block his Gift."

Olivia laughs harshly. "I said he could leave if he wanted to. He's probably too high."

"His feet are only hanging a few inches from the ground," I say. Olivia smirks. "High. Too much dust."

"Dust should enhance his Gift."

"To a point," she says, "but it's called high for a reason. Dust can take you places where your Deviance doesn't matter—where it's hard to control, but you no longer care." She looks directly into my eyes, and the grin on her face chills me. "You've never inhaled, have you?"

I shift my shoulders back. "Sure I have. It's impossible to live out here without breathing dust."

"Some, sure." She looks around, then strides over to a pile of dust that's drifted against an uneven cut in the rocky surface. She scoops some up and sashays back, hands held forward, like she's teasing me with the most precious gift in the world.

The razors have retracted into her hands, and she slides her palms into a beam of sunlight. As much as I want to look away, I can't. The sunlight makes the particles of dust sparkle and dance. They reach out to me from my aunt's palms as if they're alive, as if they know me. It's like I can see every individual grain and each is different, and the colors—which appear pale gray in a pile—stand out individually. Golds and pinks and greens and blues. Shimmering silver. Gleaming bronze.

It's the most beautiful thing I've ever seen. The most enticing. The most tempting. Why have I never really looked at dust before?

"Glory." Drake grabs my shoulder and forces me to stand straight.

I blink. My face was inches from the dust.

"Oh, come now, nephew," Olivia says. "It's not like you don't know the pleasures. Stop pretending to be so virtuous." She smiles at me. "He's not."

Drake's grip tightens on my shoulder.

His armor's still up and his fingers dig deeply into my flesh. I cover his hand with mine, but he doesn't seem to notice. "Drake, that hurts."

His head snaps toward me, and I barely recognize my brother's eyes. They're too wide, too frantic, and I see how hard he's fighting to resist the dust.

I move forward, blocking his view of her hands. "Are you going to help us save Dad or not?" I ask Olivia. "We need someone to distract the guards."

"It's just the two of you?"

"Yes." Burn and Jayma should be in position by now. I won't tell her about them unless I have to.

She lifts her chin. "I'll help you. On one condition."

"What?"

"He might not *want* to be saved. You need to understand why. Inhale some dust."

"No."

"Who told you to fear dust?" Her voice rises. "Your father? Hector lived too many years brainwashed inside that dome.

Then when he got out, he moved to another prison where dust is shunned. Here, we're free."

"He's chained!"

"Could be his choice. Maybe he's finally faced the truth."

"I don't believe that. And the women and children here aren't free, either." I gesture around. "If you are, then why all the barricades?"

"We're all as free as we want to be." She puts her mouth close to my ear. "What you don't understand is that the females have the true power here. We set the rules. You'll see when you join us."

"I'll never join you."

"You're not facing reality. Like I keep telling your dad, embrace what you are. Pining for life BTD is ridiculous. Don't you think the dust is here for a reason? Don't you see it made some of us better? We're meant to use it." She lifts the dust to my face. "You can't judge if you don't understand."

Looking at the dust, I shake my head.

"I won't help you get Hector until you try."

The dust pulls me in.

Drake grabs my arm.

I straighten. "I'll try some *after* we get Dad."

"Do it first." She steps right up against me, so close I can smell her putrid breath. So close I can see the tiny razor scars on her cheeks, on her dark lips—from her own hands.

I look into her eyes and grab hold, focusing in on her mind. *No one helped* me, she thinks. *I was expunged and alone out here for twenty years. Why should I help my brother or his kids? Hector had it easy. Time for him to get a taste of my life.* Her mind sparks with rage and resentment.

As I tighten my hold on her brain, she staggers, crying out in pain.

I close my eyes. "Are you going to help us or not?"

"You're powerful." A smile brushes over her lips. "You're right. We're family. I should help."

"Thank you." I look back toward the others.

"Aren't you forgetting something?" Olivia asks.

I turn to her.

She knees me in the gut.

I bend, sucking in air as she raises her hands to my face.

"No!" Drake yells.

He's too late. My lungs fill with dust, and my mind ignites with a thousand explosions—beautiful, exciting explosions. Lights spark and fly. Pleasure flicks and flames. Power surges and slams through my entire body.

I'm dimly aware that Drake's pushed Olivia down as my head drops back to face the sky. It's like I'm floating, but grounded at the same time. I don't remember when I've felt so alive, so whole, so free.

I raise my head and offer my hand to my aunt. She stares at her own before taking mine, and her palm is razor free as I pull her to her feet.

"Now," she says. "Now, you're ready to see truth."

Chapter Twenty-Five

RAKE AND I FOLLOW OLIVIA. WE KEEP LOW AND silent behind her clomping strides. I have to give her credit: there's nothing suspicious or tentative in the way she moves. Olivia looks like she's got her own reasons to head toward the guards.

My mind's spinning impossibly fast. Everything's changed: the sun is brighter; the rocks are sharper; the air is sweeter. Every sense is turned up to high—and it's like the dust has unleashed new ones. I can taste every scent on the breeze and see individual minerals and elements in the stone. And as we pass a group of sleeping males, I can hear their heartbeats. I smell—I *feel*— the rotting tang of their breath as they snore.

The power's incredible, intoxicating.

We approach the spot where they're holding my father. There's no movement from either guard. One's still sleeping and the other hasn't noticed us. If Burn and Jayma are near, they're well hidden.

Besides the two guards, three other Shredders are scattered nearby, sleeping. From forty feet away, I can sense everything about them, almost like I'm locked onto them with my Gift.

My Deviance seems so much stronger on dust.

Drake and I stop while Olivia continues. I spy Jayma on Burn's back as he crouches at the side of a building that's so rusted I'm surprised it's still standing. Above them, a jagged piece of metal hangs like a dagger.

That metal could slice Jayma when they rise. But I trust Burn. He'll keep Jayma safe—if he can. Olivia calls out to the guard closest to us.

"Come here." Olivia beckons for the guard to follow her behind a slab of rock.

"What do you want?" the guard asks.

"You," Olivia says. She puts one hand under her breast and the other between her legs.

I cringe. We asked her to create a distraction, but her repulsive solution will handle only one of the guards—at best.

"How about a preview?" the guard says. "Show me what you've got." He drops his weapon to the ground, and the clatter echoes through the camp. One of the nearby Shredders turns in his sleep.

Her eyes on the guard, Olivia gyrates her hips and turns as she slowly lifts her shirt. I hiss softly. Her stomach is a crisscross of raised black scars on red flesh. Some of the scars are straight and thin, like the ones on her face—and obviously made by her hands—but others are longer and deeper.

She might not want to leave this camp, but I understand why my father's been trying so hard to convince her.

Bending at the waist, she displays her backside to the guard. He reaches her in seconds and lifts her off her feet from behind. She struggles in his arms.

I want to help her, but Drake stops me.

"She knows what she's doing."

I hope he's right. Burn runs toward Dad as he lifts Jayma from his back to his shoulders.

Dad still hasn't moved.

Jayma reaches up and snaps the chain holding one of Dad's arms, and he slumps.

"We should help them," I say, and before my brother can object, I race forward and grab my dad under his arms to support him.

"Hey!" A Shredder's screech rakes my eardrums.

The other guard is awake.

"Stay with Dad," I tell Drake. "I've got this."

Drake replaces me as Dad's support while Jayma works on the second chain.

This guard is tall and thin, his skin a mass of scabs. Dark-brown blood oozes from his neck and ribs. I focus on his bulging eyes.

Almost immediately, I connect. He freezes, staring at me. I should kill him, explode his head or his heart like I've done to other Shredders, but I can't.

Shredders—at least some—were once human and could be again. They do monstrous things, but do their actions make them monsters? If so, Burn and I are monsters, too.

I don't accept that. I *won't* accept that.

The Shredder's mind is engorged with hate but shadowed by fear. This Shredder didn't ask for guard duty; he was forced. Memories flash in his mind. The images of the Shredder who seems to run the camp are so horrific I nearly gag.

I barely need to think the word "unconscious" and the guard collapses to the ground.

A scream fills the quarry, and I raise my hands to my ears.

Olivia walks out from behind the slab of rock, a wicked grin on her face. Globs of thick shredder blood drip from her razor hands. I don't want to know what she's done.

Dad is freed now, and Burn slings Hector's limp and bleeding body over his shoulder. I hurry toward them.

"We'd better get out of here," Burn says. Drake takes Jayma's hand. Cal and Morag are standing watch back by the pit's edge.

"What?" Olivia asks, striding toward us. "No thank-you? No tearful good-bye for your auntie?"

"Thank you," I tell her. "Come with us. Dad was here to get you."

She tips her head to the side, and I believe for a moment that she's considering it.

"You." She puts her hand on Jayma's forearm. "You're strong for your size."

Drake puts his hand over our aunt's. "Olivia. Let her go."

"What's your name, little one?" Olivia asks.

"Jayma."

"You'll do well here, Jayma. You've got what it takes. A small feminine body to draw the males in, but the strength to keep them from killing you."

"Thanks?" Jayma says tentatively.

"Don't thank her." I step forward. "Do you realize what she wants? What she's suggesting?" I take another step, but Jayma shakes her head to stop me.

She has the strength to pull away from Olivia, but she's not doing it—and I realize why.

"Let her go," Drake says firmly.

Blood drips from Jayma's arm, and I watch in horror as Olivia drags her palm along Jayma's skin; it's shredded and bleeding. I reach out, but Drake's already bundled Jayma into his arms.

"Why did you do that?" I stare at Olivia, trying to meet her gaze.

"It was an accident." Olivia grins. "Better give her some dust. Those cuts look deep."

Fury rises inside me. My aunt won't look at me, but I can hear her heart beating. Even without eye contact, I can sense the flow of her thick blood as it pushes through her veins.

Olivia implied that dust hampers my dad's Deviance, but it's helping mine. I focus on her heart, but while I can sense it pulsing, the organ's too hard to squeeze, as if it has a shield around it. But that could be the limitations of my power. And she won't make eye contact with me.

My father stirs. "What's going on?"

Burn sets him down. "Are you strong enough to teleport out of here?" he asks.

Dad staggers as he nods. He turns to me and he looks so weak, so fragile. Nothing like my dad. His hair is dull and matted, his cheeks sunken, his eyes bloodshot and wild.

"Go," I say. "Teleport up top. Or back to Simcoe." He should get as far away from here as his Gift will take him.

"That's enough!" Drake shouts. His armor up, he shoves Olivia's hand away from Jayma. "Leave her alone."

Jayma's eyes are glazed over, but the bleeding on her arm has stopped. Drake and Olivia must have given her dust while I was distracted by Dad.

"Drake"—Olivia raises her hands—"you two should join the camp. I know you enjoy the dust."

I'm about to lunge at Olivia—I'll kill her before I let her draw them in—but Morag shouts, "Run!"

A male Shredder has woken and is lumbering toward us.

Dad takes a shaky step, then disappears. I don't know where he teleported to, but at least that's one less person I love who's down here in danger.

Olivia reaches for Jayma, but Drake takes my friend's hand and pulls her out of reach. Morag, with Cal at her side, motions for us to join her.

We're closer to the main road than the ladders, and that route doesn't have a deep pit beside it. But going toward the main road means crossing the open area littered with sleeping Shredders. Some are stirring.

Drake leads Jayma toward Morag and Cal, but Burn runs toward the Shredders, pulling a sword from his coat. I follow him.

Burn swings the sword at the first Shredder he reaches. The Shredder ducks too late, and the sword slices into the top of his head. Burn tugs at his sword lodged in the Shredder's skull. The Shredder's elbows, wrists, and knees sprout sharp horns. He swings them at Burn. How is this Shredder not dead?

I yell, "Hey! Over here!"

The Shredder glances at me, and that's all it takes to capture him.

I grab on to his heart and squeeze. The Shredder pounds his fists into his chest, stabbing himself with the horns. He opens his mouth to scream, but all that comes out is a high-pitched whine.

His heart stops. I sense the last, heavy thud as his body goes slack and crumples to the ground, propped up by Burn's sword in his head.

Burn plants his foot on the dead Shredder's back and yanks out his weapon.

Something slams into me from the side, and I'm lifted off the ground. Another Shredder has me in his grip. The smell of death chokes me.

I kick and slam my head back into his, but this Shredder is too strong. His skin looks similar to that of the others, but it feels as hard as the special metal they use for the Comp uniforms. If my Deviance was enhanced by the dust, it's not anymore, and I can't even sense the Shredder's heart.

Burn's body expands in height and girth as he thumps toward me. The transformation happens in seconds. Rage overtakes his face.

He swings his huge arm, aiming for the Shredder's head above mine. The Shredder lunges to the side, pulling me with him. Burn misses.

Burn roars as he raises his fists above his head. If he's not careful, he'll kill me along with the Shredder. He slams his hands down on the Shredder's head, and I feel the body behind me compress on impact. But he doesn't let go. There's another slam, and the Shredder loosens his hold.

I twist and slip down through his arms, then scramble out of his reach.

Burn punches the Shredder, but his skin is too hard. The strikes seem to be hurting Burn more than the Shredder, who rises, screeching. Burn lunges for his legs and knocks him to the ground.

Burn lifts the Shredder by the ankles and swings.

Gathering speed, Burn rotates and the Shredder's body rises from the ground.

Burn lets go. The Shredder flies fifty feet and over the edge of the pit. Morag and Cal duck as the body passes over their heads.

Morag points frantically behind Burn. More Shredders are headed toward us.

"Come on!" I shout at Burn, hoping he can understand me, and I race past the women's camp toward the pit.

Drake and Jayma reach Morag and Cal first and keep running.

"Go!" I say when I near Cal. I don't wait for an answer, and I'm glad when he turns and runs along the pit beside me. This sharp drop should keep the Shredders from charging in our direction.

"Look out!" Morag shouts, and I see my assumption was wrong.

Five Shredders are lumbering straight at us. Behind me, Burn flings another Shredder into the pit, then heads toward us, covering the distance in bounding steps that make the earth shake. Olivia follows.

Jayma stops abruptly. "We can't outrun the Shredders. We have to fight." Her body's trembling. Her arm is still raw.

"You run," I tell her. "Morag and Cal, you, too. Drake and I will help Burn."

"I'm not leaving Drake," Jayma says, "and I'm not leaving you."

She tugs at a slab of rock that's imbedded in the ground. She easily lifts the rock and hurls it at the Shredders, striking one.

Burn swings his sword. A Shredder goes down.

There's a thud and another Shredder is on his back, crushed under a rock. Drake positions himself like a human shield as Jayma looks for something else to throw.

Burn leaps and lands by two Shredders. He lifts one in each hand and slams their bodies together. Then he tosses both over the side of the pit.

"He's a monster!" Cal shouts. "Jayma, throw that rock at Burn before he kills us."

Morag steps toward Cal. "Leave him alone."

A Shredder runs up behind Morag, a club in his hand.

"Duck!" I yell. My shout draws the Shredder's attention. Captured by my gaze, he swings the club down, missing Morag, and just narrowly missing himself. The weapon flies behind him.

Focused on his eyes, I grab his heart.

Screams rise behind me, but I can't look. Not until this Shredder's dead.

He's fighting me. His blood's heavy and thick. Morag brushes past me toward Burn.

Finally, the Shredder drops to the ground, and I turn. Burn is fighting a Shredder who's covered in long spikes, and I try to remember the animal from BTD that he resembles. A porcupine?

Drake punches his armored fist into the gut of another Shredder, and then Jayma smashes that Shredder's skull with a rock.

"Burn, watch out!" Morag cries.

I spin around.

A Shredder winds up to throw a spear into Burn's back.

The spear flies, but in midair it changes direction, heading for Morag instead.

She tries to catch it, but the spear drives through her chest. Her blood darkens the ground where she lands.

Burn yells, and the sound is so loud my bones shake. It's the most anguished cry I've ever heard. In two strides, Burn leaps over Morag's body and crushes the head of the Shredder who killed his mother.

Lifting the Shredder by the head, Burn swings.

The Shredder's spine severs, and the body sails through the air, landing near Jayma and Drake. Burn tosses the head in the pit.

Someone shrieks. Drake's fist is inside a Shredder's chest cavity. He pulls his hand back, dark blood dripping from his armored fist. The Shredder stops screaming.

I run to Drake and Jayma. They both look stunned. "Get out of here!" I tell them.

Drake points behind me and I see Cal heading for Burn.

A Shredder slams into me from behind, pushing me to the ground. I can't turn over to lock eyes.

The smell is disgusting and I choke for air, but instead I get a mouthful of dust.

My brain fires, like someone lit a lantern inside my skull. The heartbeat of the Shredder thuds in my head. It's louder than the screams and shouts around me.

I can feel the Shredder's blood flowing. I can sense every part of his body. I don't know whether it will work without eye contact, but I use my Gift to take hold of his heart and squeeze. The organ tightens, and I feel the blood slowly empty out of the ventricles. The heart stops beating.

It worked!

The body above me loses all its tension but not its weight.

I'm trapped. I try to draw air, but it's so hard. I can't move. Can't breathe.

Where is Burn?

My mind fades and fog fills my vision. If I lose consciousness, I'm going to be smothered. Even the dust I just breathed won't get me out of this one.

Suddenly, the weight lifts, and the difference is so extreme I feel like I'm floating. I suck in a breath and cough. Drawing in another, I roll over, shielding my eyes from the bright sunlight.

"Are you okay?" Jayma asks. She throws the dead Shredder into the pit.

"Thanks." I try to sit but fall onto my back.

"Easy." She kneels down and offers me her hand to help me up.

"Burn and Cal." I look to where I last saw them.

Burn's holding a Shredder over his head.

I rub my eyes and shake my head, trying to clear the fog. It's not a Shredder.

"What's going on?" My mind refuses to process the scene. Is this some strange aftereffect of inhaling dust?

Stumbling forward, I blink, trying to change the image.

But I can't.

It won't change.

I want to stop what I'm seeing, but I don't have time to yell or move.

Burn throws the body over the side of the pit.

"No!" I scream. "No!"

The body Burn threw into the pit was Cal's.

Chapter Twenty-Six

DRAKE GRABS ME AROUND THE WAIST AND SPINS ME away from the pit. "There's nothing you can do. It's too late."

"No!" I struggle against my brother. "Cal's not dead. Burn wouldn't. He'd never—"

"Burn's not himself, right now."

Barely hearing his words, I twist in Drake's hold and see Burn slam his fist into a Shredder, who drops like he was hit by a steel girder. Rage twists Burn's features as he pulls the spear from Morag's chest.

He lifts his mother over his shoulder with one hand. Then, holding the bloody spear in his other hand, he runs through the camp toward the main road. More Shredders wake as he thumps past them. He'll never make it out.

I tug against Drake's arms.

"We've got to go," Drake says. "Now."

He lets me loose, and after one last glance toward the pit, I race with Jayma and Drake toward the ladders. Olivia's still following. Is she going to try to stop us?

Drake reaches the first ladder and motions for Jayma and me to go ahead.

"I'll bring up the rear," Olivia says.

No time to question her motives, I scramble up behind Jayma, and then the four of us run along the narrow path to the next ladder, then the next.

Since our trail's directly below us, we can't really tell, but we haven't seen any Shredders following us—yet. Burn's rampage through camp has focused their attention. After climbing the second-to-last ladder, we spot someone coming down the final one, fifty yards ahead.

My muscles tense. We're surrounded. Then I recognize who it is.

"Dad, go back up!" I shout.

He does. We race up the final steep path, and then Jayma pushes me to go up the ladder first. Dad takes my hand near the top, pulling me over the edge.

"Thank Haven you made it out." He clings to me. "I was about to teleport back down to help." He lets me go to give Jayma a hand and then Drake.

I look across the quarry and squint. A figure—which looks like Burn carrying Morag—is on the second to last switchback of the main road leading out. A long line of Shredders chases behind. Burn's decision to run that way gave the rest of us a chance.

But if I give him credit for leading the Shredders away, if I believe he knows what he's doing right now, that means—

The full impact of what happened slams into my gut, and I double over, gasping for breath.

Burn killed Cal. Dropping to the ground, I put my head in my hands.

Jayma drapes her arms over me. "We're safe, and Burn will be fine."

"I don't care. Not after what he did."

"We don't know what happened," she says. "Not exactly."

I look up at her. "I know what I saw." But this isn't the place for shock or self-pity. I leap up. "Come on."

Olivia steps back from the lip of the quarry. "We were followed."

Jayma heads for a pile of rocks. They all look like they weigh twice what she does. Maybe three times.

She lifts one, carries it to the edge, and I watch in awe as she aims and then drops the rock down. The scream and crunch that follow send shivers up my spine, followed by a sick sense of satisfaction.

"Another one," Drake says. "Over here."

She grabs another rock, staggers to where Drake's pointing, and then releases her bomb.

Wanting to help, I tug at one of the smallest rocks, but it's no use. I can't budge it. Jayma grabs another big rock, lifts it overhead, and slams it down on the path below. Olivia and Dad are standing close together, watching.

"Jayma's a Deviant," I tell him.

"I see that," Dad says, his eyes wide.

"That should buy us some time," Jayma says. "I got all the ones at that level."

"She's a strong one," Olivia replies.

Ignoring her, I look back across the quarry. Dad puts his hands on my shoulders. "That was a huge risk you kids took. Thank you."

"Anything for family," I tell him.

Dad looks over at Olivia, who's fidgeting like it's impossible for her to stand still.

"How do we get to Simcoe?" I ask him. "Morag led us here, and Burn might lead the Shredders the same way we came."

"Don't worry." Dad squeezes my shoulder. "I know a safe way back."

• • •

Dad and Olivia walk together in constant conversation. He's got some of his strength back and is walking without her help. Watching them like this, laughing at times, arguing at others, they truly seem like twins, and I can almost forget she's a Shredder. Dad seems happy, but I wish I'd never met her. I want to forget everything that happened today.

I can't believe both Cal and Burn are gone.

Burn's alive—but he's gone all the same. I can never forgive him.

The image of Burn killing Cal loops in my mind, and I fight to block it, using my old tricks for stalling my Deviance. I rub my mom's ring, I count, I imagine being surrounded in white light. I even recite rules from Haven. None of it works.

I'm glad I'm alive, but grief tugs on my limbs. I'm so tired. Is it from sadness or the aftereffects of the dust?

Every few minutes, either Drake or Jayma glances back to make sure I'm still following. They smile or wave or pretend that they're looking at the stars, but I know exactly what they're doing. They think I might run off. I can't blame them. But I've changed since that day four months ago when I found out what I'd done to my mother.

I'm stronger. I know who I am.

We step out of the forest onto a wide expanse of rock. The moonlight highlights veins of mica in the granite—and drifts of dust. I stop and stare.

Inhaling some would give me energy, and I'd recapture the power I felt earlier today. It might even help me forget . . . I take several steps toward a drift, then turn away.

Dad's holding on to his side. One of his cuts is bleeding again. Olivia walks him over to the dust and scoops some up for him to inhale, and I don't have the energy to object. But I note that she doesn't take any herself. Probably already high.

When we get moving again, I have to admit the dust helped Dad. Still, we move slowly. Dad's route is longer, and it takes all day to walk back to Simcoe. When we get near, the forest thickens again, blocking out the moon, and the blackness closes in on me like a noose.

Dad stops. "We should wait here until the sun comes up."

"Why?" I just want to drop on a bed. "We're only a quarter of a mile away."

"If anyone approaches Simcoe at night, the guards shoot first and ask questions later," Dad says.

I want to argue—Houston told us it wasn't safe *outside* the fences at night—but I'm exhausted. I slump at the base of a tree. "Aren't there Shredders around here?"

"We'll take turns keeping watch." Dad kisses the top of my head and moves away, stopping Olivia from heading farther into the woods. After talking to him for a moment, she sits against a tree, facing back toward us.

"I'll build a fire," Drake says, and he and Jayma start gathering wood. My legs won't move.

Dad returns and crouches down beside me. "You should get some sleep. Olivia's going to keep watch first."

"I don't think I can." I draw my knees to my chest. And I don't trust Olivia.

He sits beside me.

Resting my head on his shoulder, I inhale.

My dad's scent and the sound of his heart take me back inside Haven, back to our small apartment in the Pents. I squeeze my eyes shut as a memory floods in, but it's not a moment of joy; it's one of despair.

It's a memory from the day I killed Mom.

I'm right back in the few hours between when it happened and when the Comps came. Until now, the memory was gone. I forgot how Dad held me. I forgot that I let him and that my heart, so full of pain, was soothed by his closeness, his support, his love.

At the time, I thought *he'd* killed Mom. Didn't I? I'm not sure anymore. I do know I spent the next three years building my hatred for him until it nearly consumed me, until distrust and fear took over every decision and move that I made.

But that day I let my dad hold me, and then, like now, his left hand stroked my arm while the fingers of his right drummed his thigh.

"Did you know they'd expunge you?" I ask him.

"What are you talking about?"

"That night. After Mom died. You held me exactly like this. You told me to hide Drake and not to trust anyone. Did you know what was going to happen?"

"I had a pretty good idea. But everything turned out better than I expected."

I raise my head. "Better?"

"So much better." He squeezes me tighter. "I never thought I'd see you or Drake again. I thought I was going to die. I certainly never thought we'd be reunited as a family, or that I'd find my sister. And now I've gotten her out of that camp for good."

I want to tell him what Olivia did to Jayma. How she tried to get us to stay at the Shredder camp. How she fed me dust, hoping to start an addiction. But I don't. What good would it do? Olivia's actions won't stop Dad from loving his sister—even if they should.

The fire sparks to life, and Drake and Jayma move to the other side of it. Drake leans against a rock, and Jayma lies down on pine needles nearby. He motions for her to move closer, and she smiles softly as she slides over and rests her head on his leg.

Seeing them together should make me happy, but instead, it makes me think of Scout and Cal. Both brothers are dead. And for what? Hot tears fill my eyes, and I don't brush them away.

I stare into the flames as the fire consumes the pine boughs and then dies down.

My father's breathing grows heavy. He's fallen asleep, but my mind won't stop racing, won't let me rest.

I killed my own mother, but what Burn did today wasn't an accident. He purposefully threw Cal into that pit. Is this how Zina feels about what Burn did to her brother?

Noise comes from the bushes.

I slide out from under my father's arm. He snorts but doesn't wake. Drake is slumped over Jayma. Both are sleeping. The slight glow from the embers doesn't penetrate far into the darkness, and I can't see Olivia. I creep forward to investigate.

Burn steps from behind a tree. He's back to his normal self and still carrying Morag.

"What are you doing here?" I whisper.

He doesn't look up. "I couldn't leave her with the Shredders."

He carefully sets down Morag's body. Her clothes are darkened with blood, and the shoulder of his coat looks wet. He crouches beside her, his head in his hands, and for an instant I want to take him in my arms.

Olivia steps up beside me. "You heading back to the camp?" she asks Burn.

He doesn't answer.

"You know it's where you belong," Olivia says.

Burn shakes his head. "I don't belong anywhere."

"Well, I'm heading back," she says.

"What?" I ask through clenched teeth.

She shrugs. "Back at the camp, I told Hector I'd walk with you to Simcoe. Listen to him ramble on. That's all."

"I can't believe you."

She puts a hand on her hip. "What don't you believe?"

"I don't believe you're related to my dad, never mind his twin. You're *nothing* alike."

"And? What's your point?"

"Dad risked his life for you. He loves you. Nothing is more important to him than family. Now that we're together, you're taking off? Don't you know that he'll just try to find you again? He can't bear to know that you're out there with those Shredders."

"Those Shredders?" She smirks. "What do you think *I* am?"

"You know you're not as far gone as most of them. You know that you could get off the dust if you tried, if you wanted to." I glare at her. "It would be easier on Dad if you *were* fully addicted. He might be able to write you off if you had no part of your humanity left. But instead, you're teasing him. Tempting him to help you and then spitting in his face when he does."

Olivia shifts her weight to her other leg. I can tell my words struck a chord.

"It's not his fault your Deviance was discovered by Management and his wasn't. It's not his fault you were expunged. Don't you think he'd turn back time and trade places with you if he could?"

She stares at me.

"Glory." Dad is standing a few feet away. "Go easy on her. She's been through a lot."

My cheeks burn with anger. "She's not worth it, Dad."

"Olivia," he says, "please don't leave yet. Let's talk."

I want to tell Dad that he should never talk to her again, but instead, I watch as the two of them head farther into the woods.

"I get it," Burn says.

"Get what?"

He's still crouching above his mother's body. "Can you make sure Morag's buried in the Simcoe cemetery? Jayma can carry her body the rest of the way." He stands. "I heard you loud and clear. You never have to see me again."

"I don't understand." My voice shakes as I look at Burn.

"I heard what you said to Olivia. Everything she did to your dad, to your family—I've done the same to you."

"I wasn't talking about *you*."

He turns to face me. "Every time you're ready to give up on me, every time you have a chance of being happy, I ruin it."

Wind rustles the boughs above us. He's right. He did ruin it, and this time it can't be fixed.

"I'm sorry." He backs away. "About Cal."

"Why did you do it?" My throat is tight and barely releases the words.

"I don't know," he says so quietly I can hardly hear him. "I was so angry."

"At Cal? Why?" I want him to give me an explanation, one I can accept. "Tell me. What happened?"

His shoulders rise and then drop. He looks up at me, and the pain on his face tears into me. I wish I could tell him that it's okay and that I forgive him no matter what—but it's not true.

Burn rubs his temple. "I remember being angry. I remember throwing him, but—"

"Were you jealous because he hugged me? Did you guys argue? Have you been pretending to like him?"

"It wasn't like that." His hand's shaking as he rakes his hair back.

"Then tell me. What *was* it like to kill my friend?"

"I only have . . ."—he shakes his head—". . . impressions. I remember lifting him, throwing him. But something—"

"What? What can you possibly say to explain killing Cal?"

His gaze meets mine, and we stand looking at each other for a long time. My Gift tingles behind my eyes, but I keep it in control. As angry as I am, I don't want to hurt him.

"It doesn't matter." He turns away.

I watch as he disappears into the woods, his gait heavy, his shoulders slumped.

When I can't see him any longer, something fractures inside me—a crack so deep and wide I know it will never heal. It expands the wound that was left when I learned that I'd killed my mother, and the ache spreads until it's in my bones, weighting every cell in my body. I want to lie down and give myself up to the pain. But I can't. I won't.

"What's going on?" Drake steps up beside me. "What's Morag's body doing here?"

Trembling, I turn to him. Drake hugs me and I hold on tight.

When I raise my head from Drake's shoulder, Dad's standing there and I pull him into our embrace. Family. That's how I'll find the strength to bear this.

I lift my head to see that Olivia didn't leave after all. She's watching us and rubbing her bare forearm. The flesh bleeds.

"Stop that!" Dad grabs her arm, and she looks down at it as if she didn't realize what she was doing.

"Okay," she says to Dad. "I'll do it."

"Olivia," he says, "you're going to be okay. You'll see."

"Do what?" I ask.

"Renewal at Simcoe," Dad says.

Drake raises his eyebrows but doesn't say anything.

"Is it possible to recover after so many years?" I ask. "Completely?"

"Others have. Look at Morag."

"She's dead," Olivia says coldly.

"Morag's not the only one who died today." I drop my head.

Dad puts his hand on my shoulder. "Let's go back to the fire."

We add more branches to the embers, and I stay between Dad and Drake as we sit. Jayma's on Drake's other side. Olivia sits by herself and leans back as she watches me through the sparks.

"Burn brought Morag's body?" Dad asks me. "Did you talk to him?"

I nod.

"Did he explain what happened?"

"He remembers doing it. It wasn't an accident."

"That doesn't sound like Burn," Dad says. "I've known him longer than you have. I'll bet it *was* an accident."

"Killing that blond kid?" Olivia says. "Oh, he did it on purpose."

"Shut up!" I yell. "You don't know either of them. You have no idea what happened."

"I *saw* what happened." She leans forward. "I saw the whole thing. Did you?"

"What did you see?" I ask, my voice rising. "Tell me." I only saw the last moment.

"I'll tell you," she says, "if you stop yelling."

I'm breathing so hard my chest hurts. I don't think I can trust one thing that comes out of my aunt's mouth, but if she saw what happened, I want to hear it. "Well?" I say. "What did you see? Why did Burn attack Cal?"

"Burn didn't attack Cal," she answers. "It was the other way around."

"Why would Cal do that?" Dad asks.

Olivia shrugs. "I only know what I saw. Cal was jabbing Burn with a spear, provoking him, distracting him as he tried to fight the Shredders."

"You must have seen it wrong," Drake says. "I'm sure Cal was trying to help Burn."

"What I saw," Olivia says, "was Cal trying to force Burn over the edge of the pit. I can't blame the big guy for what he did. I would've tossed the kid over, too."

"Burn could have disarmed Cal," I say. "Easily. He didn't need to *kill* him."

"From where I sat, your Cal got what was coming to him," Olivia says. "He should've known better than to poke a raging beast."

Chapter Twenty-Seven

DAD TAKES A LONG DRINK OF WATER AND THEN SETS the ceramic mug on the table in the central hall of Simcoe. Olivia is in Houston's office, no doubt arguing that she should start her renewal at Stage Two or Three. Frankly, she's lucky that the guards let her into Simcoe at all. They tried to toss her straight into the Stage One pen until Dad, and then Houston, intervened.

Caroline started in Stage Three, having passed the interview questions, and according to Houston, she's making great progress already. We all slept most of yesterday after burying Morag.

"You should go back to the settlement," Dad says to Drake and me. "Olivia and I will join you as soon as we've finished the program."

I stare at my father. "What do you mean by 'we'?"

Dad's jaw twitches. "I'm entering renewal, too."

I rise out of my seat. "But you're not a Shredder."

He puts his hand over mine. "I took in a lot of dust at that camp. I have no idea how much. Once they strung me up on those chains, they alternated between hurting me and healing me with dust. I couldn't concentrate enough to use my Gift. Some time in renewal will do me good."

Fighting tears, I interlock our fingers. "I'm so sorry, Dad. Drake and I will stay here until you're done."

"No need." He attempts a smile.

"I'm going back to Concord," Drake says. "Then on to Haven."

"No, you're not," I tell him. "The FA unit is long gone."

A door opens, and a group of children tumble through, laughing and shrieking and heading for the main door out of the building. I spot Burn's half brother. Does the boy know yet that he's lost his mom? He wasn't there when we buried her.

"I'm going to Haven," Drake says over the noise. "Even if the unit left without us, I'll catch up. I know how Haven works and I know the layout. They need me."

"Your *family* needs you," I say. "You should stay with me and Dad—and Aunt Olivia. Besides, if you go fight in Haven, who will watch out for Jayma?"

"I'm going with him," Jayma says from across the table.

"What?"

"I need to do my part," she says. "We need to take Management down. And my parents are still in Haven. They think I'm dead."

My heart feels as if it's being stretched in ten directions. Part of me wants to go to Haven, but even more, I want to stay with

Dad. Why can't anything be easy? I run my finger along the grain of the tabletop.

"Stay here." Drake rests his hand on my back. "You did your part for the FA already."

The day Cal and I escaped from Haven, I was determined to return and kill Mrs. Kalin. Have I become a coward? Is it selfish to care more about my family than about bringing down Management? I know more about Mrs. Kalin than anybody, and if she's still running things inside Haven . . .

But I do *not* want to take part in a war. The things the FA and the rebels were doing—bombs, sabotage, hurting innocent people—I want no part of it.

Houston and Olivia walk up to the table. My aunt looks calmer, softer. Her hair, no longer matted, is a lot like mine except it has more curls. I can see even more of our family, even more of Dad, in her features.

"Olivia's ready to go in," Houston says. "We've agreed that she'll start in Stage Two." He turns to Olivia. "But one sign of trouble and you're off to the Stage One enclosure."

"Don't worry," my aunt says. "I'm highly motivated." She looks at me as she says this and nods. I want to believe that she means it. I want to believe that she listened to my dad and heard what I said to her in the woods last night.

"I know you can do it, Liv," Dad says. "I'm going to spend some time in Stage Three, and Glory and I will be here waiting for you when you're done."

"I'll visit you both," I say. "Every day. I'll be here to support you. Cheer you on." This is where I'm most needed.

"Wait a minute," Houston says. "There are no visitors during renewal."

"Why?" I ask.

"We've found it to be counterproductive. There's no point in your staying here. But you're welcome to, if that's what you want."

I sit down, confused again. I don't want to stay here all alone.

"Olivia," Houston says, "it's time to go." Two large men approach and take her arms.

"Good luck," Drake says.

I go over to Olivia and whisper, "Don't blow it. If you break Dad's heart, I'll kill you. You know I can."

She tips her head away and smiles, but I can't tell whether she's mocking me or reassuring me.

The men lead her away and Dad starts to follow.

"Hector!" Houston calls, and my father stops. "Someone will take you in soon."

His shoulders slump, and he stands still until long after Olivia's out of sight.

When Dad returns to the table, Houston says, "She'll make it, Hector. She's determined."

"Do you think so?"

Houston claps Dad's back. "No guarantees, but based on her interview, I think she's got a good shot."

"Thank you for saying that. Can I have a few minutes to say good-bye to my kids?"

Houston steps away, and Dad envelops Drake and me in his arms.

"We'll all be together again soon," he says. "I know it."

I try to smile but I can't.

"Glory," Dad says, "go with your brother. I don't want *either* of you going back into Haven, but I'd rather know you're together than apart."

A lump rises in my throat, but he's right. If we can find a way back into Haven, we should help.

"And don't be so hard on Burn," he says. "Next time you see him, hear him out. As long as I've known that kid, I've never seen him attack anyone unless his life was in danger."

"You're wrong," I say. "This isn't the first time Burn killed an ally. The day you were expunged from Haven, Burn killed one of the other FA soldiers sent to save you. It was Zina's brother, and—"

"I know about that," he interrupts. "I was there."

"But then why did you say—"

Dad takes my head in his hands. "Zina's been told a hundred times what really happened. She won't listen. She's enraged about Andreas's death and determined to punish someone for it. She even hates me because he died while the FA was saving me. She's so convinced that Burn is a murderer, she won't hear the truth. Burn acted in self-defense."

"But Zina's brother was part of his FA unit."

"That day was the first time Burn changed," Dad says. "Everyone was frightened of him. No one knew what he would do, and Andreas decided he wasn't going to wait to find out. He was about to shoot Burn."

"Really?"

"Yes." Dad drops his hands to my shoulders. "Talk to Burn. If he doesn't remember everything that happened that day, help him figure it out."

"I'll try. I will." But I'm not certain I'll ever get the chance. And it doesn't erase what he did to Cal.

Chapter Twenty-Eight

HOW WILL WE GET INTO HAVEN WITHOUT AN FA UNIT?"
Jayma asks. She's sitting with me at the pub in Concord. Ravenous, we came here as soon as we got back. "And how will we contact them once we're in?" She takes a spoonful of thick soup.

"We'll do it," Drake assures her. "Rolph must have left at least one communicator behind."

I frown. "Those things have a short range. They were considered old even BTD." The FA communicators have channels and little dials to turn. "We'll need to be almost in Haven before we make contact."

"Then we should leave as soon as we can," Drake says. "This place is eerie with so many people gone."

"When do we leave?" Jayma asks.

"Are you done with your soup?" He half grins.

"No," I say, "we need a night's sleep first."

Sunlight floods into the room from the door behind me. Jayma's eyes open wide.

"What?" I turn.

Burn's standing in the doorway.

Seeing me, he starts to leave.

"Burn," Greggor calls, "I already dished out your soup!" The big, fur-covered cook strides across the room and slaps Burn on the back. "Don't let it go to waste." He nods to a table in the corner.

It takes every ounce of my willpower not to watch Burn, but eventually I hear a chair scrape on the floor in the corner. Despite Dad's advice, I'm not ready to talk to Burn, but I'm glad he didn't go back to the Shredder camp. I'm glad he's safe.

"Maybe Burn will come with us to Haven," Drake whispers to Jayma.

"I hope so," she says.

The bell in the lookout tower rings and we all jump up.

"Intruders!" Drake yells.

So much for our day of rest. Leaving our food half-eaten, we head for the door.

"I'll guard the wall by the lake," Burn says, and his words tear open what's left of my heart. He's following Cal's strategy from the last Shredder attack.

Burn heads down toward the lake, and the rest of us head up the main road. The few people left in Concord join us as we race through the village to the lookout. If our odds seemed bleak the last time we were attacked, our numbers are even lower now.

The bell stops ringing. Either the guard has decided that the danger has passed, or she's already in battle—or dead.

When we reach the tower, at least twenty settlers are gathered in a circle. I duck through the crowd to get to the front.

"Captain Larsson?" My mouth drops open. Gwen has her gun pointed at the chest of my former COT instructor. I haven't seen him since he helped Burn and me escape from Haven.

Captain Larsson smiles—an expression I barely recognize on his ruddy face. "Hi, Glory." He holds his hands up in surrender.

"You know this guy?" Gwen lowers her gun slightly.

"Yes, he was my Comp trainer." He's wearing civilian clothing. A rumble goes through the crowd.

"He's a Comp!" Terry, one of the tower guards, grabs Larsson's arms and binds them behind his back.

"I told you. There's no need for that." Someone steps out from behind Larsson.

Cal! The breath rushes from my lungs and I run forward. Jumping, I throw my arms and legs around him. "You're alive!"

He hugs me tightly, then sets me down. His cheeks are bright red. "Yeah, and lucky to be that way. Our FA unit ran into Larsson on the way into Haven. He tried to convince Rolph to turn back, but he wouldn't. So we came back to warn everyone here."

"Warn us about what?" My mind spins with questions. "And how can you be alive? I saw Burn throw you into the pit."

"Burn?" He rubs his head. "What pit?"

"At the Shredder camp." Fear grabs my gut. I back away from him. "This isn't Cal!" I yell. "It's Zina."

"No." He shakes his head. "It's me."

"Prove it," Drake says. "The person Burn killed looked like you, talked like you."

"When were you at a Shredder camp?" Cal asks. He shakes his head. "*Zina* went to a Shredder camp. Rolph sent her to sneak around there, impersonate Shredders, and warn us if they were planning another attack."

I raise my hands to my head. Zina's solo mission. This makes so much more sense. "Burn didn't kill you."

"Of course not."

I look directly into Cal's blue eyes, and the truth seeps through my shock. These are the eyes of the boy I've known and loved my whole life. I was so wrapped up in saving my dad, I got fooled by Zina—again.

"Burn didn't kill you," I repeat softly. "He killed Zina."

• • •

Cal, Jayma, Drake, and I sit in the first row of seats in the Assembly Hall. Gwen and Terry, the other tower guard, guide Larsson onto the platform in front of us and sit him down next to the table. In spite of my plea, the rest of the group refused to untie Larsson after they heard he's a Comp. They barely trust Cal. There are too many of us in Concord who once lived in Haven.

It looks like everyone left in Concord is here, and the room sizzles with tension.

I stand and raise my hands to quiet the crowd. Once the noise dies down, I turn to Larsson. "Tell us everything."

"The day you, Burn, and Cal got out of Haven," he says, "things were looking pretty good for the joint FA and rebel front. The first wave of the invasion plan worked."

"What was the plan?" I ask. "Everything going on in the Hub that day looked like chaos to me."

Larsson clears his throat. "The FA and rebels moved into the Hub together on the President's Birthday, spreading the word to every employee who'd listen. We told them that they were free. That it was okay to fight Management. That better days were ahead." He pauses for a breath.

"Thousands of employees converted to our side that first day. The next day's rebel meeting was massive. We couldn't fit everyone on the factory floor. But over the next few days, Kalin took control of every communication screen in Haven. Not only the big ones in the Hub but *every* System screen, every announcement screen. She confiscated all privately owned TVs—even from Management."

"Who besides Management *has* a TV?" Drake asks.

"True," Larsson continues. "But the point is: she placed screens *everywhere*, and her speeches are playing constantly on a loop. It's impossible to escape them."

"What is she saying?" I ask. I suspect I know the answer, but everyone else here needs to know, too.

"She's saying that the rebels and the FA are terrorists out to destroy Haven and hand it over to Shredders." Larsson leans forward in his chair. "It didn't help that a few of the FA soldiers looked like Shredders to the people inside."

"That message isn't new," Drake says. "That's what Management said about the rebels even before Mrs. Kalin became President."

"True, but Kalin's claiming that the former President *welcomed* the invasion, knowing that the resulting casualties would be an opportunity to downsize, cut costs, and improve the ration shortages."

Mrs. Kalin can twist anything, I think. *Worse, she can make people believe her lies.*

Larsson goes on. "Kalin claims that she –and only she– can keep Haven safe. She told them that she's close to finding a cure for the dust but needs more test subjects. Volunteers."

"She's brainwashing people into submitting to her barbaric experiments," I say.

Larsson nods. "The Hospital was swarmed, so they instituted a lottery to select which employees got to volunteer first."

"I don't understand," Gwen says.

Questions arise from around the room: How could she sway so many people like that? Kalin's claims are crazy. Why does anyone believe her? What are the other members of Management doing? Why would anyone volunteer to go into the Hospital?

A woman in the middle of the room shouts, "Why didn't our people tell everyone that she's lying?"

"Because Mrs. Kalin can control minds," I explain. "She can plant thoughts. It's her Deviance."

"Using the screens?" Drake asks.

"Her Deviance works with eye contact," I answer. "It must work with a screen, too." *Would that work with mine?*

I climb onto the platform and stand next to Larsson. "Mrs. Kalin believes she's better than everyone else. She calls herself Chosen, but she doesn't mean what we do. She claims she's destined to lead what's left of humankind, and she plans to kill anyone who tries to stop her."

"How do you know all this?" Gwen asks.

"Because she tried to get me to join her. My Deviance affects my mind, not my body. So by her twisted definition, I'm Chosen, too." I can sense the collective reaction in the room: suspicion.

"How do we know you're not under her control?" Terry asks. "How do we know you're not controlling us?"

Gwen looks at me with fear in her eyes. She's thinking of that night in her tower.

"I'm not. I can't plant thoughts."

Drake jumps up. "Kalin couldn't control Glory's thoughts. Otherwise, she'd still be in Haven." He turns to me. "Otherwise, you'd be working with her, right? But you're immune."

"Actually, her Deviance did work on me at first, but I figured out how to sense when she's in my mind. It's hard, but I can block her." I look at Larsson. "And you can block her, too?"

"No," Larsson answers. "But on the President's Birthday, when I watched you with her on the balcony, I suspected what she was doing. I avoided the screens, which wasn't easy, believe me. I tried to get others to look away, but for most people it was too late. And for the rest . . ."

"What?" I ask.

"She holds public executions for anyone who speaks out against her. She has them killed in the Hub."

Killing people resistant to her power is the job Mrs. Kalin wanted to give me.

Terry rounds the table, his boots clunking on the wooden platform. "We just sent another unit in. Are you telling me they might be brainwashed already? And how did you end up with Cal?"

234

Sweat drips down Larsson's forehead. "I intercepted the FA unit as they were coming in. I warned Rolph. Told him not to go in." He shakes his head. "Rolph disagreed, but Cal understood. He brought me back here to warn the rest of you."

"What about the rebel leaders?" I ask. "What are they doing to stop her?"

Larsson's expression is grim. "Most of them are dead. Adele, Sahid—they avoided the screens, but the other rebels turned them in. Adele and Sahid were dragged into the Hub and killed by people they thought they could trust."

"Why didn't the crowd try to stop them?" Drake asks.

"Stop them?" Larsson shakes his head slowly. "The crowd *cheered*. Even the smallest word against Kalin gets you killed."

The room's so quiet we can hear the lake lapping against the shore a hundred yards away.

Sahid is dead. Adele is dead. Maybe Rolph, too. Everyone who was on our side is either dead or under Mrs. Kalin's control.

"What about Sahid's son, Joshua?" I ask. He and Adele were the first rebels I met. Josh is just a kid, like me.

"I haven't seen Josh in almost two weeks," Larsson says. "I expect he's either dead or in the Hospital."

The murmurs in the crowd turn to shouts: "Larsson's a Comp. We can't trust him! This is a trick to keep us from sending more soldiers."

"We don't *have* any more soldiers," I shout back, but I doubt anyone hears me over the din.

"Hey!" I hold up my hands and the noise lessens. "Larsson may be a Comp, but I trust him. He took a big risk in coming here. He has nothing to gain from telling us any of this."

Gwen faces Larsson. "Why haven't you killed Kalin?"

"No one's seen her in person since the President's Birthday. She's in hiding, controlling everyone through the screens."

"Everyone?" Terry asks. "Haven has over three hundred thousand employees."

"If we can stop the screens from broadcasting her messages," I say, "her mind control will eventually wear off. It did for me." *And for Cal,* but I don't want to bring him into it. There's enough distrust in the room already.

Larsson stands. "Even if we can stop the broadcasts, Kalin's ideas have spread through Haven like an infection. If ideas are repeated enough they become ideologies, taken as truth."

I nod. "It's like the old Management propaganda: Haven Equals Safety."

"But it's worse than that," Larsson says. "Haven employees repeated those slogans, but most of the lower-level employees never believed them. Did you?"

I shake my head.

"Of course you didn't," Larsson says. "Employees repeated the slogans to make their lives easier, and because they didn't see another way out."

"Isn't it the same thing now?" Gwen asks.

"No. Kalin's not just *saying* these things; she's planting the ideas in people's heads." Larsson taps his forehead with his fingers. "They think her ideas are their own. They'll do anything she says."

"Still," I say, "if we stop the broadcasts, it will help."

"Agreed," Larsson replies.

"How do I get to Kalin?" a deep voice says from the back of the room. "I'll kill her."

I crane to see through the crowd. Burn is standing near the door. Has he seen Cal? Does he know?

"We've sent people to try to reach her," Larsson says. "It's impossible to get close enough without coming under her power."

My knees shake as I say, "It needs to be me."

"No, I'll do it!" Cal leaps onto the platform. "I already know what she can do. I've been through it, too, and recovered."

"Watch out! It's Zina!" Burn yells, pulling a spear from his pack as he charges toward Cal. I step in front of Cal just as Burn thrusts his spear. The point stops inches from my neck.

"Burn, it really *is* Cal."

"How do you know?" The intensity in Burn's eyes is hard to read. I think I see hope, but I also see uncertainty.

"Trust me." I reach up to move the spear point away. "You didn't kill Cal—you killed Zina."

Cal steps from behind me. "I was in Haven. My FA unit left the same day you guys took off. People here saw me go with them."

Burn glowers. "I can't believe she fooled me again."

I know how he feels.

"Rolph sent Zina to the camp," Cal says. "She was already there when—"

"She saw another chance to prove you were a killer." I touch Burn's shoulder, but he pulls away. "She provoked you. She cared about hurting you, about proving her point, more than she cared about her own life."

Burn stands still for a moment. He looks relieved, but not as much as I expected or hoped. "So where do I find Kalin?" he asks. "I'll rip her head off."

"I can get in to see her," I say. "I'm her daughter."

"No you're not." Drake jumps forward. "Did she plant that thought in your head, because you're *not* her daughter"—he takes a step back—"are you?"

"No." I smile at Drake. "Of course not. But she *wants* me to be. She even filed the adoption paperwork with HR. Kalin will see me." I'm sure of it. Caroline was sent here to find me. "I'll convince her that I'm on her side, then use my Deviance to kill her."

"It's too dangerous," Cal says. "We should send a sniper to shoot her. I'm a good shot."

"But Larsson told us she's never out in the open," I say.

"I'll take you in," Larsson says to me. "It's risky, but Glory might be our only chance. If Kalin agrees to see anyone, it'll be her."

"Then we'll mount a team to take you in." Cal turns to the crowd. "Who will volunteer?"

About a dozen people raise their hands, including Jayma and my brother.

"Where is everyone else?" Larsson asks. "We need combat-trained fighters. Ever since the wall around Haven was breached, the Shredders have spread. There's no way to get to the tunnels without crossing over Shredder-infested territory."

"You and Cal got out," Drake says.

"Barely," Larsson replies as Gwen unties his wrists. "And we had a tank for part of the way. It ran out of fuel."

238

"This is everyone," I tell him. "Most people, especially the ones who could fight, already went to Haven with the FA."

"If this is it"—Larsson scans the volunteers—"our top priority is protecting Glory. We can't let the Shredders take her."

"When do we leave?" Cal asks.

"Tomorrow at dawn," Larsson says.

I scan the room for Burn and spot him leaving the Hall.

By the time I'm out of the building, he's walking up the road through Concord. He rounds a bend and disappears behind a building. When I follow, I find him waiting, leaning against a wooden rail and staring up the road.

"Are you heading to Haven alone?" I ask. "Don't."

"That's not where I'm going."

"Why did you run off?"

"I'll help you get to Haven."

"Thank you." I step closer, but he stares at the ground, refusing to look at me.

"Isn't it great about Cal?" I reach for him, but it's like he's wearing a huge "Do Not Touch" sign.

"I'm glad he's not dead," Burn says to the ground.

"You don't sound it. Don't you see what this means?"

"It means Cal is alive."

"It means more than that." I put my hand lightly on his back. He twitches. "No, it doesn't."

"Of course it does, Burn. *Everything* has changed. Zina was trying to kill you. My aunt saw the whole thing. Zina was trying to force you off the cliff. It wasn't your fault. You were defending yourself."

"You're missing the point." His voice is cold. "When I tossed Zina into that pit, I thought it was Cal. The fact that it turned out to be Zina doesn't change what I did. When I threw rocks at my mother, I knew who she was, too. And most importantly, it doesn't change how you feel about me."

"How I feel? What do you mean? I love you."

"No. You want to, but you don't." His gaze flicks up for an instant, and the sadness in his eyes nearly crushes me. "Your reaction proved it. You couldn't forgive me."

"Burn—"

He raises his hand. "I know that you want it to be okay between us. You want it to be safe, but it isn't. You'll never feel safe around me and you know it."

"No, Burn."

"Admit it. Your reaction showed the truth."

"I was in shock. I should have known it was self-defense. I should have known it wasn't Cal. That day was so crazy. I wasn't thinking clearly." I slide my hand onto his chest over his heart.

He leans into my hand. "None of that matters. I can't be trusted not to kill my allies. You know I've done it before."

I slide my hand up to his neck. "You were defending yourself that day, too. My dad told me that Andreas was about to shoot you."

"Doesn't make him less dead." His head drops forward.

"Burn," I whisper. "I wish you could see yourself the way I see you. I wish you could see the gentle, strong man who's pure goodness inside, who'd do anything for someone he loves."

He doesn't respond, but I can feel the heat of his breath on my neck. His pulse beats hard under my hand, and every inch of my body feels connected to him. I can't lose him. I won't.

I tip my face up to kiss him.

He jumps back. "Don't."

"Why?" My voice breaks. "What more do you want from me? I trust you. I promise. I thought you'd killed someone I've loved my whole life. I'm sorry that I didn't forgive you the second it happened."

"That's not the only reason I can't kiss you."

"Then what is it, Burn? What? Tell me!"

"I'm afraid!" he shouts. "Okay? I'm afraid."

"Afraid of what?"

"Afraid that I'll hurt you. Afraid that I'll kill you."

"You won't."

"You should be with Cal. Why keep—" He cuts himself off and shakes his head.

"I told you! I don't *want* Cal. Not since the first day I met you. I want *you*, Burn."

He turns away from me and walks up the hill.

"Where are you going?" I yell. "Don't go stomping off. We're leaving for Haven in the morning."

"I know," he says over his shoulder. "Don't leave without me. I'll meet you at dawn on the other side of the ridge."

He heads off for the pass at a run.

Chapter Twenty-Nine

I SCAN OUR RAGTAG TEAM GATHERED TOGETHER UNDER the early dawn light. We may be only a small group, and we might not be trained soldiers, but we're armed with sharp weapons, a few guns, and our Gifts. Drake's the youngest.

Larsson checks his Aut gun—the most powerful weapon we have—and then stows it in the holster strapped on his back. "Ready?"

"Yes, sir," Cal says, and Larsson sets off up the hill.

Drake checks the straps on Jayma's backpack before they start. Cal takes up the rear and I fall in beside him, walking slowly to put a little distance between us and the group.

Carrying way more than his share, Cal adjusts his pack full of weapons and provisions.

"Are you scared?" he asks.

"Completely." I turn to him and grin. "But this has to be done. I should have killed her the first time I had the chance."

"Hey," Cal says, "don't beat yourself up for that! Nobody who's sane ever wants to kill. Plus, she was messing with your mind. She was trying to replace your mother. She had you convinced that she loved you."

"Thanks. I'll be stronger this time." I just have to keep her out of my mind.

Ahead of us, Jayma picks up a rock to put in her pack. I want to tell her that she'll find plenty of objects to throw when she needs them, but I guess it's better if she's prepared, and the extra weight doesn't bother her. I'd guess her pack is already double her weight.

"Where's Burn?" Cal asks. "I thought he'd come with us."

"He's going to meet us."

"Did you guys work everything out?"

"No. And I'm starting to wonder if we ever will."

"Do you want me to talk to him?"

My stomach flips. "Why?" The idea of them talking about me . . .

He cracks his knuckles. "I could tell him that I forgive him for killing me—in a way. And I can make sure he understands that there's nothing between you and me anymore."

"That's a nice offer. Really." My feelings for Cal might be sisterly, but I do still love him, and I wish there was something I could do to erase the hurt I caused. "But I'm not sure anything you say will make a difference. It's me who let him down."

Cal raises his eyebrows. "How did *you* let *him* down?"

"It's how I acted when I thought he'd killed you. He thinks it means I'll never trust him."

He rubs his chin for a moment. "Oh. That's rough."

We march along in silence, listening to the voices ahead of us. The fading stars form patterns in the sky, and I understand why some people BTD believed that the stars held answers.

I wish I knew how to read them. I could use some guidance right now.

I take a sip of water. "Cal, do you know how you got Mrs. Kalin's thoughts out of your mind?"

"At first I thought that they wore off over time, but I'm not sure anymore."

"We need to figure it out."

Cal waves at a little kid at the side of the road as we pass. "I think my head cleared on the walk to Concord—after we left the tank. After I took off my mask."

"You think it might have been the dust that helped you?"

He shrugs. "I'm not positive. I wish I were."

"So do I." The odds are stacked against us in so many ways. Even if our small group can get to the dome without being captured by Shredders, even if we can get safely inside, even if we can avoid being brainwashed ourselves, even if I succeed in killing Mrs. Kalin—according to Larsson, nearly everyone inside Haven is under her control.

Like Larsson said, it's hard to reason with a large group who all believe the same thing. We might get rid of Mrs. Kalin's influence, but they might still influence one another.

We pass under the lookout tower just as the sun starts to rise, then move quickly down the ridge. At the bottom, I scan the trees lining the clearing. Larsson keeps walking and the others follow.

"Wait!" I yell. "We need to wait for Burn."

Drake shades his eyes from the rising sun. "Do we know for sure that he's coming?"

"He said he'd be here. It's barely dawn."

Larsson strides back toward us. "We can't afford to wait. Daylight's the safest time to travel."

My heart slams against my ribs. What if I never see Burn again? I can't leave things the way they are now. "We need Burn. He can defend us if we run into Shredders, and he knows all the secret routes through the tunnels."

"I know the tunnels," Larsson says. "I am a Comp, remember?"

"If the Comps know the tunnels so well, how come Burn was able to get in and out of Haven so often?"

"The Comps can't patrol *every* tunnel *every* minute." Larsson frowns, and I flash back to how cruel he was during Comp training. "That doesn't mean we don't *know* about them."

"Hey, look!" Jayma points toward the forest.

Burn is leading a group of Shredders. At least fifty of them. Larsson pulls out his Aut.

"No!" I yell. "Wait." Houston is next to Burn, and I recognize some other faces from Simcoe.

Burn has assembled an army of recovered Shedders to help us get to Haven.

"Someone better explain this," Cal says when they get closer.

"We need numbers." Burn gestures to the group. "Glory gave me the idea."

"I did?"

"These people were Shredders," he says. "But they aren't anymore. They don't breathe dust anymore. They're on our side."

"I don't know," Cal says.

Houston steps up beside Burn. "Look, if you don't want our help—"

"We need your help." I walk over to shake Houston's hand, then turn back to our group. "We can't do this without them."

"I think I've seen everything now." Larsson lowers his gun. "Let's go."

• • •

We walk through the day and most of the night. Twice we come across small groups of Shredders, but Houston and the others from Simcoe fight them off.

Larsson and Burn are walking at the front of the group, and they stop at the edge of a forest.

"After we clear these trees," Burn says, "we'll be exposed. We should wait here until morning."

"I agree," Larsson says. "The Shredder population will go up from here on."

As everyone prepares to settle down for what's left of the night, I walk over and look out onto the vast expanse of dust-covered land. Remnants of ruins poke out in a few places, but most evidence of life around here BTD has either decayed or been salvaged.

The air is chilly and I rub my arms. Houston and two from his group have taken up guard positions, and I turn back to join the others. Most are already sleeping. It looks like Jayma collapsed immediately. Drake is sitting cross-legged behind her, struggling to keep awake.

I wander over to them and whisper in his ear, "Go to sleep. Jayma's safe."

He tugs my hand and pulls me down to sit next to him. "Do you really think you can kill Kalin?"

"I do." I wish I were as sure as I sound.

He leans his shoulder into mine. "It's going to be strange to be back inside Haven."

"You're not going inside," I say. "Too risky. One glance at a screen and you'll be brainwashed."

"I won't look at the screens." Drake gazes at our sleeping friend. "Jayma's parents are inside. She's determined to go in."

"You two can wait outside until Mrs. Kalin is dead."

"I doubt Jayma will wait," Drake says. "And if she goes in, I'm going with her."

"One way or another, you should get some rest."

He stretches out on the ground near Jayma, turning to face her as if he plans to guard her in his sleep.

Cal is propped up against a rock, and when I catch his eye, he waves. I nod, then weave through sleeping bodies until I spot Burn. He's standing near the forest, facing into the distance.

The tangy scent of pine needles rises with each of my footsteps, and when I'm about ten feet away, Burn looks at me. His face is in the shadows, but I can sense the heat of his gaze on my body.

I step up next to him. As we stand there, our bodies pull toward each other. Our hands brush, and I draw a deep breath.

"You sure about this?" he asks.

"Yes." I'm not just talking about the mission.

"You don't have to do it, you know."

"I know—but I'm doing it."

He nods. "I'll take you as far as I can."

"Thank you." I know that he understands why I have to take this risk, why I need to be the one to kill Mrs. Kalin. He's the only one who hasn't tried to talk me out of it.

I gently slide the back of my hand against his, marveling at how the slight contact ripples inside me. "How are you doing?" I ask him.

"I'm fine." He moves his hand away.

"Cal forgives you, you know."

He grunts.

"Burn—"

"He told me." Burn exhales heavily. "Cal's a good guy."

"I know. But I want to be with you."

"Do you think you can always get what you want?"

"Of course not."

He doesn't respond and I can't take the silence. "Burn, I'm sorry about how I reacted."

"I know. I get it."

"Then what's wrong?"

"I told you."

I cup his face and bring it around to mine. "Look into my eyes," I say. "Any time you're afraid, all you need to do is look into my eyes."

He leans toward me and I can feel the desire building inside him. I know he wants to kiss me as badly as I want to kiss him, but he's afraid.

He looks down. "You can't use your Deviance on me tonight. You can't risk it."

"I can sense when a headache starts," I tell him. "I can feel it building. If it does, I'll stop. There's no reason to be afraid. I can keep you from changing."

Hope flashes in his eyes and it fuels my own. I have no idea if I can do what I claimed, but I want Burn to *believe* that I can. "You said I'd never be able to trust you again," I continue. "Let me show you that I trust you. Show me that you trust me."

Rising on my toes, I slide my hand up his neck and into his hair. A tremor grows inside me as he slowly relaxes his neck to let his lips drop toward mine.

He pulls back. "This won't work. We can't keep eye contact while we're kissing. If I lose control, you can't stop me."

I stroke his neck. "I'll sense it if you start to change. So will you. We'll make eye contact and I'll calm you down. Trust me. Trust yourself. Don't be afraid."

He bends down to kiss me, and something inside me explodes. When our kiss deepens, the detonation expands, touching every part of me as his hands roam my body, and mine his. My senses muddled, I can no longer tell where I stop and he starts. Burn's become part of my bones, my muscles, my heart.

In his arms I feel safe; I feel home; I feel loved. I wrap my legs around his waist, and I realize that at some point he lifted me.

"You okay?" he asks.

"Definitely."

Pressing my back against a tree trunk, he kisses my face, my neck, my lips. Then once again, he pulls away to look into my eyes.

I brush his hair from his face. "Everything's fine," I say softly. "I told you we'd be okay."

As we look into each other's eyes, the heat and hardness of his body press into mine, igniting more sparks, but a tiny amount of fear invades.

I'm not afraid that he'll kill me—I'm afraid of the power and intensity of all that I'm feeling. I'm afraid I'll lose him. I'm afraid this will be the last time I'll be in his arms.

"You two should get some sleep." Houston's voice comes from behind us, and Burn's body tenses against mine.

He carefully releases me, and I slide down until my feet touch the ground, my back still against the tree. I should probably be embarrassed but I'm not.

Houston steps forward into a beam of moonlight. "I'm serious," he says. "Sleep. Now. Tomorrow is going to be rough enough as it is."

Burn takes my hand. We find a clear spot, lie down on the pine needles, and I fall asleep, warm and safe in his arms.

Chapter Thirty

BURN STANDS CLOSE TO ME, AND WE STARE UP THE ladder leading from the tunnel—the same ladder that Burn, Drake, and I came down when we first escaped Haven. The ladder leads to a storage room in the corridors behind Management's shopping mall.

Larsson went up to make sure the coast is clear. Burn, Drake, Cal, Jayma, and I are waiting here, and the rest of our group is guarding the entrance to the tunnels and fending off Shredders. We haven't seen any trace of Comps, which leaves me with an uneasy feeling. Every second that Larsson's gone makes me question whether we were right to trust him. And if *I'm* feeling that way . . .

"You okay?" Burn asks.

I nod and try to look calm.

Sound comes from above us. We back against the walls of the tunnel, weapons out. Heavy steps clang on the ladder and Comp boots come into view. My insides go into a tight spin.

"It's a Comp," I say. "Kill him!"

The Comp takes another step. Burn leaps up, grabs the Comp's belt, and pulls him off the ladder and onto his back on the tunnel floor. An empty Comp uniform drops to the floor beside them.

Burn pins the Comp down with his knee and tries to remove the Comp's helmet so that his knife can find skin.

"It's me," the Comp says through the amplified mask.

"Wait!" I grab Burn's arm. "It's Larsson."

Burn backs off, and Larsson raises the visor of his helmet.

"Why are you wearing a Comp uniform?" Burn asks. "I could have killed you."

Larsson sits up slowly. "You nearly broke my back."

Cal helps Larsson to his feet. "What's going on up there?"

Larsson removes his helmet. "I found a Comp locker room and grabbed a couple of uniforms. I thought they'd come in handy." He bends at the waist, hands on his knees, clearly still in pain. "Cal and I can pretend the rest of you are our prisoners. That'll get us through the mall and onto the streets."

"Good plan," Burn says. "All clear above?"

"Yes," Larsson answers. "There was no one in the storage room corridors."

"As soon as we're out," Jayma says. "I'm heading to the Pents to find my parents."

"Not yet," Larsson tells her. "There will be time to find parents and friends once we complete our mission. Cal, put on the other uniform."

Cal nods and starts to get dressed.

"We stick together until we're outside the mall," Larsson says. "Once we're out, Cal and I will make contact with the rebels and FA, assuming any of them are left. Burn, you help the others find a place to hide. We'll meet at the southeast corner of the Hub in four hours and figure out how to convince Kalin to see Glory."

He looks at me. "You ready?"

"Yes." I have to tighten my legs to keep my knees from shaking.

"While we're in the mall, you're our prisoners," Larsson says. "Stay together. Above all else, keep your eyes down. The screens are everywhere. One look into Kalin's eyes and you'll be trapped."

He climbs back up the ladder, and everyone follows until it's just Burn and me at the bottom. I start up, but on the second rung, I feel his hand on my shoulder and his breath on my neck.

I turn my head and he kisses me. Releasing the ladder, I wrap my arms around him, and our kiss lifts me out of the tunnels, out of Haven. For a moment I forget what I'm facing, how much danger we're in. The only thing in my mind is the kiss, the heat, the warmth of his body against mine.

He groans deep in his chest and breaks away. I balance with my heels on a rung as he holds my head between his large hands and looks into my eyes.

"Thank you," he says.

"What for?"

"For using your Gift to calm me last night. You made it possible for me to kiss you without—"

I put a finger on his lips to stop him. I didn't use my Gift last night. I need him to know that he can control himself on his own, but now isn't the time. I lightly kiss his forehead.

"Be careful," he says.

"I will. I promise."

"Are you lovebirds coming?" Drake calls down, and Burn helps me turn back to the ladder.

Climbing quickly, I feel the weight of his steps behind me.

• • •

Larsson and Cal put everyone's wrists in restraints behind our backs. I'm prepared to convince Burn that this precaution is necessary, but he offers his wrists to Cal without question. Burn could probably break the binding anyway, if he wanted. So could Jayma.

"Burn, you go in front," Larsson says. "Glory, you're next. Drake and Jayma behind her. Cal and I will flank the group at either side."

I shake my head. "Burn can't go first. People know his face."

"They know yours, too," Larsson says. "But even if you're recognized, you're prisoners. No one will see a reason to raise the alarm or get involved."

Down the corridor, the door to the mall opens.

"What's going on?" asks a tall woman in a red dress. "Who are you? Why are you back here?" Her hand shakes as she reaches toward a button on the wall.

Larsson drops down the visor of his helmet. "Don't touch the alarm." His voice sounds so different through the mask—empty and cold. "Everything here is fully under Compliance Department control."

Her hand falls to her side without touching the button.

"Clear the corridor," Larsson says to the woman. He shoves Burn's shoulder, then mine. "I need a path to escort my prisoners."

"Must you do it through the *mall*?" The woman sounds offended, like Larsson asked her to dispose of his waste.

"We apprehended the prisoners down here," Larsson says. "How else will we get them out?"

"Fine." The woman presses her hand to her stomach. "Just do it quickly."

"Move," Larsson says to us. "You're all headed to the Hospital."

"Oh!" The woman raises her hand to her mouth. "You lucky people. You're going to be part of something wonderful. Small sacrifices yield giant leaps." She smiles. "Research is Haven's top priority. Science equals safety."

The woman opens the door to the mall and steps aside to let us pass. Burn stares at the floor. I whisper to Jayma and Drake behind me, "Look down. Don't be distracted."

As I walk through the door, the light is blinding. Looking down, I see Larsson's feet to my left and Cal's to my right. Over the murmur of voices in the mall, I hear the clomping of their Comp boots and the crunch of Larsson's Aut as he slams it against his glove.

But penetrating all those sounds is Mrs. Kalin's soothing voice. It's impossible not to hear her. Her voice seems to project from every speaker in the mall, each set on high volume.

"Good people of Haven," she says, "for the first time since the asteroid dust irrevocably altered the earth, our future is bright. Through scientific advancements, we can all live better lives: free from fear of the dust, free from fear of Shredders and Deviants.

"There is still much to learn," she continues, "but through cooperation and teamwork we can accomplish anything. Small sacrifices yield giant leaps. Whether your contribution is big or small, we will collectively progress and survive."

I can imagine how it feels to hear these convincing words over and over, while looking into her kind, brown, brainwashing eyes.

But I don't need to imagine. I *know* how it would feel: powerful and safe, as if anything's possible.

As we walk, the colors and lights from the screens reflect and bounce off the floor. The images become blurred flashes that dance over the polished granite.

"Are you looking for a challenge?" Mrs. Kalin asks. "Are you looking for a way to advance your career? Well, I'm happy to tell you that each and every Haven employee—no matter what your current work placement, whether you live in Management apartments or up in the Penthouses—everyone has the potential to make a difference. You, too, can contribute to our future success. Each and every employee of Haven is important to me." She pauses and anticipation builds inside me. "I love you all."

My urge to look up is unbearable. I stare at the lines between the floor tiles and dig my fingernails into my palms.

Hearing her voice—remembering how it felt when she loved me—I long to see her face again and feel the reassurance and comfort she offered.

But I know better, and I can only hope the others resist, too.

"The newly restructured Science and Research Department is hiring," she says. "Apply today and you can be part of this exciting work. Research is Haven's top priority, so fill out your transfer applications for the S&R Department today. Obtain applications directly from your current Supervisor or from Human Resources. Don't delay. And remember: science equals safety."

S&R must be a new department, or maybe she renamed Health and Safety—the department she ran before anointing herself President.

"Keep moving," Larsson barks.

"Even the terrorists," Mrs. Kalin goes on, "who were once working against us, now support our scientific efforts. Isn't that right?"

"Yes," says a voice that I recognize. It's Joshua, Sahid's son, one of the first rebels I met. My heads snaps up.

The walls of the mall are covered in screens that reflect off the glass and mirrors and chrome to create a tunnel of identical images. On each of them, Joshua is smiling broadly.

"I was once a terrorist," Josh says, "fighting against Management. But since Mrs. Kalin became President, there's no reason to fight. Under President Kalin, everything is different. She will save us all. Science equals safety." Joshua sounds and looks like himself, but he's got some kind of a metal band around his head.

Mrs. Kalin's image comes back on-screen. She puts her hand on Joshua's shoulder and smiles. Instantly, my eyes lock onto her face and warmth spreads through me.

She's looking through the screen directly at me. Only me. Mrs. Kalin loves me. She knows what's best for me, for us all.

No.

I blink rapidly and my mind goes fuzzy as I push her influence out of my head. I look down and catch a reflection of my own image on the back of a shiny metal bench. I stop.

It's been a long time since I looked at myself. Really looked. My dark hair hangs past my shoulders; my brown eyes are framed by strong eyebrows and heavy lashes. I look so much like my mother. Mesmerized, I can't turn away, and I'm flooded by sadness and long-buried memories of the day she died.

It's like I can feel my mother's hands tugging on my shoulders. She's trying to turn me away from something, to stop me from doing something, but I'm not sure what.

Did my mother grab me to stop me from going out that day? Is that what made me so angry? I know we argued. I know I said terrible things, but was there more? Tears rise and blur the image.

"Keep moving," Larsson repeats. "Don't even look at reflections," he whispers to me.

Mrs. Kalin's voice bombards me from all sides, and I know that I'll find comfort if I look into a screen. But I don't. I close my eyes.

I trip, and my knees slam onto the floor. I stop myself before my face hits. Cal turns to help me up but stops himself.

"On your feet," Larsson says. "We're going through those doors on the left. Only ten more yards."

I admire how he's guiding us without rousing suspicion, but I can hear the fear in his voice.

"Officers!" someone calls out.

"Halt," Larsson commands.

I carefully glance up. Larsson's talking in hushed tones to a man wearing a business suit.

"It's against the P&P for any employee below Management to be inside the mall," the man says.

"Sorry, sir," Larsson replies. "We apprehended these Deviants in the storage area. We'll be out of here in a moment."

"What are your employee numbers?" the man asks. "I'm going to report you to the Compliance Department."

"We *are* the Compliance Department, sir," says Larsson. "Responsible for enforcement of the Haven Policies & Procedures Manual."

"Don't be insubordinate," the man snaps.

"Yes, sir. Sorry, sir."

Larsson recites an employee number, and I wonder whether it's his actual number. Growing up, I never imagined anyone would dare confront a Comp. Technically, they oversee all employees, but this man is Management and clearly considers his work placement far above a Compliance Officer.

"Now go," the man orders. "Out of here immediately."

"Yes, sir," Larsson says.

I stare at Burn's legs ahead of me.

"Drake," Larsson says sharply. "Eyes down."

I turn to see my brother smiling as he stares at one of the screens. He doesn't react to Larsson's command.

"Drake!" I shake him, and when that doesn't work, I reach up and cover his eyes with my hands.

"Hey!" His armor rises and he pulls my hands down. He looks at me and I see something click in his eyes.

I start to relax. A close call.

But then Drake backs away from the rest of the group. "Help!" he yells. "Someone stop these people. They plan to kill President Kalin!"

Chapter Thirty-One

THE ENTIRE MALL CONVERGES ON US AT ONCE. A BIG man yanks my bound arms up behind me, and my shoulders scream against the strain. Five people pile on top of Burn.

"Keep calm," I mouth to him. "Keep calm." If he changes, he might be able to save himself, but he won't be able to save us all.

Burn nods and holds eye contact as long as he can, but more Comps swarm in and block my view. Larsson goes to Cal's side and pulls him away from the group. I wonder if they'll stay, or if they'll go find the rebels before they're found out themselves.

One of the real Comps grabs Jayma. She breaks the bindings around her wrists and slams her arm into him. He flies through the air, knocking down several people.

Jayma's struck by the tags from at least three Shocker guns. Convulsing, she collapses to the floor. I try to run to her, but the man holding me is too strong. Rage builds in my chest. I want to kill the Comps who hurt Jayma—I could easily make eye contact with the closest one—but I need to remember that I'm here for the big prize.

Drake's eyes are wide with alarm. Someone has cut his bindings, and he tugs on his sleeves as if he's trying to cover his Deviance. Does he even realize what he's done?

Our group is pushed and shoved—and in Jayma's case, carried—through the mall exit and into the Hub. Mrs. Kalin's voice echoes over the speakers. Reflections from the screens flash everywhere. It's so hard to avoid them.

We're forced up stairs and onto a platform. The man holding Jayma drops her unconscious body. I cringe.

"Don't look up," I remind the others, although I'm mostly trying to remind myself. Especially here in the Hub, one misplaced glance and we'll be captured by her image.

"What do we have here?"

I know that voice. It's my former roommate, Stacy, dressed in a full Comp uniform but with her visor lifted.

"Glory," she says, "I always knew you were a traitor." She grabs a megaphone and turns to the crowd. "What do we do with traitors?"

"Execute them!" The crowd shouts.

I glance around for Cal—he could always manage Stacy—but he and Larsson are gone. I hope their Comp uniforms helped them get away and they weren't taken into custody.

"We're here to volunteer!" I shout. "We want to go into the Hospital to help with the experiments." If we get into the Hospital, I might still have a chance of finding Mrs. Kalin.

"Liar!" Stacy slaps me. The weight of her glove nearly knocks me off my feet. My mind fogs and I can feel a welt rise on my cheek.

Burn shouts. He breaks free of his captors, but they've already attached Shocker tags to his body, and I can only watch as the Comps turn up their dials. His body shakes. I think he's about to change, but instead, he collapses.

Stacy raises her hands to quiet the crowd. "These traitors want to ruin everything that President Kalin has done for Haven. These *Deviants* want to kill our leader, our mother, our savior." The crowd roars. "But we won't let that happen, will we?"

The crowd cheers.

"They must all die." Stacy grabs me by the hair and tugs. "This one first."

The pain sharpens my focus as I'm dragged to a block at the side of the platform. It's stained with blood.

One of the Comps holds an ax. This is it.

Burn and Jayma are unconscious, and Drake is barely visible at the far side of the platform. He's staring up at one of the screens. I can't blame him for being mesmerized by Mrs. Kalin, but the sight hurts more than my impending death. Because I've failed, my brother's mind will be trapped by her forever.

Burn shifts on the platform.

"Kneel," says the man behind me.

"No." I turn to face him. "Take me to President Kalin."

He laughs. "You're making demands?"

"Do it, or I'll kill you."

"If you prefer, I can chop off your head while you're standing." He readies the ax.

I lock onto him with my eyes, grab his heart, and squeeze.

The Comp clutches his chest and drops the ax. He can't look away.

"Glory," Burn says. "Don't."

I look away just in time to see a Comp stomp on Burn's back and another turn his Shocker tags on again. Three Comps, protected by their heavy gloves, lift Burn to a standing position. He's limp and his legs are vibrating from the electric shocks.

I've lost eye contact with my executioner. He's kneeling on the platform, his face pale.

"Kill her!" Stacy shouts. "What's wrong with you?"

The man grabs his ax and tries to rise.

"Glory!"

It's Mrs. Kalin.

All eyes turn toward the screens, including mine.

"It's good to see you again, my lovely daughter."

It's as if she's right here, as if we're the only two people in the world.

"So it's true?" Drake says. "You're her daughter?"

Looking at Mrs. Kalin, a smile tugs at my mouth. "It's good to see you, too," I say, although I have no idea whether she can hear me.

"You came back to me," she says. "Why?"

I feel her inside my mind, trying to make me trust her again. I struggle to build a wall to block her thoughts from my own.

"You haven't answered my question," she says. "Why have you returned?"

"I'm so sorry. I was wrong to leave you. You were right about everything."

"Stop it, Glory," Burn says from behind me. "Don't look at the screen." I wish I could turn to reassure him, but I can't let Mrs. Kalin doubt her control.

"As soon as I was gone," I tell her, "I realized my mistake. I fought to get back here, and now that I am, now that I've seen you again, I can't remember why I left."

"If you're not sincere, I will be very disappointed." She stares into my eyes.

"I understand. Please, Mother. All I want to do is make you proud."

"Bring her to me."

Two Comps grab me by the arms.

Mrs. Kalin waves her hand. "Kill the others."

I strain against the Comps' hold. "No!"

Mrs. Kalin frowns. "Have you been lying to me?"

"No! I would never lie to you, Mrs. Kalin."

She wags her finger. "Mother."

"Mother, please, don't reject my offering." I gesture to the others.

"Your offering?" Her frown deepens. "Surely you don't mean these traitors? They're only a gift to me if they're dead."

"But Mother, I brought these Deviants for your experiments."

Mrs. Kalin leans back slightly. I hear her voice in my mind. *Their deaths are inevitable. They must die.*

The wall I built to keep her out is shaky, but I can still sense my own thoughts. "They must die," I say, "but why not let them contribute to science first? Research is Haven's top priority." I quote her own propaganda, but again her thoughts invade mine.

You trust me, she thinks. *You know I want the best for you. I am the one who will decide what happens to your Deviant friends.*

My head aches. I fight to support the wall in my mind. It's about to crumble. "It's your decision." I let my chin quiver. I want to blink, but I can't, and I'm no longer sure which thoughts are my own. "I want to please you. But if you don't like my present, then by all means—" I gesture to the Comp who's picked up his ax.

"You really brought these Deviants for me?" Mrs. Kalin asks. "Your brother? Your best friend? The monster who stole you from me?"

I nod. "I want to make up for what I did. I need you to forgive me. Please . . ."

"Very well," she says and looks at the Comps holding me. "Take the volunteers to the Hospital, and bring my daughter to me."

Chapter Thirty-Two

THE HOSPITAL DOORS OPEN, AND A GROUP OF MEN AND women in white coats emerge.

While the Comps who escorted us here keep their Shocker guns pointed at us, the staff brings out metal bands that they tighten around my friends' heads like crowns.

"What are the bands for?" I ask. It's the same thing I saw on Joshua.

One of the women turns to me. "The halos are for the Deviants' protection. If necessary, we use them to repress their Deviant traits until we are in controlled experimental conditions. We don't want our subjects injuring themselves."

"Is that really necessary? Does Mrs. Kalin know you're doing this?"

"Of course. The President invented the device."

"Kneel," says the technician trying to put the halo on Burn.

He does as she asks and nods to me that he's okay, but the tendons in his neck are straining. His trust fills my heart. For all Burn knows, what I told Mrs. Kalin is true.

"Small sacrifices yield giant leaps," Drake says to the tech tightening the band around his skull.

His armor's still up, so I know he's afraid, or stressed, even though he still seems to be under Mrs. Kalin's control.

The Hospital tech finishes installing Drake's halo, then pushes up his sleeves to examine his armor. The tech nods as he makes notes on a clipboard.

"Stop it." Jayma pushes against the worker trying to install her headgear, and the woman slams back against the wall.

The Comps reactivate Jayma's Shocker tags, and she crumples to her knees.

"Don't hurt her." Drake strides forward.

One of the women presses a button on an electronic pad that's clipped to her coat. Drake stops. His armor retracts. He trembles but he seems unable to move.

"What's happening?" I ask. "What did you do to my brother?"

"The halos create brain-wave interference to block emotions." The tech taps the button again, and Drake relaxes. "We've discovered that by blocking emotions we can block a subject's Deviance."

What have I done? I might have saved them from having their heads chopped off in the Hub, but for what?

"That hurt," Drake says calmly and lifts a hand to his head.

"Small sacrifices yield giant leaps," the tech says, and Drake smiles.

Jayma slumps in defeat, and they install the band on her head.

Everyone except me is fitted with a halo, and then we're led into the Hospital. The last time I was here, the corridors were quiet and nearly deserted, but now they're noisy and crowded. Many people look up from their clipboards or conversations and smile as we pass.

"Welcome," says a woman wearing a gray cap that covers her hair and ears. "Thank you for your service. Science equals safety."

"Science equals safety," I repeat.

My thoughts are back under my own control, but the Hospital workers are easy to fool. Mrs. Kalin won't be.

I crane my neck to watch as the tech at the head of our group pushes a code into a keypad to open a set of double doors. My friends are guided through, and I'm the last one in the hall. I step forward, but a man seizes my arm.

"We're taking you to see the President."

"I want to say good-bye to my friends." I pull against him. The doors are about to close.

"That's not necessary," he says.

I pull out of his grip and jam my foot in the doorway. I yank one door open.

My brother and my friends are all frozen in place, and techs have descended on each of them, stripping them to their underwear.

"Is that necessary?" I run up to the worker who's cutting off Jayma's pants. "Glory," Mrs. Kalin says.

I find her image on a screen. I must not look away. If I do, she'll know.

Small sacrifices yield giant leaps. I struggle to figure out whether that was my own thought, or whether Mrs. Kalin planted it there. Either way, the words might be true, but I don't want to sacrifice my friends.

"Your staff is hurting them," I say to her image, trying to temper the anger in my voice.

"Are you telling me how I should treat these Deviants?" Her image grows as she leans toward the camera.

"I don't want them to suffer. I don't want them to die."

"Small sacrifices—"

"Death is not a small sacrifice!"

Her lips purse. Only her head and torso are in the frame, but I can imagine her manicured fingers smoothing the fabric of her skirt.

Out of the corner of my eye I see Burn. They've chained his ankles to bolts on the floor. Bands around his wrists are chained to a pipe running the length of the room. He's not moving, and I assume that the halo is activated.

"Come to me." Mrs. Kalin smiles. "And if you like, we will discuss your friends' contributions in more detail."

I nod, fighting to make my smile sincere.

So far I've been able to block her, but the separation of the screen might be helping. I only hope I'm strong enough to keep her out of my mind when I confront her in person.

• • •

The instant we return to the corridor, the Hospital worker blindfolds me.

"What's that for?" I resist the urge to pull it off.

"The President's orders." He puts a hand on my back and shoves. "We don't want to keep her waiting."

Walking blindly through the Hospital corridors, I'm even more aware of the crowds and the noise and the smells.

"Excuse me," a man says as he jostles me. My shoulder strikes what feels like the corner of a wall.

Sharp, astringent odors sting my nose and throat as we continue, and then I detect the coppery tang of blood. Every few moments the chatter in the halls is punctuated by screams. I jump, muscles seizing, and my handler grips my shoulder.

"Release her," says a male voice that crackles over an intercom. "Step back."

The hands drop off me, and I hear footsteps backing away. Then a click. Air moves across my skin. I must be standing beside a door, and I reach out, groping, trying to discover something, anything, about my surroundings.

My hand lands on a hard, cold surface.

"This way," another man says.

I'm pulled forward, and after a few seconds, I hear the door close behind me. This new corridor is quieter and the air is different, less tinged with chemicals and fear.

We stop. Once again, a voice comes over a speaker, a door opens, and I'm passed off to a new guide.

As I'm led through the halls, I try to keep a map in my mind of each time we turn, each time we go up or down stairs, and each time I'm passed off to a new guard. I try to find audio clues or landmarks—but disoriented, I quickly lose track. Twice, I'm pulled into a space that feels like it's moving, and my best guess is that we're inside elevators. I'm inexperienced with elevators, but I'm pretty sure we go down.

After the fifth handoff, my blindfold is removed, and I squint against a light that's affixed to the wall beside me. Where am I?

The corridor is narrow and might be a tunnel. The light doesn't travel far into the darkness. The floor and walls are bare concrete. The air is cool and damp. I look up to my guide and it's no one I recognize. His cheeks are covered in red pimples, and his green eyes are so pale they seem translucent.

"Where am I? Are we still in the Hospital?"

"I'm not supposed to tell you."

I rub the goose bumps on my arms. "Where's Mrs. Kalin?"

"The President is through those doors at the end of the hall." He points ahead.

"Where?" I squint through the blackness.

"There." He flicks his wrist and a series of lights come on.

"How did you do that?" I ask.

He laughs again. "I'm Chosen. Since the President wants to see you, I expect you are, too." He reaches out his arm. A metal rod, leaning against the wall, flies twenty feet through the air and into his hand. "That's what *I* do. And *you*?"

"If I show you, I'll kill you."

His eyes open wide, then he grins. "Impressive."

My heart races as I start down the hall. With each step, my anxiety grows and I force myself to take deep breaths.

I reach for the doors, but before I have a chance to push, they swing open to reveal a space that's painted a soothing shade of blue. It's like the sky Outside on a hazy day. The air smells fresh, although I think we're several stories underground.

As I step onto a thick carpet, artwork draws my eyes, and I recognize one of the paintings from Mrs. Kalin's apartment. But I'm definitely somewhere else. Two long sofas and several chairs are arranged in a cozy square. On either side of the door, shelves cover the wall. They contain dozens of books and almost as many beautiful objects—vases and teacups from BTD.

To my right, a high-backed chair faces a wall of screens that flick between various locations around Haven.

The chair spins toward me, and Mrs. Kalin removes a listening bud from her ear.

"Hello, Glory."

She rises and slowly approaches. She walks with such elegant confidence, placing each foot almost directly in front of the other, and her hips sway as she glides toward me. Her dark-blue suit shines from some rich material, and a clear gem that's strung around her neck catches an overhead light.

I can't stop staring. Her hair is loose and the dark curls bounce on her shoulders. I remember how my mother's hair would do that for the first few days after she gave it a vinegar rinse. Tension melts from my shoulders as I look into Mrs. Kalin's eyes.

She reaches up to push the hair from my face. "Your skin is so dark. Is that what happens in sunlight?"

I nod.

"It suits you." Her thumb brushes over my cheek.

"Thank you."

"Tell me about Outside."

"Sunlight feels fabulous on your skin," I tell her. "Unless you stay out too long. Then your skin gets red, and after a few days, the top layer peels off. My skin doesn't burn much in the sun, but my friend Jayma—" I stop myself and press my lips together. What's *wrong* with me?

"Come." She takes my hand and leads me toward the sofas. "Tell me more about your experiences Outside. Every piece of information helps us build our understanding. Your research will help keep us safe."

Warmth spreads inside me. "Because of your research, everyone in Haven will be able to live safely Outside someday, even Normals, right?"

She smiles, but it's a weak smile that snaps me out of my euphoria and reminds me that I have to be careful. Her mind control is definitely affecting me, and I have to stay sharp. I can't forget my mission.

I focus on a pointed glass sculpture that's in the middle of a table in the sitting area. I also recognize it from Mrs. Kalin's apartment. She called it an obelisk.

She sits on a sofa and pats the space beside her. I sit as far away as I can.

"I'm pleased that you're back, Glory. Very pleased. And you'll be glad to hear that, while you were gone, we successfully defeated the terrorists and others who invaded Haven."

I nod.

"I was so concerned when that monster took you off the balcony." She holds my hand and looks into my eyes. "Did he hurt you?"

"No," I say. "He didn't hurt me, and I came back as soon as I could."

"Why did it take so long?"

"I . . . I couldn't get back. I tried." She doesn't believe me. I see skepticism in her eyes.

You trust me, she thinks. *I am your mother and you will do whatever I ask. You want to please me. You believe in my research.*

"I'm so excited about your research," I say. "I can't wait to help in any way that you ask."

"I'm happy to hear that."

"And you've found others who are Chosen?"

She tips her head to the side.

"The man who brought me to your door." I gesture toward the hall. "He can move things with his mind."

She smiles. "Yes. Others are Chosen, but none with your talents or mine." She squeezes my hand. "You and I, my daughter, are destined to lead."

It's time. I need to be brave. I need to do this.

Before she pulls me under her spell, I need to kill her.

Focusing on her eyes, I let my Deviance build. The thoughts she's pushing into my mind make it difficult to concentrate, but I focus in on her heart, sensing the flow of her blood, the thumping rhythm of the organ's beat.

I squeeze.

Her eyes reveal pain, and her grip on my hand tightens until her nails dig into my skin.

I am a traitor, I think.

No! She planted that thought in my mind.

It's over. She knows what I'm doing. There's no going back. If I fail to kill her, she'll kill me.

Staying focused on her eyes, I increase my grip on her heart, on her lungs, but for some reason, I don't have the power to squeeze.

I can't kill her. It would be like killing my mother all over again. That would make me a monster. It's unforgivable. I would never be able to live with myself. Besides, I love Mrs. Kalin. I would never do anything to hurt her.

I break eye contact and bend forward, heaving for breath. Raising my hands to my head, I rock back and forth, tears in my eyes. "I'm so sorry. So sorry." I turn to her. "Can you ever forgive me?"

"Of course. Children make mistakes. As your mother, it's my job to guide you and help you learn." She lifts my face and stares into my eyes. "You'll never, ever, hurt me again."

"I'll never hurt you. Not ever. And I'll never disobey you." Relief rushes through me. My breaths come fast and shallow. I drop my hands to my lap, and small trails of blood flow from the nail marks on my skin.

The fog in my mind starts to clear. Mrs. Kalin stopped me. I was almost there; she was almost dead, but she used *her* Deviance to talk me out of using my own.

I inhale slowly, pulling air to the bottoms of my lungs. I need to calm down. I need to regain control before trying again.

Next time I'll be stronger. Faster. Next time I won't let her into my mind.

"Come." She stands.

I take her hand, and she leads me behind a partial wall where there are a few pieces of wooden furniture and a bed. Sleep is tempting, and if she suggests that I take a rest, I'm not sure I'll be able to resist, but she leads me in front of a mirror that's attached to the wall.

It's long and wide enough that I can see my entire image and hers beside me. It's like the mirror I saw in the clothing store when she bought me a dress. I look down at my feet.

"Look at yourself." Mrs. Kalin puts her hand on my lower back. "Now."

I raise my gaze. My pants look dirty and shabby next to her pristine skirt. The hem of my shirt is torn and its neckline scoops down low over my chest. I cross my arms to cover my darkened brown skin. My hair's tucked tightly behind my ears.

Lastly, I look into my eyes. Nerves twist, nausea rises, and I turn my head to the side.

Mrs. Kalin grabs my chin and twists my head back. "Look at yourself, darling. Look."

I do as she says. I focus on my face, my eyes.

I hate this. I can't stand seeing my own image. It's like a thousand rats are crawling over my skin. I close my eyes.

"Open them," she says calmly. "Look into your eyes. You need to see who you really are. You need to see yourself the way I see you."

Trembling, I open my eyes.

"What do you see?" she asks.

"I—" My mouth is dry, my voice shaky. "I see my reflection."

"No. What. Do. You. See." She enunciates each word separately. I don't know what she wants me to say. I need her to trust me again, but I'm not sure how.

My heart beats so loudly it's like rocks slamming together in my chest. My blood rushes and I can hear the individual cells colliding inside my veins.

I gasp. My Deviance has amplified my senses, my awareness of everything inside me. I can't even blink. I can't look away no matter how hard I try.

Looking into my eyes, my own power has trapped me.

The heat of adrenaline burns my blood and my heartbeat's deafening. I draw a breath, and the sound and force seem a million times stronger than the rush of wind outside the dome.

"I know what *I* see in this mirror," Mrs. Kalin says. "I see an ungrateful daughter. I see a cold-blooded killer."

A chill traces through me, but my terror only makes things worse.

"Did you think you could trick me?" she asks. "Did you think I was so stupid and weak that I'd believe your lies?" She shakes her head. "For a moment, I hoped you were sincere. I was a fool. But I am glad that I didn't let them take your head in the Hub. I have a much more fitting fate planned."

I want to respond. I want to break away, but I can't. As attuned as I am to every nerve, every cell in my body, I can't seem to make any part of me work. And I can't turn away from the mirror.

"You must be so ashamed," she says, "turning against me after I took you in. After I adopted you. After I accepted you as my daughter. It's my own fault for having such an open heart.

I should have known you were a monster. You paralyzed your brother, you killed your mother, and you let your father be expunged for your crimes."

Each one of her words is like a sharp stab. I can't believe I'm not bleeding all over her soft carpet.

"And now," she continues, "after I offer you everything, after I offer you more power than you could possibly imagine, what do you do? You try to kill me." Her hand tightens on my chin, fingers digging in with bruising force. "You deserve to die, you ungrateful brat."

My whole body shakes and pain spreads through me, yet I can't look away.

I struggle for a breath, but my chest is too tight. I'm squeezing my own lungs, my own heart.

I'm killing myself.

And she's right. I deserve to die. I am a monster. I killed my own mother, and today I tried to do it again.

I spread my power from my chest to my mind.

In a flash, the image in the mirror changes.

Instead of seeing myself as I am now, I see myself at thirteen. I see myself staring at my image in a much smaller mirror with my real mother beside me.

"I hate you," I hear myself say to my reflection. "You're so ugly. No wonder Cal doesn't like you. You're ugly, ugly, ugly."

"That's not true," my mother says in the memory. "And you're wrong. Cal does like you, but you're too young for him. He's nearly sixteen." She strokes my back. "Don't be in such a hurry to grow up. In a year or two, the boys will be fighting for the chance to take you to HR for a dating license."

"I don't want those stupid boys!" I yell at my image—at her. "I want Cal. You don't understand, Mom. You don't understand anything. I hate you. I hate you!"

"Glory." My mother holds my shoulders and tries to turn me from the mirror. "Stop this. Calm down."

"No. It's not fair. If I can't have Cal, I don't want to live. I hate myself. Ugly. Ugly. Ugly." I feel my heart tightening. I feel my head screaming in pain. I feel my body shutting down.

Then, in my memory, the mirror shatters—and I remember.

I remember everything that happened the day my mother died.

My mother wasn't the first victim of my Deviance. She might have been the first person I killed, but she wasn't the first person I *tried* to kill.

Before I turned on my mother, I used my Deviance on myself.

Without knowing what I was doing, without knowing I was Deviant, without understanding the power inside me, I almost took my own life.

And my mother saved me.

It was Mom who broke the mirror. She broke the mirror to save me from myself. I see the memory in front of me as if it's happening now. I see blood dripping from her hand where she smashed our small mirror. I hear her voice. I hear Drake yelling at us both to stop.

My mother's eyes fill with pain as I yell, transferring all the hate and anger from myself to her. I see her clutch at her chest. And collapse.

I see the terror in Drake's eyes and how he dives between us as his armor rises for the first time. His legs collapse as I stare into his eyes and accidentally crush his lower spine.

Sadness flows into me. Guilt. Shame.

But also love. Love for my brother for his forgiveness, love for my mother for saving me, and love for my father for the sacrifice he made to protect me.

Their love doesn't erase my guilt, but knowing how Mom tried to save me—how she saw what was happening—my love for her expands and fills me completely.

The memory fades and the image in front of me changes.

Once again I'm looking into my eyes in the present, with Mrs. Kalin standing beside me, eagerly waiting for me to kill myself. *I deserve to die*, her thoughts say in my mind.

My Deviance comes back under my control.

I blink, then twist and kick the mirror with all my strength.

The glass shatters. Mrs. Kalin shouts. I might not be able to kill her with my Deviance—she might be able to use hers to talk me out of it every time I try—but that doesn't mean I can't kill her.

Lunging, I pick up a long shard of the mirror and thrust it into her chest.

Chapter Thirty-Three

BLOOD POOLS ON THE FLOOR NEAR MRS. KALIN, BUT I can't look at the body. I bend and put my hands on my knees. I can't catch my breath.

Come on! I think. Not now. I can't pass out. Not now. My friends and my brother need me.

I suck in breaths, fighting to maintain consciousness, and finally my mind starts to clear.

I stagger out into the main part of the room and cross to the wall of screens. Sitting in the chair, I place the audio bud in my ear but hear nothing beyond a slight hiss. I scan the controls and notice a red light at the corner of one screen that shows the corridor outside this room.

Footsteps sound in the audio bud. On the screen, the man who delivered me to Mrs. Kalin paces in the hall. Will he come inside? I might not have much time. I study the controls.

How can I find the room that my friends are in?

Without a map, it's like searching for a single grain of dust in a drift. And I need to stop the constant loop of Mrs. Kalin's recordings that are broadcasting on all the screens in Haven. We might not know if we can free everyone from Mrs. Kalin's control, or how long it will take, but removing the constant bombardment of her messages will be a start.

I shift my focus to the screen showing her image, and I shuffle through menus until I find an option labeled "Broadcast Channels." I touch the words "Transmit to All" and they fade. I'm hoping I toggled the transmit option from on to off.

Simultaneous motion on almost all of the screens catches my eyes. All around Haven, people are stopping to turn to the screens. Some people were already watching, but now everyone's attention is riveted on what I hope are blank screens.

I spot a camera in the center of the console. I don't see a microphone, but perhaps it's built in. I find the magic words in the menus: "Broadcast All."

I press it and instantly my face appears on the screen that previously showed Mrs. Kalin. My stomach flutters. I pressed the button without thinking about what I should say.

"Hello." I clear my throat. "My name is Glory Solis and I'm here to tell you that everything is going to be okay. You're going to be free. You're going to be happy. You're going to have more choices about where and how you live and what you do every day."

Some people shout and shake their fists at the screens, and I have no idea what they're saying. I choose a screen that looks like it's in a factory and switch on the two-way audio channel.

"Hello," I say. "Can you hear me?"

"Where's the President?" a man asks. "Why did you stop her message?"

"Mrs. Kalin's message won't be broadcast again. It's time to think for yourselves." It's on the tip of my tongue to tell everyone that she's dead, but if they're still brainwashed, that will cause riots.

A woman steps up beside the man. "You're her daughter," she says.

"Mrs. Kalin adopted me," I respond. "But she's not my mother." I look around at the other screens, and based on the reactions I'm seeing, my answers to these questions are being broadcast to everyone.

"Please," I say. "People of Haven. Go back to your business. And concentrate on what you really believe. Think about what you know to be true, deep in your hearts. More information will follow."

I switch the broadcast feature off and then scan all the screens, changing the feeds over and over, hoping to find the room where they're holding Drake and the others. I finally find a sequence of screens that are clearly in the Hospital, and I cycle through each choice.

Some of the images are chilling, but I force myself to search each room for my friends. Scanning room after room, I can't find the right one. Then I do.

I stand, and the chair clatters back onto the floor. On the screen, I see my brother. He's limp, in restraints, and his armor is down. An area on his chest, about four inches square, is raw and bleeding, like they cut away a section of his skin.

Not far from him, Jayma is strapped down on a metal table and appears to be unconscious. I can't see Burn. Or any techs. I have to get there. Fast. I'll figure out something to say to my guard outside.

I race for the door, but then I hear Cal's voice calling my name. I spin back to the screens.

"Glory. We're at location SE41-63. Please contact us." He repeats the words again, slowly, as if he has no idea whether or not he's being heard. I find the screen Cal's on, then press "Broadcast Private." As soon as I do, the image of Cal appears on my main screen.

"Cal!"

He looks over his shoulder. "I got her." He smiles into the camera as Larsson appears on the screen beside him.

"You did it!" Cal says. "We saw your broadcast."

I nod. "But I need to find the others. They're in one of the research rooms in the Hospital. They're hurt."

"We'll come. I knew we shouldn't have left you guys alone."

Larsson shakes his head at Cal. "Glory, you have to find them yourself. Cal and I have other business. Remember, taking out Kalin was only Step One."

Cal frowns but doesn't argue.

"Where are you?" Cal asks me. "Are you hurt?"

"I'm fine. And I'm not sure where I am. Somewhere below the Hospital, I think. I was blindfolded and led a long way."

"Are you alone?" Larsson asks.

"For the time being. But it won't be long before someone comes in."

"We found a group who aren't affected by Kalin's mind control," Larsson says. "Some of them never looked at the screens; others seem immune."

"That's great. What's the plan?"

"Cal suspects that dust exposure helped him when he was brainwashed. We sent maintenance workers up to the vents. As soon as you appeared on the screens, we gave them the signal to reverse the flow."

"Reverse the flow?"

"We're going to let some dust into the dome and see if it helps."

I scan the other images. In a few areas, closer to the perimeter of the dome, people are shouting and pointing at the vents above them.

"It won't be long before there's widespread panic," Larsson continues. "Cal and I need to head out and help keep the peace."

"People are already noticing the dust," I tell them. "In the Hub, they're rushing the exits, pushing one another, covering their mouths with their clothing."

"You need to say something," Larsson says. "Calm them down."

"No. You do it. They won't listen to me and I have no idea what to say."

"I can't. Not from here. We'll spread the word on the streets, but the broadcast—it's got to be you." He leans closer to the camera until his image fills my screen. "You can do it, Glory."

A noise distracts him. When he turns back to me, he says, "We've got to go. Aim for our originally planned rendezvous. If you're not there, we'll try to find you." He spins away from the camera.

I'm left all alone.

Someone pounds on the door to the room.

I press "Broadcast All" again, and my image appears on the main screen.

"Don't be afraid," I say into the camera. "The very small amount of dust that's entering Haven is perfectly safe. Management lied to us. Humans—even Normals—can tolerate dust in small quantities. It's one of the discoveries that Mrs.—that President Kalin made in her experiments. Don't panic. The dust will help you think more clearly."

"President?" The guard's voice comes through a speaker near the door. His image is on a screen above it. "Is everything okay?" he asks. "Do you need my assistance?" I wait, hoping he'll leave.

"Please respond, President Kalin," he says. "If you do not respond in ten seconds, I will sound the alarm."

An alarm sounds, but from the look on his face, he didn't do it. A huge bang comes from out in the hall.

And something crashes to the floor—inside the room.

Mrs. Kalin staggers around the corner, holding one hand to her bloody chest. Her other hand is holding a gun.

Chapter Thirty-Four

YOU'RE NOT DEAD!" BLOOD RUSHES IN MY EARS.

"Do you think I'm ever without dust?" Mrs. Kalin says. She stumbles. The laser light from her gun flicks around the room, but she quickly recovers and trains it on me.

She removes her hand from her wound and grips one of the couches for support.

"You don't want to kill me," I say, keeping my voice even.

"You have no idea what I want."

I focus on her forehead. "Then shoot me."

She steps forward, leaving a bloody handprint on the pale-yellow sofa.

I move in front of the door. "Is that gun even loaded?"

She reaims and fires the gun.

I jump at the blast. Stuffing from one of the chairs explodes, and the acrid smell of the spent shell fills the air.

The door flies into the room and slams into me, knocking me facedown, the door on top of me.

"Mrs. Kalin?" the guard calls.

"I'm fine! Keep her down."

The pressure from the door increases, and it gets harder to breathe as I watch Mrs. Kalin's high-heeled shoes walk toward the panel of screens. She's going to turn her messages back on. She'll undo all we've accomplished.

I can't let that happen, but I can't move. Whether the man's using his own weight or his Deviance, the door has me pinned.

I feel the alarm's vibrations through the floor, but something else is repeatedly slamming the concrete, and the intensity increases with each crash.

There's a roar. The man shouts. I hear another crash, and then the pressure from the door releases.

I start to slide out from under the door, but I decide to use it as a shield until I know what's going on. To my left, the man lies in a heap, buried under the shelving unit. Books, broken glass, and pottery are scattered around him. He groans but isn't moving. I look toward Mrs. Kalin and see Burn. He's changed.

She points the gun at him, but Burn leaps toward her and swats the gun away.

He picks up Mrs. Kalin and flings her. She arcs through the air, slams into the ceiling, then drops straight down.

I stare at her body. The point of the obelisk sculpture is jutting out through her chest. Her head turns to the side, and blood drips from her mouth.

This time, dust won't save her.

Burn strides over, his footsteps shaking the room.

I step between him and the bodies. "Burn. Calm down."

His face twists with anger and he swings one of his arms. I cringe, fighting the urge to duck. He stops himself and lets his arm drop to his side.

I climb onto a chair so that I can look into his eyes. But I don't use my Gift.

"It's over," I tell him. "She's dead. And you saved my life. Thank you."

I see understanding in his eyes and the shift begins. First his skin softens, then his height and bulk diminish. I step down off the chair, and his hands, still large, land softly on my hips.

One of my hands drifts down from his face to his bare chest, still hard and broad even now that it's back to normal. I hold my palm over his heart as he breathes heavily.

"What—"

"Shh," I tell him. "Wait until you're ready. Deep breaths. Look into my eyes."

His eyes are the last thing to change back. Warmth returns to them, and in spite of everything that's just happened, a smile spreads on my face.

Burn's bleeding in a few places, and from the precision of the cuts, I'd guess they were inflicted by the Hospital workers.

"Do you need dust?" I ask.

He shakes his head.

"We have to get the others." I peek into the corridor. "Were you followed?"

"I'm not sure."

"How did you find me?"

He scans the room for weapons and takes a shard of the broken mirror. I take Mrs. Kalin's gun. Burn looks vulnerable without his coat and with only one weapon.

"I'm not sure how I got here," he says. "I think I was chasing someone."

I look back at the fallen bookcase with the man buried underneath. Part of me thinks we should help him, but we can't risk it. "Let's go."

We head into the corridor, and at the end, I push the door open slowly, trying to see what or who is on the other side.

"Glory?"

I jump back, but Burn holds the door open.

The boy who said my name is Ansel, a classmate from COT.

"What are you doing here?" I ask.

"That big Deviant was rushing through the halls and shouting your name." Ansel, who's almost as short as I am, looks up at Burn. "I knew he'd saved you on the President's Birthday, so I led him here."

"How did you—" I have so many questions, but they can wait. "Can you take us to my brother and our friends? They're—"

"I know where they are," Ansel says. "Come on."

The corridors are even louder than before. No one seems to realize that Mrs. Kalin is dead, but it won't be long. Ansel finds us white coats to wear, and I hold up a clipboard, using it to shield my face.

On the way, there's evidence of Burn passing through—smashed windows, injured workers—but no one seems to recognize him now that he's back to his normal size and dressed like them.

We turn a corner and I rush to the door where we left the others, but it's locked. Remembering the code, I type it in.

All of the techs are gone except one who lies unconscious, or dead, in the corner.

Drake is suspended by his wrists from a pipe high above us, not moving. Blood trails from several patches on his body where it looks like his skin was taken.

I head toward him, but then I see Jayma. She's in some kind of metal box, the walls of which are closing in on her from all sides. She's pushing back against the force, and I can hear the machinery grinding against her. She's weakening. The second she slips, she'll be crushed.

Burn leaps over to her and tries to pry apart the sides of the machine, but even with both of them working together, the walls won't stop.

I find the control panel on one side, looking for an emergency release, but I can't find it. I try my pass code from Comp training and gasp when the System jumps to life.

Burn yells in frustration, and I worry that he'll change again, but he doesn't. I find the Science and Research Department menus and what appears to be a list of devices used to test Deviant limits.

There's one called the Crusher. That has to be it. I switch it off.

The second the machine releases its force, Jayma collapses. Burn lifts her and carries her onto a table. I rush to my brother.

"Drake." I stroke his face, but he doesn't wake up. I find a chair to help me reach his outstretched wrists. As I release the bindings, his body slumps onto mine, and my chair tips back.

Burn catches us both before we fall to the floor.

"His halo," Burn says, and I find the button at its side to release it.

Drake groans as the halo comes off. His armor instantly rises, his skin now cold and hard against mine.

"Is he okay?" Jayma sits up on the table.

"He's unconscious." I check his pulse.

Jayma looks exhausted and bruised but otherwise okay. "What happened?" she asks me. "Is—is it done?"

"Yes."

Burn grabs something from a cabinet.

"What's that?" I ask.

"Dust."

"Give it to them."

I support Drake's head as Burn puts a small amount of dust under his nose.

"It's not working."

"Since he thinks we're traitors," Burn says, "maybe it's best if he stays unconscious?"

I shake my head, and Burn gives him another pinch of dust. Drake's eyes open. "Jayma!"

"She's okay," I tell him. "How are you feeling?"

His armor retracts and the wounds on his chest bleed. His eyes are unfocused.

"Get some bandages," I tell Ansel. He looks stunned but does as I say.

Drake rubs his temples. "My head is cloudy. I can barely remember—"

"Don't try right now," I tell him. "Rest."

Jayma inhales a tiny bit of dust. "Wow, that feels good." She jumps off the table and stares at the dust container. Burn moves it behind his back.

"Careful," I say.

"Yeah." She rubs her arms. "I'm going to be sore tomorrow."

"No kidding," Burn says.

"What now?" she asks.

"Time to get out of here." Burn finds his coat and shoves the dust container in one of the pockets.

"Cal and Larsson released some dust into Haven," I tell the others. "They're hoping it will help the employees clear Kalin's thoughts from their minds."

"Cal and Larsson?" Ansel asks. He's checking the pulse of the lab tech, who appears to be alive.

Suddenly I'm not sure whether we should be so trusting. "Ansel, what do you think of President Kalin?"

He looks down and slides one of his boots along the floor.

I walk toward him. "It's okay, Ansel. You can answer honestly."

He guides me away from the unconscious worker. "I'll tell you what I think," he whispers. "I think everything she says is *insane*. And the things they do in here are horrific." He gestures around us.

"Do you work in here?" I ask. He's wearing a white coat.

He nods. "After you left, I flamed out of COT. My dad got me placed here as part of the President's in-house security team, and right away I knew something was wrong."

Ansel's dad is in Management. He got Ansel into COT, too. "Do you look at the screens when you listen to Mrs. Kalin's speeches?" I ask him.

He shrugs. "It's not like you can avoid it."

"But you don't believe the things she says."

"No. But everyone else does—even my dad—so I keep quiet. I argued with one of my coworkers the first day I was placed on the President's detail, but I quickly realized it wasn't smart." His cheeks turn pink. "Instead, I help people when I can. Try to ease people's suffering." He looks to the side. "But I hardly do anything. I see horrible things in here every day and do nothing." He looks up at me. "I wish I was brave like you."

"You're plenty brave," I tell him. "I wonder why you're immune to Mrs. Kalin's Deviance."

He steps back awkwardly and bangs into the wall. "She's a *Deviant*?"

"Yes. She can plant thoughts in other people's minds."

"But not mine?" He looks confused and proud at the same time.

"Some people can resist her," I say. "You're one of the lucky ones. I could block her, but only sometimes." Maybe Ansel could do it because he has a Deviance he doesn't know about yet? "We still have so much to learn."

"Wow. This explains so much. But"—he straightens—"how do we stop her?"

"She's been stopped." I lean in close. "She's dead."

"Oh." Ansel exhales loudly. "So everything's okay now?"

"It's a start."

Burn walks toward us. Ansel takes a step back but relaxes slightly as Burn wraps his arm around my shoulders.

"Mrs. Kalin's ideas," Ansel says, "are they still planted in everyone's minds?"

"Cal and Larsson are trying to fix that," I tell him. "Will you help us?"

Chapter Thirty-Five

ANSEL FINDS LAB COATS FOR JAYMA AND DRAKE, AND we all stride purposefully out of the room, chatting and referring to our clipboards. No one pays us any attention—even though Burn's brown coat hangs out below the white one—and we march directly to the main entrance of the hospital.

As I put my hand on the door, someone bangs from the outside. I yank my hand back.

"I wouldn't go out there," a woman says from behind me.

"Why?" Ansel asks her. "What's going on?"

She points to a screen on the wall. It shows the scene outside, where an angry mob is shouting and banging, trying to get in.

"They've turned against us." The woman raises a trembling hand to her cheek. "Don't they know that science equals safety?"

I back away from the doors and motion for the others to follow. "It looks like the dust might be working out there," I whisper, "but maybe the dust isn't getting inside this building." It makes sense that the Hospital is better sealed.

"How do we get out then?" Jayma asks. "If that mob thinks we work here, they'll kill us."

"I know where the back entrance is," I tell them. "On our way out, we'll ditch these white coats."

• • •

The streets leading to the Hub are filled with people. Many are covering their faces, clearly terrified of the dust, and it's hard to know if they're still under Mrs. Kalin's mind control. At least Drake seems to be free of her, but he's still confused about what happened.

When we reach the designated corner of the Hub, neither Cal nor Larsson has arrived.

"Do you think they're okay?" I ask Burn.

He nods slowly.

Drake looks around the Hub and scratches his head. He spins back toward us. "How did we end up in that research room?" he asks. "Did I—" His shoulders droop. "Did I turn us in?"

I step forward, but Jayma rushes to his side. "You were under her influence. It's not your fault."

"I'm so sorry," he says. "I can't really remember."

Jayma rubs his back and looks up at me. "Glory, we'd all be dead if it weren't for you."

"And Burn," I say. "And Ansel. We all did our parts."

Looking up to the inside of the dome, I try to figure out whether the vents are still blowing in dust. The air is hazy, but it's no worse than on a day when one of the factory filters malfunctions. I'd forgotten how bleak it is inside Haven. How gray.

"Attention!" a voice calls from the speakers in the Hub. The screens flicker on, and Larsson and Cal appear.

"Attention, employees," Larsson says. "The President has been removed from office. Management is no longer in charge."

Silence falls over the Hub.

Then, one by one, people start to clap until the air is filled with cheers.

On screen, Cal smiles, but Larsson keeps his usual stern appearance and holds up his hands.

"Things will be different from now on. We have a lot of work to do, many things to learn, but if we work together we can accomplish so much."

A murmur flows through the crowd. "Who's in charge?" someone shouts.

"Us!" someone else responds. "Kill everyone in Management!"

Cheers rise.

"There will be changes in leadership," Larsson says, "but we hope that all Haven employees—including Management—will work together as we rebuild our city." He steps to the side and gestures for someone to join him. It's Mr. Alast, the Senior VP of Human Resources.

"I realize I was following the P&P without thought," Alast says, "especially since Kalin took over. But it's time for change." He nods toward Larsson. "If we all work together, we can reform the P&P and rebuild our lives."

Cal steps up to the microphone. "The first order of business is food. I know your rations have been severely restricted these past months. Starting in one hour, food will be available in the Hub's ration store. Please line up in an orderly fashion. There's enough for everyone." He grins. "In fact, some of you will be surprised at a few of the treats we have."

Larsson steps back into view. "Glory, Burn, Drake, Jayma— if you're seeing this, we will rendezvous in twenty-four hours."

The screens flicker off and everyone in the Hub talks at once. But there are no riots. No further shouts for anyone's head. A line forms in front of the ration store.

"I need to find my parents," Jayma says.

"I'll go with you." Drake reaches for her hand.

I hug them both. "Keep each other safe. And don't be late for the rendezvous."

"Worrywart." Drake lightly punches my upper arm. "You just take care of yourself." He kisses my cheek.

I watch Drake and Jayma disappear into the crowd. When I turn back, I find Ansel and Burn deep in conversation.

"What's going on?" I ask.

"Burn's telling me about what it's like Outside." Ansel looks amazed. "I'm going to find Larsson and Cal and help out at the ration store."

"Good idea," I say. "And if you're interested in going Outside, meet us back here in twenty-four hours."

Ansel rubs his temple. "I'm not sure I'm ready for that. But I'll come back to say good-bye."

When he leaves, I look at Burn. "What now? Should we go help at the store, too?"

He shakes his head. "Let's go find someplace quiet."

. . .

Lying back on a rooftop with my head resting on Burn's arm, I stare at a cluster of LED lights. I spent the first sixteen years of my life inside Haven, thinking that the dome was the sky and these lights the stars. Or, at least, not believing that I'd ever have the chance to see what these were created to imitate.

And now, I never want to be inside here again. I'm done with Haven and can't wait until my family is reunited, so we can start our new lives together.

The memories of my mother's death flood back, and the LED stars blur through my tears.

Burn turns onto his side. "What's wrong?"

"I was just thinking about my mom."

His breath catches, and I reach up to cup his cheek. "I'm so sorry you didn't have more time with Morag."

"Me too."

We look into each other's eyes, and I'm glad he didn't deny his feelings. I know how hard it was for him to face his mother and then lose her. If I have any say in the matter, he'll never feel abandoned again.

"Thank you," he says, his voice deep and thick.

"For what?"

"For everything."

I start to object, but he presses his lips to mine, and I forget what I was going to say. But it doesn't matter. With his arm crooked behind my neck and the heat of his body against mine,

I feel as if anything's possible; I can do anything, be anything, accomplish whatever I want.

Burn's hand traces up the side of my body, leaving a trail of tingling fire, and he breaks the kiss. "Everything still okay?" His breathing is heavy and his words vibrate through me.

"Better than okay."

He leans over me, but I place my fingers on his lips to block them.

"Too fast?" he asks. "Do you need more time to make sure I don't change?"

"That's not it." I smile. "Not at all. I need to tell you something."

He nods.

"Last night when we kissed, I didn't keep you from changing."

He tips his head back. "Did I change and forget?"

"No." I stroke his cheek. "What I mean is that I didn't do anything to stop you from changing."

"Yes you did." His eyebrows draw together. "Of course you did. Last night we—How else—"

"You did it on your own, Burn."

He pulls away a few inches, and the gap feels like a canyon.

I reach for him. "I don't think it was passion that made you change the other times we kissed."

"That's crazy. When we kiss, I definitely feel passion. Believe me. Especially last night."

"I could tell." I smile for a second. "Me too. But I don't think passion was the emotion that made you change the other times. I think it was fear."

"Sorry, Glory. You might be pretty terrifying to some people," he grins, "but I'm not afraid of you."

"Maybe you should be." I pinch his upper arm.

"Ouch. Okay, okay, I'm terrified."

I slide closer. "I'm serious about this. Remember when you said you were afraid to kiss me?"

"So?"

"My Deviance is only triggered by negative emotions—fear, anger, hate—and I think it's the same for you. I think you were afraid of hurting me. Afraid of the other things you were feeling." I pause. "I was afraid of that, too."

He frowns. "But what was different last night? We kissed longer than we ever have before."

"You *thought* I was helping you, so you weren't afraid. Because you weren't afraid, you didn't change."

He slips his arm out from under me and sits up.

I sit, too. I want to wrap my arms around him, but I wait.

"I think you're right," he says quietly. "Except that, before, I wasn't just afraid that I'd hurt you." He looks down. "I was afraid you'd hurt me."

"I'd never hurt you." I put my hand on his back. "I can feel my Deviance coming on."

"That's not what I mean." His eyes fill with tears. "I've lost everyone I've ever loved."

"Burn." I slip into his lap. "That's not going to happen. You're not going to lose me. I promise."

He holds me tightly. "I want to believe that, but what if I can't control my fear? I'm too dangerous."

I caress his neck. "That's for me to decide, not you."

He shakes his head.

"Come on, Burn. You're not the only one who's dangerous. You know perfectly well that I can kill you. And I'm afraid of losing you, too. But now that we both know what triggers our Gifts, we can sense them. Your control will improve. Mine did."

"I don't know . . ."

What can I ever say to convince him?

"I have the answer!" I keep my expression serious.

"Yeah? What's that?"

"Practice."

A slight smile creeps onto his face. "Practice?"

"Yes. Lots and lots and lots of practice. We need to kiss as often as possible." I tip up my palms and shrug. "I'm sorry, but it's the only answer."

Laughing deep in his chest, he rolls me back against the rooftop and presses his lips to mine.

Chapter Thirty-Six

JAYMA STANDS OPPOSITE HER PARENTS, HOLDING HER mother's hands. Her dad is carrying a sack filled with their belongings, and it's easy to see that both of her parents are frightened. A lot of people who've chosen to leave Haven are frightened, and even though there are close to fifty people in this narrow corridor, the mood is hushed.

It's been a month since Mrs. Kalin's death. After our first rendezvous, we all realized that we needed to stay until we were certain that every employee in Haven was out from under Kalin's control. Some members of the FA went back to Concord right away to bring the good news. I hope the news got to Simcoe, too. I hope Dad knows that Drake and I are safe.

"You've got dust masks if you need them," Jayma tells her parents. "But once we get a few miles from Haven, you won't need them very often."

Her mom pulls Jayma into her arms, and her dad wraps his arms around them both.

I walk over to Cal. "You ready?"

He beckons for me to follow him and we turn a corner, away from the group.

"Strange being back here again, isn't it?"

"In Haven?" I ask.

"No, this hall." He leans against the wall. "This is where we were when I was almost expunged for giving you a false alibi for Belando's murder."

"That seems like ages ago." But it's barely been two months. I was his dating partner then, and Cal risked his own life, hoping to save mine.

"Listen," he says. "I need to tell you something. I'm staying in Haven."

"For how long?"

"Maybe forever."

"No." I grab his arm, then let go. "How can you stay in here now that you know what's Outside? Why would you stay? Is this because of me and Burn, because if it is, well, we can make sure we never touch each other when—"

"It's not about you, Glory." He smiles gently. "In fact, you're one of the reasons my decision to stay here was hard. I'm going to miss you—Burn, too."

"Then why?"

"There's so much to do here. I feel useful. Working with Larsson and Alast, I've accomplished so much. I feel like I can make a real difference here."

"But—"

"As soon as people are allowed to come and go freely from Haven," he continues, "the population will grow. Especially if Shredders can recover and might want to live inside. Houston's helping us set up a renewal center and contributing his knowledge to the research.

"Even though her motives were messed up, Kalin and her staff were actually close to developing an antidote to help Normals like me cope with the dust. They're also researching why it changed some people's DNA, and how it heals, and a bunch of other stuff. We just need to make sure the scientists no longer hurt people."

His eyes are filled with excitement, and he gestures with his hands as he talks. "And that democracy system they use to run things at Simcoe—I *love* that idea."

"It does sound fair," I agree.

"Really fair. And guess what? Hidden in the Exec Building, we found some old books and public records from the city that was here BTD. It turns out democracy was the system then, too! This city used to have a Mayor, just like Simcoe's. And a council of some kind. I think that's what we should do from now on. Everyone I've talked to agrees. Mr. Alast thinks I should head the committee to organize it all."

Red spots rise on his cheeks, and he straightens his shoulders. "Maybe some day I'll be the Mayor."

"You'd make a great Mayor." Happiness for Cal starts to fill the void opened by the thought of missing him. "I'm so proud of you."

"Thanks." He runs his hand down my arm. "That means a lot to me."

Burn clears his throat, and I turn to see him standing at the corner.

"Are you ready?" he asks me.

I nod.

"Good luck." Burn reaches for Cal's hand.

"You too," Cal says as they shake. "Take good care of her." He points at me. "And you take care of him."

Unable to stand it, I lunge forward to hug Cal.

"I'm going to miss you," I say. "So much."

"I'll miss you, too, Glory."

Chapter Thirty-Seven

I SPOT DAD WHEN WE'RE HALFWAY UP THE RIDGE, AND I start to run, leaving Jayma and her parents to follow behind. Drake beats me, but within seconds the three of us are wrapped in one another's arms.

"You finished renewal!" I say.

"Yup. Only took me two weeks."

"That's great, Dad," Drake says.

Dad pulls us tighter. "I'm so proud of you two."

I press my head against his shoulder. I'd be happy to stay here for the rest of my life, but Dad pulls back and gestures to the rest of the group.

"Welcome to Concord!" he yells. "We have a meal ready for everyone at the Assembly Hall."

As we walk, he tells me about how things have changed since we left. The absence of the FA in Concord left a gap in leadership, and although he's too modest to say so, I can tell by what Dad's saying that he's been filling that gap.

"We're planning a vote," he says. "Concord will choose a leadership committee, and anyone over the age of ten can help choose who's on it."

"That's sort of like what they're doing in Haven," Drake says.

"Cal's organizing it for them," I add.

I can barely contain my happiness as the three of us catch up on our way to the Hall.

My smile drops away when I see Olivia standing near the entrance. I look over to my dad and he's beaming.

"Come on," he says. "Say hello."

"Did she quit renewal?" I ask.

"No. She passed with flying colors. Everyone was impressed at how fast she got through it." His voice is full of pride.

I turn back to look for Burn, but he's busy talking with someone. Jayma's talking animatedly to her parents and gesturing toward the fields and the lake. Her father already looks less tired and wan. Her mom, too.

Unable to think of an excuse, I cautiously follow Dad as he leads us to his sister. I will not let her spoil this day.

"What about Caroline?" I ask.

"She's great," Dad says. "She's gone back to Haven, hoping to talk her husband into moving here."

Olivia's hair is shining and clean and falls in two braids. Below a brightly dyed shirt, a skirt flows down to the top of her boots. All these details make her seem gentler and kinder than the woman I met before, but the biggest difference is in her eyes.

"Glory, Drake," she says. "Hello. I'm your aunt, Olivia."

"We've met," I say coldly. Drake bumps me with his hip and frowns.

"I know we met." She looks down to her feet, then up again. "But I was hoping to start over. I wasn't my best self before. I hope you'll give me another chance."

"Of course we will," Drake says and hugs her.

I cross my arms over my chest.

"Don't be rude, Glory," Dad says.

Olivia nods. "It's okay, Hector. Give her time." She shows me her palms so I can see that her razors are retracted.

Dad wraps one arm over my shoulders and then pulls Drake and Olivia toward him with the other. As the four of us stand close, joy spreads through me like fire.

"This is everything I wanted," I say, choking on tears. "What's left of our family is together, and nothing can ever separate us again."

There's only one thing missing.

I break away and look for Burn. He's standing alone about twenty feet away, and when our eyes meet he waves.

I practically skip to his side and grab his hand. "My family's back together."

"I'm happy for you."

My heart breaks for Burn. How could I be so insensitive? I rise on my toes and hold his face between my palms. "I'm sorry. I shouldn't be flaunting this—"

He raises a hand. "It's fine. I'm fine."

"Great. Because you're part of my family now, too."

He raises his eyebrows. "Don't you think you're rushing things a bit?"

I drop my arms. "What's wrong?"

He grabs my hands and pulls me closer. "Nothing. Everything's very right." He bends down to touch his forehead against mine. "But we've got all the time in the world. Let's take it slow and enjoy the ride."

"But I want you to know that you belong. That you're loved. My family is your family."

He pulls me against him. Nestling in his arms, I turn to watch my family joke and laugh.

Everywhere around us there's joy. Although being Outside is still new for the Haven employees who joined us, everyone seems happy as they file into the Assembly Hall for the welcome meal—Normals and Deviants alike.

Although it will be a hard habit to break, I never want to use the word "Deviant" again. So much of what they taught us in Haven was wrong.

As soon as I was old enough to think for myself, I knew that Haven didn't equal safety. And maybe there's no such thing as safety. Not in this world. Not anymore.

But at this moment, for me, family equals safety; Burn equals safety; love equals safety.

And if I trust my heart, my instincts, my strength, I know I'll always be safe.

Acknowledgments

Glory and The Dust Chronicles have been part of my life for about three-and-a-half years, and it's bittersweet to be wrapping up Glory's story. Writing a trilogy carries extra challenges and rewards, and I thoroughly enjoyed creating three complete stories inside of one larger story.

And as always, I couldn't have done it alone.

First, I'd like to thank the readers and fans of this series. A big thank-you to EVERYONE who has read The Dust Chronicles, especially those who've posted reviews at Amazon or Goodreads. And a very special thanks to Team Burn: Nicki, Elly, Guida, Crystal, and Anabel. You ladies rock!

Authors write in isolation, creating stories and characters we can only hope will resonate with others, and every moment of stress, hard work, and angst becomes worth it when a reader posts a great review or contacts me. I invite every single reader to sign up for my mailing list on my website.

In my writing camp, a multitude of thank-yous to Molly O'Keefe and Ripley Vaughn. You two are not only my trusted critique partners, pushing me to get better every day, but also my counselors, my strategists, my advisors, my drinking buddies, and my very best friends. I love you guys.

Also invaluable is the support and help and education I consistently get from my various writing communities, including #torkidlit, Toronto Romance Writers, CANSCAIP, Backspace, SCBWI, Blue-boarders, and the monthtowrite girly-whirlies.

Young adult and romance authors are the most supportive and generous people I've ever encountered, and I couldn't possibly list all the fellow writers who've impacted my career, but a special shout-out to Diana Peterfreund and Kelley Armstrong for generously agreeing to read advance copies of *Deviants* before it came out.

I'd also like to thank my fabulous agent, Charlie Olsen, and everyone at InkWell Management for all their support and guidance. I still pinch myself some days, marveling that I have such a great agency and agent in my corner.

On the publishing front, a special thank you to Robin Benjamin for helping me make Glory's final episode better than I could have made it on my own. Your insights and keen eye for detail were much appreciated. And thank you to everyone at Skyscape and Amazon Publishing including Courtney Miller, Amy Hosford, Timoney Korbar, Katrina Damkoehler, Paul Barrett, Erick Pullen, Andrew Keyser, Deborah Bass, Louise A.

Hutner, and Erica Avedikian and to Terry Goodman for being the first one to believe in Glory.

Finally, thank you to my friends and family for all your support. I'm so much stronger having you all in my corner.

About the Author

© *Marti Corn 2014*

Maureen McGowan always loved writing fiction, but sidetracked by a persistent practical side, it took her a few years to channel her energy into novels. After leaving a career in finance, she hasn't looked back. Aside from her love of books, she's passionate about films, fine handcrafted objects, and shoes. Maureen grew up in various Canadian cities. Her previous career moved her to Palo Alto and Philadelphia before she settled in Toronto, where she attends the Toronto International Film Festival each year. Visit her online at www.maureenmcgowan.com.